MURDER IN AMSTERDAM

Murder in Amsterdam

(DeKok and the Sunday Strangler *and* DeKok and the Corpse on Christmas Eve)

by

BAANTJER

translated from the Dutch by H.G. Smittenaar

INTERCONTINENTAL PUBLISHING

ISBN 1 881164 00 4

Printing History:

1st Dutch printing:	1981
23rd Dutch printing:	1998
1st American printing:	1993
2nd American printing:	1996
3rd American printing:	1999

Cover Design: InterContinental Publishing
Cover Painting: Judy Sardella
Typography: Monica S. Rozier

Library of Congress Cataloging-in-Publication Data
Baantjer, A. C.
  [De Cock en de wurger op zondag. English]
  Murder in Amsterdam / by Baantjer ; translated from the Dutch by
H.G. Smittenaar. — 2nd American ed.
      p.   cm
  Contents: DeKok and the Sunday strangler — DeKok and the
corpse on Christmas Eve.
    ISBN 1–881164–02–0 (alk. paper)
    I. Smittenaar, H. G.   II. Title.   III. Title: De Cock en het lijk
in de kerstnacht. English.
PT5881. 12.A2C6313 1996
839.3'1364—dc21   96–36722
                                                                                    CIP

MURDER IN AMSTERDAM

DeKok and the Sunday Strangler

by

BAANTJER

translated from the Dutch by H.G. Smittenaar

INTERCONTINENTAL PUBLISHING

Printing History:
   1st Dutch printing: 1965
   2nd Dutch printing: December, 1978
   3rd Dutch printing: May, 1980
   4th Dutch printing: October, 1983
   5th Dutch printing: November, 1984
   6th Dutch printing: April, 1987
   7th Dutch printing: June, 1989
   8th Dutch printing: March, 1990
   9th Dutch printing: April, 1991
   10th Dutch printing: June, 1991
   11th Dutch printing: August, 1991
   12th Dutch printing: September 1992

1st American edition: 1993

1

With hands folded in the small of his back, Inspector DeKok of the Amsterdam Municipal Police, Homicide, stood in front of the window of the bare, inhospitable detective room of the old, renowned police station at the Warmoes Street in Amsterdam. His stance was comfortable, legs spread apart, slowly rocking on his heels. The view was obscured by the water that streamed along the outside of the window. Of course, it was raining. Morosely he stared at the gleaming rooftops of the buildings across the street.

Diagonally below him, in the narrow Corner Alley, the drain pipes were blocked again with the offal produced by Moshe, the Herring Man, who had his stall on the corner. From there he dispensed the so typical Dutch snack. Tourists would gape and shiver in wonder as the herring man deftly scaled a raw herring, divested it of head and intestines, whereupon the customer would just as deftly pick the cleaned herring by the tail, briefly slide it through the raw onions and then, with head bent far back, would let the fish slide down in two, maybe three bites, leaving only the tail. The Dutch consumed tons of the fish, each year.

The alley always stank of rotted fish, mingled with the stench of stale beer and liquor. The stink would permeate the police station and surrounding buildings. In the police station, the aromas were additionally mingled with the sickening, sweetish smell of the disinfectant chemicals, used to regularly clean the cells in the basement.

DeKok was in a foul mood.

The Commissaris (a rank equivalent to Captain) had recalled him from a well deserved vacation in the provinces. And as soon as he had returned to the City, it had started to rain.

While on vacation he had enjoyed continuous days of clear skies and revitalizing sunshine. He had savored the long quiet walks over the heather, accompanied only by his old dog, Flip, a good natured boxer. The sun had tanned him and in the quiet, uninhabited expanses of the heather along the eastern border of the Netherlands he had slowly, but surely, started to forget all about crimes and the more sordid aspects of his job. The old inner city of Amsterdam, crammed with alleys, narrow streets, canals and bridges, had become an unreal world, a fantasy land. A land in which he had been roaming for more than twenty years, as if in a dream. A nightmare.

Then, suddenly, the telegram had arrived and everything had changed. The old inner city, the alleys and canals, the petty and major crimes had become reality again. Again assumed a sobering substance.

While he and his wife packed their suitcases, dark clouds had gathered in the west and it was raining buckets when his old car crossed the city limits of Amsterdam. His wife had remained silent and the faithful boxer in the back seat had whined softly.

DeKok was definitely in a foul mood.

Why could they not leave him alone? He wanted to get away from the corpses, the revolting, sickening crimes that took the full attention of the media and stood out in the harsh glare of publicity. As he got older he found he preferred to deal with the lesser crimes, the misdemeanors almost, the petty crimes that he could solve on his own, settle in his own inimitable manner, sometimes dispensing rough and ready, but always acceptable justice.

In the early days he would consider it an honor when a difficult, or important case had been assigned to him. But no more. He had paid his dues.

There was now a newer generation of detectives, young, athletic men, in their early thirties, who knew everything about computers, the modern, technical advances and the latest developments in forensic laboratory research. They carried on among themselves. They had long debates about the psychology of crime, argued at length about the influence of genetics and environment. Discussed input, output and throughput, whatever that was.

DeKok did not participate in such conversations. He was regarded as a sort of museum piece, from before the war, World War II, which most of the younger generation knew only from books. In those days it had been enough for a detective to be possessed of a good working brain. That was all.

He had actually started his police career just after the war, in the forties, but he seemed much older now. Then, everything was different. Society did not seem as complicated and crime was more understandable. He tried to keep up with things, but it was not easy. His ideas and opinions were not so easily malleable anymore. The changed morals seemed strange to him. The so-called sexual revolution was no more than hedonism gone wild, freed from every restraint. That, too, was so different from the strict moral upbringing that had characterized his youth.

He managed to get by on the reputation he had gained with his bigger successes in the past and the younger officers respected him, mainly because of that reputation.

DeKok snorted.

Now he had been recalled from a well earned rest because of the sickening murder of a prostitute. The "boys" had been working on it for more than ten days and had not made any progress at all. And now he was expected to solve the puzzle, quickly, almost in passing. It struck him as a challenge, a provocation. It was like a fixed race. If he solved it, it was no more than was expected. If he failed, his reputation would be out the window. Gone, would be the mystique, the magical aura that surrounded him. Because, in a way, he had become a myth among the younger generation. But the myth would be destroyed if he failed. He looked at his watch. Almost ten o'clock. Vledder would be here shortly, with the records.

Vledder was another of the young officers. A tall, blond guy, with a pleasant, open face. DeKok liked him. He was less stubborn than the others, less of a know-it-all, less opinionated. And he was sensitive to the shortcomings in people; including his own. Vledder was supposed to brief him on the case and was supposed to fill him in on the gruesome details. That had been the decision of the Commissaris.

DeKok turned around. He heard footsteps in the corridor. A few moments later, Vledder entered with a smile on his face and a number of folders under his arm. With outstretched hand he approached DeKok.

"How was your holiday?" he asked cheerfully.

"All right."

"I apologize for asking for you."

"You?"

Vledder nodded.

"Yes," he answered, "it was my idea. We weren't getting anywhere fast. We'd reached a dead end. In short, we're stuck. Then I proposed to the Commissaris to get you involved. You have a lot of experience in this sort of cases."

DeKok's face became more melancholy. The wrinkles in his forehead deepened. His eyebrows vibrated slightly. It was generally assumed that DeKok's eyebrows could live a life of their own. They could perform feats that no other eyebrows could hope to equal.

"Well, you haven't done me any favors," he sighed.

Vledder looked at him with surprise.

"Sorry," he said hesitatingly, "I'd rather thought that you would welcome the opportunity to prove what you're capable of. As far as I know, you haven't handled any big cases, for a while."

Slowly Dekok rubbed his thick fingers through his gray hair. Meanwhile he cocked his head and looked at the disappointed face of his younger counterpart. He looked for signs of insincerity. He failed to notice any.

Vledder apparently meant exactly what he said. Slowly a smile spread over DeKok's face.

"Never mind, my boy," he said in a friendly tone of voice. "Let's see what you got."

Vledder seemed relieved. He opened the folders and took a thick stack of photos from them. Carefully he spread the photos on the top of the desk and placed them in sequence. It was quite a series.

12

"I had them make color photos as well as black-and-whites," he said, cheerful again. "It seemed the thing to do. The photographs accurately depict what we found, and the order in which we found it."

He developed a slightly priggish tone as he continued.

"The murder was committed during the night between the third and fourth of July on the premises owned by Molly of the Lights. She operates a sort of informal brothel. We have, so far, been unable to determine the exact time of death, but suppositions have been raised that the time must have been close to one o'clock in the morning. The victim was a thirty five year old prostitute who worked under the name of Fat Sonja."

He pointed at one of the photographs.

"Look, that's how we found her."

DeKok leaned forward and looked. The photograph showed the nearly nude figure of a relatively young woman, reclining on a wide sofa. Her only clothing consisted of a soiled corset, with broken stays. It had been a pitiful attempt to force her body in a more tempting shape. But the corset had been unable to hide the shapeless fat of the body. Excess rolls of flesh pressed out from under the curled-up edges of the garment. Fat Sonja had fully earned her disparaging nickname.

There was also a close-up of the face. A horrifying photo. The flash of the camera was mirrored in the dead eyes, bouncing off the retinas. The result was a strange, frightening image of a corpse with awareness. The big mouth below the flat nose with wide nostrils, was frozen into a sad grimace. Scratches and the traces of strangulation were clearly visible on the lower part of the neck. The reddish purple of subcutaneous bleeding and bruises contrasted sharply with the cream-colored skin.

DeKok sighed.

"Poor Sonja," he murmured sadly. It came from the bottom of his heart.

"Did you know her?" asked Vledder, looking at him.

"I've spoken with her, from time to time," nodded DeKok. "She was the mother of three children. Her husband left her about five years ago. I found out, when she was a bit in her cups and in a confiding mood. I believe, he had another girl, somewhere."

"And . . .?"

"Well, that's when she stopped caring about anything, but her children and became a prostitute. Every week she sent a money order to her sister in Rotterdam, who's taking care of her children."

"The sister will miss the money," said Vledder gravely.

"And the children will miss their mother," agreed DeKok.

Silently they looked at the photographs.

"Did she ever see the children," asked Vledder.

"Yes, regularly. Considering the circumstances, she was a very good mother. Whenever possible she would visit them and she'd take the kids on little trips. Often to the beach, she had a small summer cottage near Seadike. The days she spent there, with her children, were the highlights of her life."

He paused momentarily.

"Of course," he continued, "the children had no idea what their mother did for a living. They're still too young to worry about that. They were just happy to see her and looked forward to going out, to the beach. They didn't ask any more. Why should they?"

"Who could possibly profit from her death?" sighed Vledder.

"At first glance, nobody." DeKok shrugged his shoulders. "After all, she was no more than the residue of a failed marriage. That's all. Perhaps it'll do so some good to ask her runaway husband a few questions. I don't know. But sometimes, in a case like that, there are some problems over custody. Things than can lead to bitter quarrels and sometimes escalate into pure hatred. I've known cases where it was hard to believe that the parties were once married and must have loved each other." He cocked his head at Vledder and asked: "Have you found the husband? Have you tried?"

Vledder shook his head.

"So far we've been unable to locate him," he answered.

"He wasn't at the funeral?"

"That . . .eh, that, I don't know," stammered Vledder.

DeKok looked at him probingly.

"Didn't you go to the funeral?"

"Oh, yes," nodded Vledder, "I went. But . . . eh, but I only watched the sealing of the casket."

Reprovingly, DeKok shook his head.

"Let me teach you just one thing, my boy, even if I don't ever teach you anything else. Always be on the alert during the funeral of a victim. Believe me, that's extremely important. Usually, though not always, the perpetrator will be among the public. Sometimes they watch from a distance. But they seldom, if ever, fail to attend. I can give you plenty of examples of that. Sentiment plays a greater role in crime than many people suspect."

"If I ever get to investigate another murder," answered Vledder, a bit timid, "I'll not forget it."

"Excellent, really excellent," smiled DeKok. "Other than this," he gestured vaguely at the desk, "do you have any particulars?"

Vledder shook his head.

"Not really," he said glumly. "As you can see from the photos, everything else in the room is more or less normal. Nothing remarkable. The clothes are neatly arranged on the chair, in the order in which they were taken off. The furniture has not been moved. As far as we've been able to determine, there was no fight, no struggle before the strangulation took place. Except for the marks in the neck, the killer left no traces, no clues whatsoever. There wasn't even a partial fingerprint. It's a sad case. There are no clues, no progress, no suspicions. No hits, no runs, no errors. The case is at a dead end. Stuck!"

DeKok rubbed his hand over his broad chin.

"Then we have to revive it," he said thoughtfully. His eyebrows moved in a peculiar manner. Vledder knew that there were people on the force, who swore that DeKok's eyebrows lived a life of their own; could not possibly be part of the man. DeKok's eyebrows could, apparently without him being aware of it, take on the most peculiar shapes and make the strangest movements. He had heard it many times. Now he watched the phenomena and believed the stories he had heard.

"Yes," repeated DeKok, "yes, we've got to get it going again, revive it, that's all."

"Revive?"

DeKok nodded emphatically.

"A case is only dead if there's no longer any interest in solving it, if nobody mentions it any more. Therefore we must first take care that people are going to take an interest in Fat Sonja's murder. People have to talk about it. In the train, in the bus, at home, over coffee. Perhaps there's somebody, somewhere, who remembers something that may help us in our investigations."

"You're right,"nodded Vledder, "but how do you propose to revive an old case like this? The papers won't even mention it any more."

"What do you think of this?" grinned DeKok. "What about some big headlines in the papers along the lines of *Husband of murdered prostitute still at large. Almost immediately after the discovery of the mysterious murder of Fat Sonja, etcetera, etcetera. . .."*

"You should have been a reporter," smiled Vledder, chuckling at the sight of DeKok's grinning face. DeKok's grin was almost as famous as his eyebrows. It was undoubtedly his best feature. His craggy, somewhat melancholy face would light up with boyish wonder when he grinned.

"Yes," continued Vledder, "You definitely have a talent for writing sensational copy."

DeKok ignored the remarks and picked up the telephone. He reached a number and Vledder understood he was talking to somebody from the press. DeKok gave an exhaustive report. He added that the investigations were continuing and under the highest priority. All available personnel was being mobilized, according to DeKok.

Vledder listened attentively.

After DeKok had replaced the receiver, he asked:

"What *all* available personnel?"

Again DeKok's face was transformed by his inimitable grin. He looked jovially at Vledder and said:

"That's us, my boy. You and me. After all, that's how you wanted it. You'll have the opportunity to watch me at close range. Remember what they say: Don't tease an old dog, he may have one bite left!" The thought seemed to amuse him.

Open mouthed Vledder stared after him, as he waddled over to the peg reserved for his old, much abused raincoat. The twisted belt, so twisted it resembled an old rope more than a belt, was tightened nonchalantly around his ungainly frame. A youthful fire sparkled in his old gray eyes. Finally, Vledder found his voice.

"Where are you going?" he asked.

"Where are *we* going," corrected DeKok. "Just put the stuff away, for the time being. You and I are hitting the road and our very first stop will be at Molly's, Molly of the Lights, that is."

Vledder shrugged his shoulders.

"I already interrogated her," he volunteered.

DeKok nodded understanding.

"Of course you have," he smiled. "I know that. But our visit isn't going to be official. No, no, not at all, at all. We're just going to visit, no more."

* * *

Old Molly, or as she was better known, Molly of the Lights, an obvious reference to her occupation in the Red Light District. She had started her career as a prostitute herself and was thoroughly familiar with the world's oldest profession. She had saved her money, unlike so many, and when it had grown to a modest, but significant capital, she had purchased an old brownstone near the center of Amsterdam's well-known Red Light District.

At first she had been burdened with a high mortgage at an exorbitant rate of interest, but that had not lasted long. Soon, she had earned enough to pay off the mortgage and became a respected and well-known brothel keeper, one of the foremost Madams in the District. When taking the word 'good' in its relative meaning, Old Molly could be considered good as well, at least, so it was said, she was a 'good' woman. She took care of 'her' girls.

Of course, like any Madam, she watched the pennies. But that, so to speak, was part of her job. From an easy chair near the window, she kept an eye on the arriving and departing clients. Her estimating ability was almost magical. She had an uncanny knack of guessing how much a particular client was willing to spend for his visit to the ladies. A single glance at clothing and attitude, was generally enough. No doubt the ability was invaluable in her business. After all, there were no receipts, no cash register, no records.

The prices, too, were flexible. It was, as Molly used to say: 'whatever a fool wants to spend.' And the fools were the men who visited Molly's establishment. Molly's share was fifty percent. She did not break her head over complicated calculations. She simply estimated the amount that was her due and the girls handed it over, generally without any grumbling, because Old Molly was seldom wrong. Even then, she was never far wrong.

She received the two detectives with the suspicion of somebody used to living on the edge of the law. There was an understanding between her and the law. Although brothels, as opposed to prostitution, were not, in the strictest sense legal, they were tolerated. There was a smile around her mouth, but the eyes did not participate. They remained alert. Without much ceremony, DeKok pulled a chair from under the table and sat down as if he had come for dinner. After a little hesitation, Vledder followed his example.

"Wadda you want?"

"Coffee," answered DeKok tersely, "and with as little arsenic as possible." Old Molly did not appreciate the wisecrack. She looked daggers at DeKok. Her bright eyes flashed with suppressed anger. She went to the kitchen.

"I'll see what I can do," she countered in passing. "After all, I'm used to take care of the slightest whims of our boys in blue."

"How nice," grinned DeKok.

As soon as she had left the room, he got up and seated himself in her chair, next to the window. Intently he looked through the sheer curtains. Outside the wooden window frame, an ingenious set of mirrors had been mounted. Much like rear-view mirrors of a car. The mirrors enabled him to see both sides of the canal in either direction. All coming and going traffic could be scrutinized at leisure through one, or more, of the mirrors. DeKok observed male figures, hesitatingly passing from one window to the next, observing and evaluating the female charms that were displayed behind the glass in various states of undress. Red and pink direct and indirect lighting attempted to gloss over the inevitable imperfections and helped to display the 'merchandise' in their most alluring form. It was this lighting in the rooms and behind the windows where the prostitutes waited, that had given the neighborhood its name of Red Light District.

He discovered a more horizontally placed mirror that covered the entrance to Molly's establishment. As long as Molly occupied her seat, nobody could enter, or leave, without being seen. That, in combination with the other mirrors, made it the perfect stake-out position.

DeKok was still seated in her chair when Molly returned with the coffee.

"Wadda you want in my chair," she snarled.

DeKok's eyebrows performed one of their incredible ripples.

"Looking," he said in an exaggerated polite and friendly tone of voice. "Just looking," he continued, "trying to verify how you must have seen Sonja's killer enter . . ." He paused for effect ". . . and then saw him leave again," he concluded.

"I seen nuttin' I tole you," she called out. The cups rattled on the tray she was carrying. "I tole them and I tole them, I ain't seen nuttin'."

DeKok nodded slowly.

"That's what you said, all right," he answered slowly. "I read the reports, of course. But I sincerely hope you don't think I believed them. Not a word of it, as a matter of fact."

He looked at her. Cocked his head a little.

"Dear Old Molly," he said soothingly, "we're all grown up now and we've known each other for a long time. Let's not play hide-and-seek. You *always* know exactly what happens in the house. You *always* know exactly who comes and who goes." He made a clicking sound with his tongue, made a bewildered gesture, pursed his lips and then continued: "And now, just this once, when a murder has been committed on your premises, you don't know? Come on! No, no, no, Molly, you just simply cannot expect me to be *that* stupid."

She shuffled her feet, a bit embarrassed. She put the tray down and rubbed the back of her neck.

"I weren't feeling good," she said reluctantly. "I were feeling real poorly. I went to bed early." She shuffled over to the mantel piece and picked up a little box. "Here, lookit, powders from the doc. Strong powders. Gotta take 'em every day. Ask the doc, iffen you don't believe me. Ask 'em, I tell ye. You'll see, he'll tell ye. I'm sick."

DeKok looked at her with astonishment.

"Sick . . .?" he asked suspiciously. "You . . . sick?" his voice dripped with sarcasm. "Well, that's a first. It must be the first time in your life. As long as I've been in the District, you've never missed a single day. Just let me take a look at that box, a moment."

"There's no labels," she said hesitatingly.

DeKok grinned.

"Let me see it anyway."

Her hand shook as she passed the little box to DeKok.

DeKok looked at the box.

"It's a prescription from July 5th," he said deprecatingly. "The day *after* the killing. Is that what made you sick, all of a sudden?"

She lowered her head.

"I were all upset," she whispered.

DeKok nodded, feigning understanding and sympathy.

"Yes," he said then, sharply. "Yes, no doubt, *after* the killing, but not before. You knew damn well that the police wasn't going to believe your story about a mysterious illness. That's why you went to see the doctor the next day and complained about a headache, or something." He pointed at the box in his hand. "That's all these are, just headache powders."

She looked at him, with cunning stubbornness.

"I seen nuttin'," she repeated emphatically.

DeKok turned his head and took another look at the array of mirrors. Then he stood up, sighed deeply, crossed the room calmly until he stood next to her and softly stroked her black hair.

"You're allowed," he said amicably, "you can hide your gray hair with black dye. There's no law against that." He raised a thick forefinger in a threatening gesture and changed his tone. "But," he continued, "but if you're hiding a murderer from me . . . you . . .eh, you old harridan, then you're in a heap of trouble. I'll make your life so miserable, you'll regret the day you ever saw me. I'll personally see to it that you'll be put out of business. In addition, I'll keep a comfortable cell reserved, just for you." He tapped her gently on the forehead. "Has that penetrated into that little, cunning brain of yours?"

"You ... eh, you shouldn't threaten an old woman," she swallowed.

DeKok ignored her. He could be infuriating that way. What he did not want to hear, see, or know, could be so blithely ignored that nobody was ever sure whether it was on purpose, or just a momentary lapse.

He sat down at the table and slurped comfortably from the coffee cup. It was a most uncivilized sound. When he had drained the cup, he stood up.

"Come," he addressed Vledder, "let's go."

He turned once more, before leaving the room. With the doorknob already in his hand, he threatened:

"I'll be back tomorrow. If I were you, I'd go to bed early tonight. Perhaps a good night's sleep will refresh your memory."

"You gotta do wadda you gotta do," she screeched, "I ain't seen nuttin'!"

DeKok nodded resignedly.

"Yes, yes," he said, wearily, "I've heard that tune several times, now. Try to change the record for tomorrow."

Followed by Vledder he stumbled his way down the stairs. Downstairs, in the room where Fat Sonja had been killed, a different whore had already been installed. The open places were rapidly filled, as usual. Plenty of applicants to serve the unending stream of customers.

DeKok entered the room and looked around. Nothing much had changed. The interior was almost identical to that depicted in the photographs Vledder had shown him. Only the corpse was missing.

"You've got guts," he told the girl.

"Why is that?" she asked.

He shrugged his shoulders nonchalantly and gestured around, pointing at the wide sofa.

"There's an old saying," he said slowly, "that a murderer will always return to the scene of the crime."

2

With the heels of his shoes resting on the edge of his desk, DeKok leaned backward on the rear legs of his chair. His upper body was hidden by an outspread newspaper. Only his tousled gray hair could be seen to stick up from behind the upper edge of the paper. He read the reports of his statements to the press, from last night. The various editors had done their work well. It had turned out as an exciting story about a nationwide manhunt with hard-working police officers in hot pursuit. DeKok read with relish. The admiring tone of the articles pleased him. He was due a little advertisement. The force could use the positive publicity as well.

Close to ten o'clock, Vledder entered the large detective room. His face was serious.

"Good morning, DeKok," he greeted.

"Good morning, my boy," was the jovial answer.

"There's a man, outside in the hall and . . . eh, he's furious."

"So . . . ?"

Vledder nodded, as if to emphasize the presence of the man, or the level of his fury. DeKok could not be sure.

"Yes, he's the husband of Fat Sonja," announced Vledder.

"Furious, you say?"

"Yes, he asked for the Commissaris, but he hasn't arrived yet."

DeKok grinned, as if in anticipation.

"Let him cool his heels a little longer."

Calmly he poured himself another mug of coffee and resumed his comfortable position.

"What did you learn from Doctor Rusteloos, at the lab?"

Vledder shrugged his shoulders.

"Not much. Some cartilage in the windpipe had been crushed and the neck bone had been broken. Compression of the neck artery caused excess blood pressure in the brain which quickly resulted in unconsciousness. Other than that, there were a few vague bruises to either side of the belly, just above the hips."

DeKok nodded his understanding of the details.

"The strangler must have been a powerful person. Probably the perpetrator straddled the victim, knees along the outside of the body, and hands to the throat. The pressure and strength required to strangle the victim must have been responsible for tightening the large muscles, ergo, bruises near the belly as the legs of the assailant tensed with the exertion."

Vledder eyed him with admiration.

"But that's almost exactly what the doctor said. Nobody can call you stale."

Flattered, despite himself, DeKok smiled.

"Well," he said modestly, "after all, it isn't exactly my first murder."

He stood up and stared out of the window. The windows were smeared from yesterday's rain. The rooftops glistened in the weak sunlight, just barely breaking through the low hanging clouds. Below, Moshe, the Herring Man, was in the process of moving his stall into position. DeKok opened the window and sniffed.

"Fresh pan-fried flounder, today," he murmured. "At first I thought it would be kippers again."

He closed the window and turned slowly to Vledder.

"Ask Sonja's better half to enter, please."

"You think he's cooled down enough?"

DeKok grinned.

"We'll see,' he said.

Vledder left the room. A moment later he held the door with an inviting gesture to allow an elegant man to enter. The man was about forty and his fury did not seem to have abated. With a red and excited face, he strode into the room. The sound of his footsteps echoed angrily off the walls, resembling a dragoon about to take possession of an enemy fort. He carried a rolled up newspaper as a sword in his right hand.

"I'll file a complaint!" he yelled, "I don't have to stand for this!"

He lifted his makeshift sword.

"This is an insult," he carried on, "a grievous insult, slander! I've got nothing to do with that slut, that whore!"

Calmly DeKok sat down on his chair behind the desk and looked at the man with contempt.

"You, eh, . . . you mean, Sonja," he said hesitatingly, feigning misunderstanding, "the mother of your children?"

If possible, the man's face became redder still. His wide nostrils trembled above a thin mustache. For a few seconds he was speechless, then he found his voice again.

"Here . . . , " he screamed angrily, ". . . it says here that the police wants me for murder. How *dare* they! How can they be allowed to write that? It's . . . it's an insult, that's what it is! An insult, slander, defamation, libel!"

"You know how newspapers are," answered DeKok, shaking his head disapprovingly. "Sometimes you wonder where they find the nonsense to write about."

He made an inviting gesture at the chair next to his desk.

"But, please, sit down, mister . . . eh?"

"Branders."

DeKok smiled.

"Mister Branders. All that excitement is bad for your health. I had a colleague once . . ."

"To hell with your colleague."

DeKok looked at him with well played astonishment.

"He was a good colleague," he said apologetically, "and a . . . eh, a good father. Really. You see, he had a wife and she left him. She left him and . . . left him to take care of their three small children. Really, we were all upset over it. After all, he couldn't really take care of three children on his . . ."

"I . . . I couldn't care less," yelled the man, impatiently, "I'm here because . . ."

DeKok sighed and rubbed his face with his hands.

"I meant to say," he continued, as if there had been no interruption, "that his wife left with a younger man. Yes, a younger man. I remember it well." He made a vague gesture. "Oh, mind you, she wasn't much of a wife, you know. We used to say, among ourselves, you understand, we used to say: 'Jansen's wife has no character at all, at all. She's no more than . . .'."

The man showed clear signs of restlessness.

"Cut it out," he screamed, "quit it! What do I care about your damn colleague? I'm here to file a complaint, to lay a charge! To charge the man responsible for this newspaper article. That's all! I have no wish to listen to your babbling about the wife of one of your colleagues! You hear me?"

The expression of indulgent sympathy on DeKok's face changed suddenly. His eyes narrowed and his eyebrows performed one of their incredible gymnastics. He looked suddenly very frightening.

"You call that *babbling*, Mr. Branders?" The tone was threatening.

"Yes . . . yes," answered the man, a bit subdued and obviously shocked by the changed tone and expression.

DeKok raised his heavy body from the chair and stood up. His face resembled an overloaded thundercloud, just before the storm broke.

"I'll tell you something, Mr. Branders," he hissed bitingly, "I NEVER babble. Do you hear me? I *never* babble! But if your dull brain doesn't comprehend what I'm trying to say, then I'll tell you straight out that, in fact, you're guilty of poor Sonja's killing." He remained silent for a while, as if catching his breath, then he stretched an accusing finger toward the now subdued, almost cowering man and said: "Yes, you, Mr. Branders!"

"Me . . . ?"

DeKok nodded emphatically.

"Yes, my fine feathered friend, you! You left her at the time she needed you most. You left her without any income. You left her to care for three small children. You left her and never looked back. You left her and didn't even bother to tell her where you went. She was past history. She didn't interest you any more, because you'd found a new love. Oh, no doubt, one much more attractive and above all, much younger than your own Sonja who had been pregnant three times in less than four years and had gained a little weight."

He paused to catch his breath.

"And then, of course, Mr. Branders, there were the children . . . such a bother. They cried when they had a tummy ache and all that noise was really too much for your delicate sensibilities, wasn't it?" His voice dripped with sarcasm. "Isn't that so, Mr. Branders?"

The man did not answer.

DeKok sighed.

"Sonja, *your* Sonja, became a prostitute. And you call her a whore and a slut. But you don't stop to think, you don't realize at all, that it was a form of protest. A protest against what *you* did to her!"

He opened the drawer of his desk and took out the most revolting close-up of Sonja's corpse. With a gesture of barely controlled fury, he pushed the picture toward Branders.

"Look," he said grimly, "take a good look. That . . . that's what you've driven her to. *That's* what you're responsible for. That's the face of the girl who, full of hope and love, accompanied you to the Town Hall, more than twelve years ago."

Eyes wide in shock, the man looked at the photograph.

"She was strangled," continued DeKok, ". . . strangled by a set of weak, characterless hands . . . *your* hands, Mr. Branders!"

As if paralyzed, the man dropped the photograph. His mouth fell open and his eyes became wider. Scared, trapped, he looked around. Sweat beaded his forehead. The room was suddenly charged with unbearable tension. Vledder observed from a distance, his face was pale. DeKok's face was a mask of steel.

"N-no . . . n-no," stammered Branders, "I-I . . . d-didn't kill her!"

DeKok looked at him dispassionately.

"Just in case," he said sneering, "you misunderstood me again, I only meant it figuratively."

Suddenly the man laughed nervously. It was a strange sort of neighing sound. An idiotic grin spread around his lips. He still did not seem capable of comprehension.

"Not me," he said, confused, "not me!"

DeKok put his hands in his pockets. For a while he stared at the man. A look full of contempt. Then he released a deep sigh.

"Vledder, please show the gentleman the door."

Without another word, the man rose and, with bowed head, followed Vledder. He still neighed like an idiot. When he reached the door, DeKok called after him:

"If you still have complaints," he said laconically, "the office of the Commissaris, my boss, is on the same corridor, two doors down."

* * *

Vledder came back after a few minutes. He found DeKok still standing behind his desk. Hands in his pockets. A melancholy, almost sphinx-like expression on his face.

"Sir Husband has left," said Vledder mockingly. "He fled the premises as a thief in the night. He didn't look left or right. It was as if the devil was chasing him."

DeKok nodded thoughtfully.

"Perhaps the devil *was* chasing him," he said mysteriously.

Vledder looked at him searchingly. His sharp eyes took in every detail. His gaze drifted from the gray hair at the temples and searched every wrinkle in the craggy face.

"*You* were that devil, DeKok," he cried accusingly. "I've never in my life seen anybody break down so completely, so quickly. How could you do it. How could you treat him so and how could you bring yourself to show him that horrifying picture of Sonja? It was . . . it was . . . eh, inhuman!"

DeKok shrugged his shoulders.

"Perhaps I'm a little old-fashioned," he said resignedly. "I don't know. Perhaps I don't fit into today's society. I *do* have rather orthodox opinions regarding love and marriage. A man who deserts a woman with three small children cannot count on any sympathy from me. I don't care what the supposed motives might have been. There's simply no excuse. It's a matter of responsibility. As far as I'm concerned, Branders is directly responsible for the death of his wife."

"But he didn't kill her."

DeKok sighed wearily.

"No, of course not, not in a judicial way. You can't report it and no judge would consider the case. But if he hadn't left her, she would never have wound up as a prostitute and the children would still have their mother."

"Yes, but . . ."

27

DeKok raised a hand.

"I know exactly what you're going to say. Branders could not have foreseen what was going to happen. You're right. He couldn't know. But that does *not* relieve him of the responsibility."

DeKok sat down and poured himself another mug of coffee.

"For want of a nail, the shoe was lost, for want of a shoe the horse was lost and . . . eventually . . . for want of a nail the battle was lost . . . ," he murmured. "Cause and effect," he added.

He slurped loudly from his coffee.

"You know, Vledder," he continued after a while, "during my career I must have handled hundreds, maybe thousand of crimes. I'll never know the exact number. I never kept track. But regardless of the case, I've never limited myself to just the case, the act. You see, the actual fact, the crime, is no more than the inevitable result. There's always a chain of events that leads up to the crime. That chain is started somewhere, a seed is planted. And when you start looking for that beginning, you'll find, sooner or later, a point at which somebody, either because of love, or the lack of it, out of hate, or an excess of it, for profit, or whatever, somebody, somewhere, at some time, shirked his responsibility toward his fellow man. Either consciously, or subconsciously, it doesn't matter. But there, there you'll find the originator of the crime, the person morally responsible. And in the drama surrounding poor Sonja, it was Branders who was the one responsible. *He* started this particular chain of events. Morally, he was the perpetrator."

Vledder looked thoughtfully into the distance, without really seeing anything.

"But the 'moral' perpetrator cannot be punished, he hasn't done anything illegal," he said, after a while. "But," he continued, "he's undoubtedly guilty. Is that what you mean?"

DeKok nodded, draining the last of his coffee.

"Yes, and that's why you need a devil to punish him."

"You?" asked Vledder, smiling.

"No," DeKok shook his head. "No, not me, but his conscience. And I hope sincerely that he'll have to struggle with that particular devil for a long, long time."

* * *

Vledder leaned forward and picked up the photograph that Branders had dropped. He placed it on the desk. DeKok looked at it. The dead face of Fat Sonja stared at him. He turned his head.

"Put that picture away," he said a bit irritated, "that face gives me goose bumps."

The old Commissaris, close to retirement, entered the room at that point. With outstretched hand he approached DeKok.

"Well, you old sleuth," he smiled, "returned from the wilderness, I see. Welcome back to civilization."

DeKok grinned.

"As you see," was the laconic answer. "I must say that the end of my vacation was a bit sudden," he added.

The Commissaris nodded in sympathy.

"We need you," he said seriously. "You see, DeKok, I've a funny feeling about Sonja's murder. I mean, the circumstances are such that I fear it might be a long time before we catch the killer. There's not a single clue, no apparent motive. As far as we've been able to establish, the poor girl had no enemies."

DeKok rubbed his chin.

"Robbery?"

"Nothing has been stolen." The Commissaris shook his head. "Apparently no attempt was made to look for either money, or valuables. The perpetrator didn't even bother to look in the nightstand where Sonja kept her earnings. The money we found in the room is roughly in accordance with her earnings for that day, at least according to Old Molly of the Lights."

"And that's the one who would know," smiled DeKok.

"Yes," agreed the Commissaris. "yes, Old Molly wasn't born yesterday. I wouldn't mind exchanging my salary for her income."

"Me too," smirked DeKok. "If offered, I'd take half of what she makes in exchange for mine."

"You think she makes that much money?" asked Vledder.

DeKok pushed his lower lip forward.

"You can bet on that," he said. "She's got four girls in the house at all times. I'm sure to be on the low side if I estimate her income at several thousand a week."

29

"Come on," said Vledder doubtingly.

"Absolutely, my boy. Figure it out for yourself. Let's say that each girl takes in about three hundred a day, and that's low. Four girls in three shifts, is at least three thousand per day. Prostitution doesn't have a five-day, forty-hour work week. The rooms are occupied *all* the time, so you multiply that by seven. And she gets half of everything. As you'll see, a few thousand per week is a very low estimate. She probably *clears* at least a quarter of a million per year, maybe more, much more."

"Goodness," said Vledder, "one would be tempted to start a brothel of one's own."

"Goodness has nothing to do with it," quipped the Commissaris. They laughed heartily.

"What are your plans for this afternoon?" asked the Commissaris, getting back to business.

"My wife is buying a dress this afternoon," nodded DeKok vigorously.

The Commissaris looked at him with astonishment.

"Yes," said DeKok. "And I'll have to go with her. You see, she appreciates my opinion very much. I've been married more than twenty years and she's *never* bought anything without me."

"Oh," said the Commissaris, completely taken aback.

His face spoke volumes, but he did not comment any further. Abruptly he turned on his heels and marched out of the room.

DeKok looked after him with a friendly grin on his face.

With difficulty Vledder was able to suppress an outburst of loud laughter. His face became red.

"You really have to go shopping with your wife?" he asked, after the Commissaris had closed the door behind himself.

DeKok nodded with a straight face.

"Yes, but that doesn't mean that you're going to have the afternoon off. Not at all, at all. I have a small wish list. First, you're going to visit Old Molly and ask her if she's remembered anything, overnight. I don't think you'll have much success, but we can't neglect it. Then you'll have to unearth a list of all known psychotic and unstable characters who, at the time of the murder, might have been running around without supervision. Then you'll contact the Harbor Police and get a list of ships that were in port during the

30

night of the murder. I'll assume that you've already checked the hotel registers and the more usual sources of information?"

Vledder nodded.

"Anything else?" he asked with only the vaguest hint of sarcasm in his voice.

"No," answered DeKok blithely. "No, that's all, for the moment. If something special turns up, give me a ring. I'll be home after five."

He smiled to himself.

"That is . . . that depends, on whether my wife succeeds in finding what she wants. Sometimes . . ." He made a slightly desperate gesture. "Anyway, otherwise I'll see you on Monday. I hope you won't need me. You see, I don't like working on the week-end."

He put his coat on.

"So long," said Vledder.

* * *

If DeKok had known about the thoughts of the man near the police station, he would have been a lot less self-assured. The man stood in front of a small, nondescript book store and looked at the display in the window, only paces from the entrance to the station. But DeKok did not know about the man, nor his thoughts. It was better for his peace of mind, but he might not have gone shopping with his wife, had he known. He simply had no idea.

The man looked at the colorful display in the window. The magazines showed good looking, fresh-faced women. The faces laughed at him from above gray, featureless strips of paper, wrapped around the magazines. Beautiful women. Too bad, that the obnoxious, ubiquitous ribbons of paper prevented him from seeing anything else; the smooth shoulders, the pert bosoms and further down. Too bad. As if hypnotized he lingered in front of the window. He could not get enough of the view. The paper bands intrigued him. He wanted to know what was hidden behind them.

His hands felt deeply into the pockets of his old-fashioned suit and found a few wrinkled bank notes. The value of the notes was a mystery to him, because he never handled money.

31

Hesitatingly and with a hollow feeling in the pit of his stomach, he entered the little store.

3

DeKok had tired feet.

Lazily, slouched down almost on his back, he sat in his old, comfortable easy chair and wiggled his toes. All afternoon he had followed his wife through town. In one store and out another. His wife had inexhaustible energy when shopping, especially when shopping for a new dress.

She still had a good figure, for her age. DeKok was well pleased with it. It was just a bit annoying that his wife had a tendency, during these hunts for just the right dress, to forget her age. Her first inclination was to look at dresses primarily designed for younger women and it was hard to convince her that she should look for something just a little more sedate, less provocative.

Just why he had to suffer this cross, this expedition from one boutique to another, from one department store to the next, had never been very clear to him. After more than twenty years of marriage he could still not discover the reason. But he had, by now, accepted it as one of those many feminine riddles he was powerless to solve. She told him that she appreciated his opinion. But obviously it was no more than an excuse to get him to come along. She never listened to his advice, or his opinions in the matter. Only after she had made her final choice would she ask him if he liked it. He always answered 'yes', tired, exhausted and grateful for the approaching end of the torture.

Comfortably he stretched his legs closer to the open fire, because the evening was chilly.

His wife placed a cup of coffee at his elbow.

"You'll have to take Flip out, in a while," she said.

DeKok nodded and thought about his tired feet. Flip, his faithful boxer was already sniffing around his chair. The dog seemed possessed of an internal clock, designed to let him know the important events of his days: mealtimes, and when DeKok was ready to take him out. Flip placed his wrinkly face on the arm of the chair and gave DeKok a soulful look.

Absent-mindedly DeKok caressed the dog's head.

"Just a moment," he murmured. "Just a little patience, let me finish my coffee."

There were those who declared that DeKok resembled his dog and there were others who maintained the opposite. It was only a joke. But the jokers were not completely wrong. There were certain similarities.

"Are we going back to the provinces, this year?"

DeKok shrugged his shoulders.

"Depends how long this case is going to take," he said.

"See any light yet?"

He shook his head, a bit depressed.

"Not much. The killings of prostitutes are very difficult. Because of their profession, there are seldom any witnesses."

He made a languid gesture, open to many interpretations.

"After all, what does she do, a little whore like that? She sits and waits. In the diffused light of her red, or pink, lamp she displays herself behind the window of her room and waits. She's for sale and waits for customers."

He closed his eyes momentarily, stroked the dog.

"Then," he continued wearily, "a man approaches. He stalks along the facades of the sparsely lit canals and slips quickly inside the house. Nobody sees him, nobody remarks upon him. The whore closes the curtains. What happens next, nobody knows, nobody sees. Everybody knows: as long as the curtains are closed, she's with a customer. There's no time limit. Some customers are back outside after five minutes and some stay more than an hour. It depends on the price. Only if the curtains remain closed for an extended period of time, some of the neighbors may start to wonder. Even then, one is hesitant to investigate, because one doesn't want to be responsible for 'spoiling the business'. If, eventually, the body is discovered, the perpetrator has an

33

enormous lead. He's been absorbed by the great army of the nameless, the lonely and the lecherous that regularly visit the District."

He rubbed his hands over his craggy face, drained the last of his coffee and carefully replaced the cup.

"It's even possible that *one* man, at a number of different addresses, can kill four, or five, or more prostitutes in a single night. Before the first murder is discovered he can be back home already, who knows where, even Rotterdam, or somewhere else out of town. If you look at the crowds in the District, it is almost inconceivable, but it's possible. It can happen."

He sighed deeply.

"When the work room of a prostitute hasn't been cleaned," he continued, "for maybe three or four days—and that happens more often than you think—you can find the fingerprints of maybe fifty, or sixty different people. When you realize that every person has ten fingers, you come to the realization that the Dactyloscopic Service has trouble getting any definite results."

He sighed again.

"The murder of a prostitute is the most difficult, most frustrating case a policeman can be asked to solve."

His wife smiled tenderly.

"And that's why they recalled you from your vacation?"

DeKok looked into his empty cup, replaced it.

"Ach," he said, yielding to the inevitable, "perhaps the Commissaris was right. The young detectives, the new generation, have little chance of getting anywhere. They're professional enough, technically, that is, but they're just not familiar with the inner workings of the District. The Red Light District is almost a world on its own. They don't know how to cope with it. They don't *feel* it. Perhaps, because of my past experience, being more familiar with the folks in the District, I can discover something, get a little farther."

With a last regretful look at his empty cup, he rose from his chair.

"Come on, boy," he addressed Flip, "let's go see if we can find you a few attractive trees along the way."

"I'm going to bed," said his wife, "it's already way past midnight."

"Keep my spot warm," nodded DeKok.

He went to the corridor and took the dog's leash from the peg near the door.

Obediently, Flip stretched his neck.

* * *

He had just returned from his walk with the dog, when the phone rang. He walked into the living room and looked at the old-fashioned pendulum. Almost one o'clock. With a slow movement he lifted the receiver.

"Is that you, DeKok?"

He recognized Vledder's voice. It sounded nervous. Hurried.

"Yes."

"Come to the station, at once."

"Why?"

"Another whore has been killed."

DeKok swore emphatically and in detail.

"Don't do a thing," he said, "until I get there. I'll be right over."

Angrily he threw the receiver back on the hook.

"Something the matter?" called his wife from the bedroom.

He went toward the bedroom door.

"No need to keep my spot warm anymore," he said grimly, "I've got to go out again."

She asked him something, but he did not hear it. He grabbed his raincoat and hat in passing and left the house. His small car, not usually that cooperative, started at once. With a determined look on his face he engaged the gears and raced through deserted streets to the station.

The old, renowned police station was a mass of a confusion. There was a lot of nervous activity. The space behind the barrier seemed too small. In the corner, near the telex, a number of high ranking officers were juggling for position. "Uncle" Jack, the graying, wizened desk sergeant who had been responsible for the night shift since time immemorial, was getting irked with all the

35

fuss. His voice trembled with ill concealed annoyance as he gave his orders to the uniformed constables who, because of the high ranking visitors, stood at attention in front of the railing that separated the public part of the large room from the restricted area.

Behind the backs of the attentive constables, DeKok tried to slip past unnoticed, up the stairs to where Vledder was waiting for him. If at all possible he steered clear of authority, especially the high ranking ones that seemed to swarm like flies after sugar, whenever a murder was committed. They were useless. They were just in the way.

He did not make it. Before he had even cleared the wall of constables, he was spotted by his old Commissaris.

"DeKok!"

The constables looked around and parted, giving him a clear view of the group near the telex. Like a schoolboy, caught with his hand in the cookie jar, he stood his ground and grinned sheepishly.

"Yes, sir?"

He shuffled closer to the railing. He knew everybody was watching him and with difficulty he suppressed the urge to make a derisive remark.

"We were waiting for you," said the Commissaris. "The gentlemen considered it well advised to keep away from the scene of the crime, before you had a chance to go over it. They didn't want to spoil any eventual clues."

"Excellent," replied DeKok, "really excellent. Most considerate."

"Of course, we roped it off," continued the Commissaris, "and nothing in the room has been touched. The young man who discovered the body, is in the Waiting Room. He'll have to be heard more closely. If you'd be so good as to take a look at the scene, we'll join you shortly. We're waiting for the D.A."

DeKok nodded with a straight face. Privately he enjoyed the situation. The Commissaris was placed in an unenviable position with all those people looking over his shoulder. The quasi formal tone that the old man used on such occasions, amused DeKok no end. Therefore he joined in the game.

"At your service, sir. Any further orders, sir?" It sounded mocking, but only to those who knew DeKok really well. The Commissaris winked carefully.

"No, DeKok, carry on."

"Uncle" Jack grinned broadly.

DeKok hastened to the detective room. Vledder was pacing the floor, hands wringing in distress.

"Oh," he exclaimed, relieved, "you're finally here."

DeKok looked at him closely.

"What's the matter my boy?" he asked. "Don't you feel well, you're so pale."

"Dammit," answered Vledder, "another murder. We've gotten nowhere with the previous one ... and now, a second corpse."

DeKok placed a fatherly hand on the young man's shoulder.

"Cheer up, my boy. You must never show your uncertainty. Never let them know you're at loose ends. A discouraged detective doesn't get any respect. Make believe you know exactly who the suspects are. Pretend it's only a matter of time before you'll tap the killer on the shoulder and invite him to follow you to the station. Believe me, at least eighty percent of our work is no more than show. Just plain theatrics."

DeKok took him by the arm.

"Come on," he said, "let's hurry. Before long we'll have the *Thundering Herd* to deal with."

Vledder knew that this was DeKok's special name for the army of specialists, consisting of the coroner and his assistants, the photographers, the fingerprint people, the forensic staff and other experts that always gathered when a murder was committed. This time, he knew, it also included the group of top brass gathered below.

They went on foot, along the familiar alleys and canals. The station was, after all, right on the edge of the District. Along the way they met a group of curious reporters.

"Do you have any suspects?" asked one.

DeKok slowed his pace momentarily.

"You can expect the arrest of the murderer within the week," he said evenly.

37

The man looked at him with surprise.

"Within the week?"

DeKok nodded.

"Yes, but for further information, I'll have to direct you to my boss, the Commissaris. You understand, that at this stage . . ."

He waved carelessly and walked on. Vledder looked at him. A smile on his face.

In front of Aunt Dina's brothel they found a number of constables, hard put to keep the curious at a distance. There was quite a crowd for such a late hour. But then, the District really never slept.

One of the constables addressed DeKok:

"Downstairs. It's Pale Goldie, strangled, just like the last one. What was her name again, Fat something?"

"Fat Sonja," supplied DeKok.

"Yes, Fat Sonja. Well, this is exactly the same. But Fat Sonja was wearing a corset, this one isn't wearing anything."

"Has the doctor been called, or just us?"

"No, the doctor has been called, he'll be here shortly."

Carefully DeKok and Vledder entered the indicated room.

It was a small room. No more than ten by twelve feet. There were two low chairs and a small table between them. To the left, against the wall was a small sink with a hospital type bucket, the kind that could be opened with a foot pedal, underneath to receive the used condoms. A wide assortment of yellowed prints, depicting scantily clad women adorned the walls. A sofa was pushed up against the wall on the right. Goldie was spread out on the sofa, nude and motionless. The stringy, blonde hair formed a disordered wreath around her head. The pale face which inspired her nickname, looked gray.

DeKok, who had seen hundreds of corpses in his long career, was certain. Pale Goldie was dead. He did not have to search long for the cause of death. The marks of strangulation on the long, skinny neck were abundantly clear.

He walked over to the bed and placed the back of his hand against the cheek of the dead girl. The body was still warm. His sharp gaze roamed over the naked skin. But, apart from the streaks caused by the strangulation, he could not detect any other marks on the body. Just below the right knee was a small wound, but that was from an earlier date. A scab had already formed over it.

He looked again around the room. It was all so normal. Even his trained eye did not see anything that would be worth a second glance. There was nothing extraordinary, no clues, nothing that could serve as a starting point for discovering the killer. The only thing visible was the normal interior so common for the working room of a practicing prostitute. He had seen so many, all more or less the same.

He let his attention wander to Goldie's clothes. Neatly folded, they were placed on one of the low chairs. Especially the finely meshed nylon stockings caught his attention. Carefully he inserted a hand inside the stocking and spread his fingers. The delicate weave did not show any damage. He could not discover a hole, or a run. Then he looked at the brassiere. It was a frivolous piece of clothing, but there was not a sign of any sort of violence. The straps were whole and the elastic centerpiece was not abnormally stretched out.

Vledder occupied himself with making a sketch of the interior.

"What do you think?" he asked.

DeKok shrugged his shoulders.

"See any differences between here, and the murder of Sonja?"

Slowly Vledder shook his head.

"Just the corset," he said.

DeKok nodded silent agreement.

"What else?"

"No, other than that, no differences. Here, too, no signs of a struggle. No damage. If the naked lady on the sofa wasn't so obviously dead, you'd say that nothing had happened."

DeKok sighed. It was a depressed sound.

"She never had a chance to defend herself against her attacker. I looked at her fingernails. They're almost sterile. I also haven't found any trace of blood, which means that the killer remained undamaged and most probably has no scratches on his face, or whatever."

Dejectedly Vledder shook his head.

39

"No hint of any kind," he commiserated. "This just isn't our lucky day."

"No," agreed DeKok. "Lady Fortuna is a willful person. But what do you expect, Lady Luck is, after all, a woman."

At that moment the doctor entered, followed by the photographer. The fingerprint experts could be seen just outside the door. The small room started to get crowded.

"As soon as the rest of the 'herd' arrives, it will be strictly standing room only, in here," muttered DeKok.

"Beg your pardon?" said the doctor.

"I wondered if she was dead," lied DeKok.

A bit irked, the doctor gave him a long, hard look.

"Oh," he said, finally. "Yes, well, let's have a look."

He pulled out a stethoscope and approached the corpse. His examination did not last long.

"She's dead," he announced.

DeKok and Vledder nodded with wise faces.

As soon as the doctor was out of the way, Bram, the photographer, started to take his shots. The light of his flash attachment lit up the room in discouraging detail. Kruger, of the Dactyloscopic Service, the fingerprint unit started to prepare his paraphernalia.

"Can I get started?"

DeKok nodded assent.

"Go ahead," he said. "Do the best you can. If we can't solve this one, either, there's going to be a storm. You'd better . . . eh, we *all* better prepare ourselves."

"If there's nothing, I can't find nothing," protested Kruger. "But if you're so set on getting some fingers, I've got an archive full of 'em. You can have mine, if you want."

DeKok grinned. It remained his best feature.

"You'd fail miserably as a murderer," he laughed, shaking his head. "Your wife told me that the turkey you bought for Christmas, is still walking around in your garden."

Vledder laughed also and Kruger started to hunt moodily for invisible fingerprints that could not be found.

The detectives forced their faces back into a serious expression when the rest of DeKok's "Thundering Herd" arrived, accompanied by at least double their number of high ranking officers. The brass entered the little room reluctantly and stared at the corpse.

"The investigation is in good hands," lectured the Commissaris. "Inspector DeKok has a great deal of experience in this sort of case."

Go ahead, pour it on, thought DeKok. You know as well as I that only a miracle will enable us to solve this case.

Happily the gentlemen did not linger long. They were gone within twenty minutes.

The Commissaris released a relieved sigh.

"Glad that's over. Thank God, they're gone."

"I feel for you," said DeKok with a mocking grin.

The Commissaris smiled, but did not pursue the tender subject. His glanced around the room.

"Well, any progress?"

DeKok shook a melancholy head.

"No, sir. I don't know what to think. It just isn't logical." He paused, then continued: "I mean, how would you classify this murder. It's so . . . so senseless."

"It could be a crime of passion," opined the Commissaris.

DeKok pursed his lips.

"It's possible," he admitted cautiously. "But a number of ingredients are missing, I think. For one thing it's too serene."

"Serene?" wondered Vledder out loud.

"Yes, serene. There's not a trace of anger, of violence. Look at the body. Except for the neck there are no signs of a fight. No bruises, no blood. Look at the room. As you mentioned earlier, if it wasn't for the corpse, you wouldn't find anything unusual. There's also no sign of foreplay."

"Foreplay?"

DeKok nodded, raising a finger in the air.

"Yes, there's no signs of foreplay. And there's otherwise always foreplay. A sex crime, a crime of passion, a lust killing all require something to bring the killer to a climax. To get him high enough to commit the killing, so to speak. That's almost always accompanied by violence. It is, of course, possible that this foreplay was only in the killer's mind. It happens, sometimes. But seldom.

41

Something had to happen before the killing took place. But there are no signs of that. So what happened? What went through the mind of the killer?"

DeKok took a step in the direction of the low chairs.

"Take a look at the clothing," he said. "Everything is so neatly folded and draped over the chair, that undressing could only have been done with the greatest calm. From the way things are folded and from the order in which they were placed on the chair, it's easy to determine that Pale Goldie must have undressed herself. If a man undresses a woman, guided by lust, arousal, with mounting excitement, it becomes a totally different picture. Usually clothing is then found strewn helter skelter around the room. But even the fine mesh of the stockings show no holes, no tears, no runs. It really seems as if Pale Goldie performed a calm and deliberate strip-tease number and that the perpetrator watched from a distance."

"But she's been strangled," observed Vledder.

"Yes, my boy, but that happened later, after Goldie displayed herself invitingly on the sofa."

DeKok rubbed his hands through his gray hair.

"It isn't going to be easy to find the killer. It's going to be even more difficult than normal, because he looks so innocent."

"What!?"

DeKok's face looked serious.

"Yes," he answered listlessly. "Yes, it'll be extremely difficult. You see, prostitutes have at least one advantage over us. They *know* men better than we can ever hope to learn. I mean, they understand them and are quick to see their intentions, judge their desires. But yet, they didn't defend themselves against the killer. There is no sign of a struggle at all, at all. Neither Fat Sonja, nor Pale Goldie, had any suspicions of the killer. They trusted him. They thought he was completely harmless."

For a while they stared in silence at the dead girl on the sofa.

"We better have them take her away," whispered DeKok finally.

Impassive attendants of the coroner's office tied her to a stretcher and carried her off.

DeKok watched them leave, a determined look on his face.

4

"Aunt" Dina was sitting comfortably behind the table in her dining room. With the tip of her apron, she wiped her gleaming lips and pushed the dirty plate away.

"A nice little chicken," she said, smacking her lips. "I always get them from Hans, around the corner."

Vledder and DeKok stared at the remnants consisting of little more than a few pieces of skin and gnawed bones.

"Every night," she continued happily, "I treat myself to a little chicken. Boiled, roasted, fried, I don't care. I just have to have my chicken. After all, I don't have to watch my figure, anymore." She caressed her abundant bosom with her greasy hands and laughed at her own joke.

"Woman," cried Vledder with loathing, "how can you eat at all? Not an hour since a girl was killed under your roof."

She shrugged her fleshy shoulders and pulled an indignant face.

"For that I should deny myself my little chicken?" she marvelled.

Vledder was at a loss for words.

"But . . ." he started.

But that was as far as he was able to go. Full of unexpressed emotions, he remained silent.

DeKok pushed him gently aside.

"Have you seen, or heard, anything particular tonight," he asked pleasantly.

She shook her head.

"I never see anything, or hear anything, or know anything," she answered.

DeKok looked surprised.

"Come on, Aunt Dina," he said, "you must know what happens in your house . . . eh, your brothel."

An angry glint flickered in her small, piggish eyes.

"This isn't a brothel," she answered sharply.

DeKok's eyebrows, without any volition from himself, rippled dangerously.

"Ah, excuse me, but what would you call it?"

A cunning look came in her face.

"I just rent rooms," she said with a sardonic grin. "Just rooms, for girls who have no place of their own."

"How considerate," smirked DeKok. "And please tell me, how much rent do these poor, homeless girls pay you?"

"A tenner," she spat. "A tenner a week. Ask them yourself."

DeKok grinned.

"Yes, plus tips. No doubt you trained them well. I'm sure the girls will give the right answers." He sighed. "Anyway, we'll discuss that subject some other time."

"You must do what you can't keep yourself from doing," she answered spitefully.

"Absolutely," agreed DeKok, changing his tone of voice. "But you can count on this: you're going to be very sorry if you don't start giving me the right answers and right now."

Suddenly he took a step forward and gripped her by the upper arm with a fist of steel.

"Get up," he hissed, "and first take those gnawed bones to the kitchen. They make me sick."

Angrily she pulled her arm out of his grip.

"Keep your hands to yourself," she yelled. "Don't you dare get familiar, I don't like it. Never did!"

She hefted her gross body from the chair and took the plate to the kitchen.

DeKok remained silent until she returned.

"How long has Pale Goldie been with you?" he asked.

"Almost a year," she answered moodily.

"Never noticed anything particular?"

She shrugged her shoulders.

"Ach," she said, "I'm not at all surprised."

"How's that?"

"Well, she was always swearing at everybody, even at her best customers. She cursed them before, during and after. She just didn't know how to be a whore. She wasn't at all suited for the job."

"You mean . . .?"

She sighed deeply.

"You've got to be able to handle men, you've got to have a feeling for what they want. Even if you can't stand them, you've got to ignore personal feelings. But she couldn't do that. She was always antagonizing them. That had to go wrong, sooner or later. A whore can't afford a big mouth, you can't talk back. You can't insult your customers. They'll stay away, or . . ."

DeKok nodded his understanding.

"But this time she seems to have been extremely cooperative. She undressed herself completely."

Aunt Dina grimaced.

"Perhaps she was turning over a new leaf."

"Why?"

"Well, she never did that before. The guy must have really shown her a lot of money."

"How much, do you think?"

She spread her fat, greasy fingers.

"A hundred at least, maybe more."

DeKok smiled at her.

"I thought," he said innocently, "that you didn't know what happened in the house?"

She reacted angrily.

"I don't," she yelled. "The girls just rent from me. But what they do in their own rooms, is their own business. That's none of *my* business. As long as I get the rent. I don't care what they do." She calmed down a little and then continued: "But, of course, sometimes they tell me things. Especially Pale Goldie. She was always talking about the men she received and always foul mouthing them, cursing them."

"She ever tell you about a man who wanted her to take off all her clothes?"

She shook her head.

"That's the first time I hear that. I mean, about Goldie. Other girls don't mind so much, they almost do it without being asked. But I never thought that Goldie went that far."

DeKok nodded to himself and stared at her for a long time.

"Why were you so defensive, at first. You don't have anything to hide from us, or do you?"

She lowered her head.

"Well, it's no joke, you know," she replied, sorrow and irritation mingled in her voice. "It's no joke when something like that happens in your house. Poor girl."

The last words seemed to indicate some compassion. For the first time she sounded human.

"But woman," interrupted Vledder, "if that's how you feel, how can you, in God's name, get any food through your throat, let alone a whole chicken. It's, it's enough to . . . make you sick!"

She sighed with a melancholy face.

"Do *you* know what people do when they're depressed?"

She rubbed her still greasy hands over her eyes.

"Maybe Goldie had a big mouth, a foul mouth, but she was a good girl. At first I didn't even want to rent to her. I thought it would be a shame. Such a girl, in that kind of work." She made a despondent gesture. "But what can you do? If she doesn't rent here, she'll rent somewhere else."

"Did she make a lot?"

She shook her head slowly, as if in thought.

"Ach, no. Not really. I told you, she didn't know how to do it. She didn't know her job."

"Yeah, it's a profession, after all," grinned DeKok.

* * *

They walked back to the station, along the narrow canals and through dark alleys. Groups of women gathered on the corners of the streets and alleys. This second murder, the killing of Pale Goldie had shocked the neighborhood. The air seemed impregnated with a silent threat. Even the trees along the water seemed to whisper about a mysterious killer, a killer who stole silently from one window to another, who strangled his victims and then disappeared without a trace, into the night.

The pimps, too, were nervous. They talked to each other in whispers. Vledder and DeKok could hear the murmur of their hoarse voices. But the conversations and arguments stopped when the two detectives passed by. Silently they would look at the twosome. Nobody addressed them.

"They're afraid," said Vledder.

DeKok nodded in agreement.

"Yes. If this keeps up, the whores will be afraid to keep working. They'll be too scared. These murders are killing the business as well. That's what the pimps are afraid of."

"What kind of woman *was* Pale Goldie?" asked Vledder. "Did you know her? According to Aunt Dina she was a bit strange, I'd say."

"Yes," answered DeKok, "I knew her."

He sighed and walked on, apparently deep in thought. After a while, as if there had been no interruption, he continued:

"I knew her quite well, as a matter of fact. She was the daughter of a former policeman."

"What. . .?" cried Vledder, he was stunned.

DeKok looked at him sideways.

"Don't let it shock you, my boy," he said soothingly. "That sort of thing happens. In the Quarter you'll find them from all walks of life. It's fashionable, nowadays, to blame the parents when somebody's life turns out to be a failure. Undoubtedly, so *they* say, it's the way they've been brought up. I'm not so sure about that. No, not sure at all, at all. I know, for instance, that Goldie was blessed with excellent, loving parents and she had the best sort of upbringing one could wish."

"Well, was . . . she . . . eh, a bit strange?"

"No," sighed DeKok, "just rebellious."

"Rebellious? In what way?"

"For one thing, she hated, really hated, so-called 'decent' people, the middle class, the so-called 'pillars of society'. To her they were all hypocrites. She was always going on about the so-called gentlemen who don't want to bother their own wives with their wishes and fantasies and therefore used whores. The men weren't good enough and the women thought themselves too good, according to Goldie. You see, as a rule, every prostitute hates the men who use her. They look down on them. It's a sort of defense mechanism. In most cases the sharp hatred dulls over the years. They accept their position and try to get as much profit out of it as possible, as quickly as may be, while their looks last. But

Goldie was different. She would never really have become a real prostitute."

"But she received men?"

"Yes, my boy, but that's not the same thing at all, at all. In my book a woman doesn't become a prostitute until she's accepted the situation as inevitable. Goldie never did that. She couldn't. Every time, whenever she gave herself to a man, she had to win a battle with herself first. She had to convince herself. No matter how strange it may sound, but every time she had to wrestle with her own sense of rightness, her feeling of decency. And because, every time, she lost that battle with her conscience, she took it out on the world, especially her clients. She cursed the men she received and she cursed the money they paid her. But in reality she cursed herself, her own cowardice, her lack of will power, her inability to give up prostitution."

Vledder sighed.

DeKok's face assumed a melancholy expression.

"Believe me, my boy," he continued, "Nowhere in the world will you find as many instances of human tragedy as within the District. This outwardly glittering world of sex and frivolity hides more suffering and broken dreams than you can imagine."

"But . . . ," cried Vledder, "nobody is forcing them!"

DeKok grinned mischievously.

"You sound like a revivalist on Sunday," he chuckled.

"It is," answered Vledder.

"What?"

"It is Sunday."

DeKok nodded thoughtfully.

"Yes," he said, "Sunday! Let's hurry up. That boy, the boy who discovered the body is still waiting for us at the station."

* * *

DeKok stared eastward, across the peaked roofs, where the first graying of the day hesitated. He had his hands folded in the small of the back and bounced slightly on the balls of his feet in an effort to alleviate the leaden feeling in his leg muscles. The boy was seated behind him. Whenever he focused his eyes to look in the window, rather than through it, he could see him sit there. On the chair, next to his desk. Vledder was a bit further away, with his back leaning against a wall.

The boy was nervous.

He had been waiting for a long time. Seated on a hard bench in the back of the waiting room. A peculiar institution, that. The waiting room in a Dutch police station. One was not, technically, under arrest. One was supposedly just waiting. One could walk around, use the vending machines, smoke, talk, visit the lavatory. But one could not leave until someone in authority had decided that the waiting was over. No matter what the reason for your visit to the station, once you had been shown to the waiting room, you could not leave until someone told you to go.

Or until someone had talked to you. Or until you talked to someone.

Finally, after an eternity it seemed, the two detectives had come to fetch him. Two plain clothed policemen. A young sporty guy and a older man with a good natured face and a pair of eyes that could penetrate to the bottom of your soul. At least, it felt that way.

They had taken him upstairs and placed him on a chair in the middle of a large room, full of desks and telephones. He had expected to be buried under an avalanche of questions, one after the other, without let-up. But that did not happen. The young detective leaned against the wall and the older man was looking out the window. Had been looking out of the window for more than fifteen minutes, without uttering a sound. What were they waiting for? He had his story ready. He had already told them his tale, downstairs. He had told the desk sergeant, how he happened to pass by, how the door of the room had been open and how he had looked inside, just curious. Then he had seen the lady, just a coincidence. That is how it happened.

A bit scared, despite himself, he looked around. Why did they not say anything? He had to go home. His parents worried if he was out this late. Finally the older man turned around.

"My name's DeKok," he said slowly, "DeKok with . . .eh, kay-oh-kay. How are you?"

The boy stood up, a bit shy, and shook hands with the gray sleuth. For a moment DeKok held the hand in his.

"A weak hand," he said, "for such a big guy. How old are you?"

"Twenty two."

DeKok nodded, as if he had expected that all along.

"Then give me a proper hand. Shake it. You must have some strength in your fingers."

The boy attempted a firmer grip, but DeKok shook his head.

"That wasn't much better," he said sadly, "I would have thought you were a lot stronger than that."

He released the hand for the second time and gave the boy an appraising look.

"How much money do you have on you?"

"About twenty five guilders."

"Your money?"

The boy nodded.

"How often do you visit the girls?"

The boy did not answer at once. His adam's apple bobbed up and down. He swallowed hard.

"Well, how often?" prompted DeKok.

"Eh, . . . about, . . . eh, once a month."

"Always the same girl?"

"Yes."

"Goldie?"

"Yessir."

DeKok sighed.

"Then why all the lies, my boy?"

With a tired gesture he picked up a piece of paper from his desk, looked at it and then looked at the boy.

"I have here," he said slowly, "a report from the desk sergeant. Apparently you told him that you happened to pass by, that you happened to see the open door and that, out of curiosity, you happened to look inside."

He looked at him evenly.

"Is that right?"

"Yes, sir."

"It was, therefore, no more than a series of coincidences?"

"Yes, sir."

"Cut that out. And stop with the 'yessir, nossir'. I'd much rather hear the truth."

"Yes, eh . . ."

"You were going to see Goldie?"

The boy nodded reluctant assent.

"I was waiting outside, under a tree, until she was ready."

"So, there was a man there, before you?"

"That's what I thought, yes, the curtains were closed."

"And then?"

"I kept waiting until the man would come out and she'd open the curtains."

"And?"

"Nobody came out and the curtains remained closed."

The young man rubbed the back of his neck.

"You see," he went on, "it took so long. I wasn't used to that. Not from her. It usually didn't take that long. Usually she'd be finished in a few minutes, fifteen minutes at most. Well, when I didn't see the curtains open, saw they remained closed, and saw nobody come outside, I thought, at first, that she had quit. Was through for the day, that is. It *was* rather late, after all. Almost one o'clock."

DeKok nodded to himself.

"So, why didn't you just leave?"

The boy blushed.

"Well," he whispered, "I . . . eh, I had been waiting a long time and . . ."

DeKok looked at him with an expressionless face.

"And you really needed to go?"

"Yessir. I had the money."

DeKok sighed.

"All right," he said wearily, "And then?"

The boy moved restlessly in his chair.

"Then, I wanted to ask her if, perhaps, she'd receive me anyway. The door wasn't open, as I told them. The door was closed. I knocked, but there was no answer. Then I pushed against the door, it was unlocked. I opened it just a little and called 'Goldie' and then a little louder, 'Goldie'. But there was no answer. And then . . ."

He stopped and worried nervously with his neck tie.

"Well," urged DeKok.

"Then I stuck my head a little farther around the door and I saw her there. She was all naked. I didn't know that she was dead. At first I thought that she was just asleep. That's why I called her again. It wasn't until I got closer that I saw the marks on her neck."

The boy lowered his head and sobbed softly.

DeKok let him be for a while, then he asked:

"Did you touch her?"

The boy shook his head wildly.

"No, no. I was too scared. I . . . eh, I just stood there for a while. Then I ran outside. I was upset, confused. I ran along the canal. I wanted to go to the police station, but I ran the wrong way. Lucky for me, I saw a constable. I grabbed him and wanted to drag him along. The constable must have thought I was crazy, or something. But after a while, he came along."

He grinned without mirth.

"Well, you know the rest," he concluded.

DeKok nodded. He rubbed his hand through his hair and walked over to the window. It was markedly lighter outside. He could see the length of the Corner Alley to the houses on the cross street at the end. For a long time he stood there and looked at nothing in particular. Then he opened the window and inhaled deeply, filling his lungs with the fresh, as yet unsullied morning air.

Still with his back toward the boy he asked:

"Why do you visit the girls, my boy? Don't you have a girl friend?"

"I'm engaged to be married."

"Engaged?"

"Yessir."

"No doubt, I think, you're engaged to a *nice* girl?"

The boy nodded emphatically.

"Yes, sir. Very nice and proper."

DeKok snorted contemptuously.

"Too proper to discuss the facts of life with her, is that it? You don't dare to discuss it with her, eh?"

"No, sir."

DeKok turned around and walked slowly closer.

"You were going to drop the 'sir'," he said amicably.

"Yes, no . . . eh,"

"Excellent," said the DeKok, "really excellent." He placed a fatherly hand on the boy's shoulder. He paused for a moment. Then he said:

"Then, this afternoon, you go and visit your proper fiancee and confess everything."

Obviously confused, the boy looked at him.

"Everything?" he asked.

DeKok nodded. His face was serious.

"Everything. Perhaps she knows a solution to your problems. Clandestine trips to the whores are no solution. There's no satisfaction in that. No fulfillment. It's just shameful. And the result . . .?" DeKok shrugged his shoulders. ". . . the result is an empty feeling inside. No more. In addition, it has nothing to do with sex, real sexuality, or love. It's just dirty."

He gripped the boy by the lapels of his jacket and pulled him slowly up, out of the chair.

"Talk to her," he said encouragingly.

"Yes, sir."

DeKok nodded.

"That's the way, my boy, very good. Go on downstairs and ask the desk sergeant for a car to take you home. Tell him I said so."

"Yes, sir. Thank you, sir."

DeKok's eyes blazed with a dangerous light.

"And . . . ," he added, almost hissing the words, raising a threatening finger, "if *sir* ever sees you again in the District, than *sir* will most personally and immediately break both your legs, understand?"

The boy looked genuinely frightened.

"Yes . . . yes, sir," he stammered and fled from the room.

DeKok shook his head sadly.

"It isn't easy," he sighed, "to be truly adult."

Vledder smiled.

"Are you sexually frustrated?" he mocked, "Do you have sexual hang-ups? *Don't* see Dr. Ruth! Visit the police station at the Warmoes Street and let Inspector DeKok solve your problems. Satisfaction guaranteed."

"Go to hell," wished DeKok.

The gray sleuth rubbed his eyes with both hands. It was a gesture of utter weariness. He looked tired and exhausted. The creases in his face looked deeper than normal.

"What's our next step?" asked Vledder.

"Sleep," he whispered, "sleep. A long, long sleep. I'm dog tired and worn out. Frazzled."

"What about the boy?" asked Vledder.

"As suspect?"

"Yes."

"Not likely. Not the type. But just to be on the safe side, check his alibi. Find out where he was when Fat Sonja was killed."

Vledder nodded.

"Anything else I can do, tonight?"

DeKok sighed.

"Pray for their souls."

He placed his ridiculous little hat firmly on top of his head, took his raincoat under one arm and strolled out of the room.

Vledder watched him leave. Perplexed.

5

It drizzled. A miserable, ground soaking drizzle.

With his hands buried deep in the pockets of his raincoat, DeKok walked leisurely through the Red Light District. The collar of his coat was turned up against the brim of his shapeless hat, to which he was very much attached.

He looked more like a retired seaman, than an experienced, dyed-in-the-wool detective, a detective who had paid his dues, over and over again. He walked along in his typical, a bit swaying, some said waddling, gait. The slick bricks of the pavement gleamed in the feeble glow of dripping street lights. The water in the canal stank. In the bend, near the bridge, floated an old mattress. Thick drops, from the trees along the canal, smashed themselves to spray on his head and shoulders. He gazed upward. The old, old facades of the 16th Century houses looked deserted and gloomy. He had come home tired and depressed and had gone straight to bed.

The Commissaris had called around three and invited him for a conference at the station. Only half awake he promised to come, but had not gone. He did not care for conferences. They never contributed to any results and inevitably degenerated into senseless suppositions and unusable plans. DeKok did not care for plans, either. He had his own methods for conducting an investigation. But after the phone call he did get out of bed and prepared a nice meal for his wife. It reconciled him with life in general.

At the corner of the Barn Alley he stopped, looked carefully all around and then he slipped quietly into the small bar on the corner. It was a ritual, dating back to his time as a very young constable. Then, his visits to bars were completely clandestine and he had to be constantly on the alert for roaming sergeants and controlling officers. But that time was far in the past. He had been a detective for more than twenty years. Nobody controlled his movements, but the ritual remained.

As soon as the heavy, leather bordered curtains closed behind him, all conversation in the bar came to an abrupt halt. In the silence he strode toward the bar and hoisted his heavy body on a barstool.

Little Lowee placed a glass in front of him and took the bottle of French cognac from under the counter. The bottle was especially reserved for DeKok.

"Back from vacation?"

The little barkeeper poured with the experience of years.

"What a business, ain't it, all them murders. We're all *that* worried about it."

DeKok pulled out a handkerchief and dried his face. He nodded slowly, eyeing the glass.

Behind him, the other visitors to the small, intimate bar, stared at his broad back. He could feel their penetrating glances. His face was expressionless. He pushed his lower lip forward and calmly took the first sip from his glass. Then he emptied it all the way. Then he wiped his mouth with the back of his hand and slowly turned around on the stool. He looked at the collection of somber faces. He knew them. They were all old acquaintances: the varied population of the Red Light District, the taunting pimps, those slimy traders in sex and flesh and the whores in their provocative and brightly colored clothes.

Blonde Annie was closest to him. He stretched out his hand and placed the tips of his fingers against her neck.

"Are you the next one, my child?"

He grinned in a friendly way.

The girl uttered a low screech and stepped back in fear. To her overactive imagination it seemed as if a glowing coal had been pressed against her flesh, instead of DeKok's cool fingers. She placed both hands around her neck and stared at him. Her big, blue eyes mirrored dread.

"I . . . , me . . . ," she stammered.

DeKok nodded slowly.

"Yes," he said. "You . . . or somebody else."

"Macho" Pete, her pimp, pushed his wide shoulders forward. Threatening, he placed himself in front of DeKok. His face was distorted by fury.

"I don't like those kind of jokes," he yelled pugnaciously. "you better cut it out. You're scaring the shit out of the broad."

"Is that so?" queried DeKok, glancing up at the hulking figure of the pimp. "Is that so? Why, are you so certain she's *not* the next victim?" Pensively he rubbed his chin with one hand. "It would be an interesting thought," he contemplated. "Now that you mention it, I wonder. How come your Annie wasn't among the first two?"

Macho Pete was speechless. Dumbfounded he tried to tuck his shirt into his pants and grinned sheepishly.

"Yes . . . ," remarked "Apeman" Anton suddenly, as if struck by an idea all his own. "Yes," he gripped Pete by an arm, "now that you mention it, why my Goldie and not your Annie?"

They looked at each other menacingly.

Little Lowee, from behind the bar, smelled danger. Quickly he walked around the bar and pressed his slight body between the two giants.

"Don't you understand!" he yelled. "Don't you understand, idiots! He just wants to scare the shit out of *you!* He wants to wake you up. He wants you to *know!* Ain't two murders enough for you?"

Slowly the words penetrated the thick skulls. They turned from each other and looked at DeKok, who, apparently totally disinterested, slurped from his second cognac. It was an uncivilized sound.

"So, what can we do about it, already?" asked "Macho" Pete.

"Try to prevent a third killing," nodded DeKok pleasantly.

Suddenly a loud voice echoed through the smoky room.

"It's a sign from Heaven!" proclaimed the voice. "God's finger points the way!"

Near the door, just inside the heavy curtains stood an old man, with a long, gray beard.

Father Matthias.

* * *

Father Matthias was a self-proclaimed missionary and as such accepted by the Quarter. When he did not raise his voice, but engaged in normal conversation, man to man, or, more in line with his calling, man to woman, it was a delight to listen to him. His deep voice spoke of God, the Father who loved His children, including whores.

His actions were not supported, or condoned, by any official church organization, because he was considered too bizarre. With his wavy gray hair and imposing beard he resembled the traditional image of an Old Testament prophet. Instead of a shepherd's staff he carried an umbrella and instead of a long robe, he wore a stained black cutaway coat with tails and striped trousers that were several lengths too short.

57

Father Matthias did not offer help in words alone, but also in deeds. Whenever one of the prostitutes indicated that she would like to leave the slippery, downward path into sin, he was always ready to help during the initial, difficult period of adjustment with practical advice and money. He lent her enough money to get started in a new life. The loans were seldom, if ever, repaid.

Usually the women could not stay away from the life and would reappear in the Quarter after just a few months. Father Matthias would express sadness, but would never ask the money back. This, and other types of charities, soon depleted his reserves.

But Father Matthias was given the freedom of the house in any brothel. Nobody ever tried to stop him, or hinder him. Only if his preaching lasted a little too long, would the Madam, gently, but insistently, remove him from the premises. Because charity and God's Word are good, but it should never interfere with business.

* * *

DeKok listened intently.

In the slovenly, smelly bar on the edge of the District, on the corner of the Barn Alley, Father Matthias spoke about Sodom and Gomorrah, the two cities that had earned God's wrath because of their moral and sexual depravity. As punishment both cities had been wiped off the face of the Earth. It seemed a most appropriate sermon to DeKok.

Father Matthias was an inspired speaker, in full command of an extensive arsenal of Bible texts, which he used gratefully and without hesitation. It was remarkable how the visitors to the bar were spellbound by his rhetoric. These people, who regularly broke almost all of God's Commandments, were mesmerized by the old man who testified to the Word of God.

DeKok was not a particularly religious man and he watched the phenomenon with a certain amount of healthy skepticism. His cool, calculating policeman's brain found the picture incongruous. He watched the faces of the audience and searched for an explanation. It was fear, he speculated, fear, stimulated by the murders that had taken two of their number already. If they had been committed by the same person, then there *had* to be a connection. Fat Sonja and Pale Goldie were both prostitutes and both had been strangled. Thus far that was the only obvious connection. There were simply no other coinciding factors. Their ages were not the same and also the physical types could not have been more different.

DeKok reflected.

Although he did not believe it himself, there was a possibility that the killer was a sexual deviant, a sadist, who could only achieve orgasm by murdering, by strangling his partner. But if that was indeed the case, his search would have to concentrate on a person with such a pronounced sexual abnormality that he would be either locked up already, or so well hidden in society that the discovery would be almost impossible. How large was the circle of suspects? Almost all men who regularly visited prostitutes had some sort of aberration. But *that* violent? It would have been discovered sooner, surely.

Father Matthias continued his sermon. DeKok tuned out. The words became a soft background murmur. They washed around him without being noticed. His attention was focused on the old man's audience.

Fat Sonja and Pale Goldie had both been strangled on a Sunday. A strange coincidence, thought DeKok, these Sunday murders. A Sunday strangler.

Suddenly he looked closer at the graybeard, his long hair waving around him, his arms gesticulating in the air. Suddenly he saw the old man in a different light. Father Matthias and the Sunday killings. Was it a coincidence? His brain went into high gear. Accepting, inspecting and rejecting a number of theories. Sunday was the Lord's day. Coincidence? God's wrath? Sodom and Gomorrah? Coincidence? DeKok was shocked by his own thoughts. Could Father Matthias have been helping God? Did he hear voices? Did he consider himself to be the instrument of God's vengeance? He sighed. It was almost a blasphemous thought.

Lost in thought, DeKok slurped softly from his cognac. It was a most uncivilized sound, but subdued. He liked cognac. A moderate amount stimulated his thought processes. It helped him think.

When Father Matthias stopped speaking, he left his rough audience in a brooding state of confusion and introspection. DeKok paid his check, slid off the barstool and wended his way to the exit. He passed through the heavy curtains and stood outside. It was still raining.

DeKok peered down the quiet canal quays. Only here and there was the gloom penetrated by the reddish light of a window. A few vague figures moved slowly from one lit window to the next.

A little further down the street he observed the silhouette of an open umbrella and fluttering coattails.

He waited a moment and let the distance between him and the apparition increase slightly. Then he pulled up his collar, pushed his hat further down on his head and waddled in the direction of the disappearing shadow.

DeKok was a master in stalking somebody through the inner city of Amsterdam. Even at night, when he did not have the protective camouflage of crowds, he could follow anybody through the quiet, empty streets without being noticed. He used porticos, lobbies, doorways, trash cans, parked cars, store windows and other obstacles. He was like a chameleon. "See, without being seen" took on an entirely new meaning, when applied by DeKok on his native grounds.

But all his tricks and experience were not necessary this evening. The man he followed was not aware that he was being followed. Did not even think of the possibility. He did not look around, did not look left, or right. Stubbornly he plodded on. The umbrella cocked at an angle in front him, he passed through the High Street in the direction of the Dam, the large square in front of the Royal Place. He crossed the wide expanse, paved with cobble stones. DeKok followed at a distance. Past the palace the man disappeared into the Town Hall Street. For an old man, he maintained a considerable pace.

He stopped under a tree on the West Market. His back rested against a tree. The old man seemed tired, suddenly. Hesitatingly DeKok approached.

Unexpectedly a young man appeared from the shadows behind the church. A muscular, powerful young man. He walked slightly bent over with a slow, ponderous, pigeon-toed gait. He carried a parcel under one arm. He approached the old man and unrolled the parcel. It was a blanket.

Engrossed, DeKok watched.

Carefully, with a tender gesture, the young man placed the blanket around the old man's shoulders. Then he placed his arm protectively around the old man and led him gently away.

DeKok followed the pair.

They climbed the stoop of one of the old houses which leaned against the church. Their progress was labored. The old man must have exhausted his reserves. They stopped at the top of the stoop. The young man felt in his pockets, leaned forward and opened the door. Together they entered.

From the shadow formed by one of the supporting buttresses of the church, DeKok watched the house. He saw a light go on behind the door. A little later the hulking figure of the young man was briefly visible behind one of the windows. He closed the curtains.

* * *

Carefully DeKok emerged from the shadows and strolled away. His rolling, waddling gait made one think of a drunkard on his way home. The suppressed cursing sounded like the incoherent babbling of the habitual tippler. But he cursed his job, the rotten job that caused him to follow an old man in the rain.

It was still raining; a fine drizzle that slowly penetrated his raincoat. The warmth of the cognac glowed in his stomach, but he feared it might not be enough to counteract the next cold. He decided to return to Little Lowee and have one for the road.

Before crossing the Dam Square, he stopped under the portico of the Royal Palace and shook out his hat. A couple was lost in a deep embrace within the shadows formed by one of the pillars. DeKok sighed. How can they do that, he thought, in this weather.

It was still and quiet along the canals. The rain discouraged the lecherous and the needy customers of the District. The women displayed boredom, as well as female pulchritude behind their windows. They were reading books, or were knitting. DeKok wondered what he could possibly hope to find along the canals at this hour. He really could not adequately explain, even to himself, his reasons for crossing and re-crossing the District. Without a goal, aimlessly. His thoughts were in disorder. There was no system, no rationality to his thoughts. He only knew that he *had* to find the murderer, and soon, before more accidents could happen. It was a desperate feeling. He had not been joking in Little Lowee's bar. He meant what he said, there. The killer would not be satisfied with the first two victims. One of the girls would be the next target. But who?

He stopped on the opposite side of a canal, across from Aunt Dina's establishment. He rubbed his hands over his wet face. What decided the killer. How did he make his selection? What influenced him for one, rather than another? It was not a matter of chance encounters and spur-of-the-moment action. The murderer did not have to wait for the right opportunity. He had a choice. No matter which whore he visited, the circumstances were always ideal. Because of their profession, the victims placed themselves in a defenseless position. Naked, on their backs, they were unable to protect themselves from a strangler. DeKok pressed his lips together. Did the murderer follow an impulse, or did he have a system? If so, what kind of system. The thought hammered around in his head. What decided the choice!?

Just as he was ready to move again, he heard a low whistle from above his head. He looked up. The rain penetrated past his eyelids and blinded him. Then he saw the head of a woman emerge from an opened window on the floor above. He could not discern any facial features. He oriented himself quickly and realized it had to be Barbara, "Boobs" Barbara. She motioned to him. DeKok pushed the door open and climbed up the stairs.

"Come in," said a warm voice.

DeKok handed her his wet hat.

She pulled up her nose.

"You better take that dirty coat off, as well," she said, "and wipe your feet."

DeKok obeyed willingly.

She put his wet stuff away and threw him a towel. DeKok dried his face and pulled a comb through his bristly hair. The room had been cozily decorated. It was also nice and warm. A big, black tomcat occupied the space directly in front of the fire place. The cat lifted its head slightly, winked and went back to sleep. The cat was used to many visitors.

"What are you looking for on the canal?" she asked.

DeKok lowered himself into one of the easy chairs.

"A murderer," he answered.

She placed herself on the long couch opposite him. She looked adorable in a man's shirt over a pair of tight fitting jeans. The long blond hair cascaded down to her shoulders and encircled the elfin face with the pale, healthy skin. She pulled her knees under her chin and placed her arms around her legs. Her blue eyes laughed at him amiably. He avoided her gaze. The tenderness he read in the eyes confused him.

"I saw you standing there," she said. "That old hat gives you away. I would have recognized you anywhere."

DeKok smiled tentatively.

"Is it important for you to recognize me?"

She shrugged her shoulders slightly.

"Why would a woman be interested in being able to recognize a particular man anywhere?"

DeKok did not answer. He knew what she meant. He had known her for years and this was not the first time she had hinted at the affection she had for him. It always gave him a strange feeling inside. He did not understand it.

"I'm working on the murders," he said evasively.

"Yes," she said, "I know. I saw you in action across the canal, last night. You never, even once, glanced in this direction."

There was a slight reproach in her voice.

DeKok sighed again.

"If you keep on like this," he said sadly, "I better get going."

The expression on her face changed suddenly.

"Oh, no," there was more than a hint of despair in her voice. "Please stay. On nights like this, when even the trees weep, I feel so lonely, lonelier than ever."

DeKok looked at her for a long time.

"Why don't you give it up? You're still young. Find a decent, hardworking man."

A faint smile played around her lips.

"A good man is hard to find. There are precious few like you."

DeKok shook his head.

"You weren't going to mention that again."

She unfolded her arms and placed her feet on the floor. She hitched a little closer to the edge of the couch. Her face was serious.

"Why not? Why shouldn't I talk about it. Why do you always silence me when I want to tell you. Is it so bad? I've always longed for a big, strong man. A man like you. A man with a hungry look in his eyes when he looks at my hips."

He scratched the back of his neck. It was an embarrassed gesture. He caught himself doing it often, but was unable to stop the habit.

"Perhaps . . . ," he said slowly, hesitatingly, "perhaps I can hide it better. Or . . . perhaps I'm not that hungry, anymore."

She looked at him probingly.

"So why are you here?"

"You called me. Remember?"

She nodded cheerfully.

"This time. But what about the other times, when I didn't call you?"

DeKok rubbed his face with both hands.

"Come, Barbara, let's stop this. I'm old enough to be your father. When I come to visit you, to talk, then that's . . . because you're a nice girl and because . . . I . . . eh, hope to see you quit this life, one of these days."

She stretched out a hand and stroked the sleeve of his jacket.

"Why do you want me to quit. Why do you insist on it? What possible benefit could you gain from it? Why should you care, whether I sit here, or another girl? What difference does it make to you?"

DeKok sighed.

"You're being difficult, tonight. It's probably the weather. The continuous drizzle tends to make people melancholy. I understand your loneliness. Of course, you're lonely. You have no customers and you're bored. That's why you play me with me, declare your love for me . . . as a diversion." He shook his head. "But that's hardly fair, Barbara. I don't think I deserve that, do you? I don't know how often I've stopped by, over the years, just to talk. Just to talk about things in general, not your 'business', just things. I knew you liked that, needed that, because in your heart you're revolted by what you do, by the neighborhood."

He paused and sighed again, sadly.

"All right, stipulated, I like you. But what does that mean? If I came to visit you for the same purpose as those 'hungry' men you talk about, you would, inevitably, despise me just as much. You see, and I don't want that. I don't want you to learn to despise me."

She lowered her head and did not answer. Finally, after a long silence, she looked up. There was a tear on her cheek and her mascara was smeared.

"You don't blame me, do you?"

Her lips trembled.

DeKok smiled tenderly.

"But of course not, my child, how could I?"

He placed a hand on her knee.

"Come on," he said amicably, "See if my coat has dried out a little."

She stood up and walked to the other room, the room with her bed. With a thoughtful look he saw her go and contemplated the exciting curve of her hips. He rubbed his face and stood up as well. Wearily he came to his feet. She helped him with his coat.

"Have a talk with Father Matthias," he said, "or contact your parents. I'm sure they'd be happy to receive you with open arms."

She smiled cheerlessly.

"I'll think about it," she promised,

He accepted his hat from her and stumbled down the stairs. It was still raining. DeKok sighed deeply. He did not look back.

* * *

The next day DeKok did not appear in the station. His chair remained empty. The familiar silhouette of his imposing figure in front of the window, his dominating personality, had, over the years, become so much an essential part of the atmosphere in the large detective room at the Warmoes Street, that his absence was immediately felt as something tangible, as if a vital part of the interior was missing.

65

Young Vledder worried about it. Without DeKok he felt unsure of himself and at a loss as to what steps to take next in the investigation which, no doubt, had to be pursued. In DeKok's wake, following him, it all seemed so simple, so devoid of problems, a piece of cake, a kid's game of questions and answers.

After a few hours of DeKok's continued absence, Vledder had called and reached Mrs. DeKok on the telephone. She had told him that DeKok would not be in the office that day. That was all. He had not dared to inquire further. DeKok was not coming in and that was it.

The Commissaris was in a bad mood. He walked around with a sulky face. Several times he had asked for DeKok and Vledder had tried to pacify him and explain DeKok's absence with a number of excuses. But the old man had seen right through the excuses. His mood had not improved because of it. Yesterday, without so much as a by-your-leave, DeKok had ignored the conference that he, the Commissaris, had personally arranged. He simply had not shown up. It annoyed the Commissaris greatly.

Everybody knew that DeKok was stubborn and intractable, a loner, who simply refused to be led by superiors and who ignored established procedure and authority as it suited him. It was well known. If DeKok had not in the past, often and brilliantly, proven his remarkable gifts as a sleuth, his career with the detective force would have long since been terminated prematurely. But deep down the powers-that-be were wary of the old, experienced Inspector. As a rule he was allowed to go his own way. It was generally for the best.

But the Commissaris always had trouble accepting what he termed DeKok's buccaneering ways. It undermined his authority, he felt. It was utterly irritating that in retrospect DeKok always had an acceptable explanation and a good reason for his unorthodox methods. That, more than anything, kept his superiors uncertain and apprehensive about his behavior. There had been many who had attempted to limit his freedom of action, to guide it into hierarchical procedure. They always succeeded, but never for long.

Whenever DeKok was confronted with his lack of discipline, he always showed sincere remorse and obedience, and as of that moment did not take any action without official permission or sanction, or without a direct order. The result was that he showed no initiative at all and the case slowly, but surely bogged down in a morass of administrative red tape.

Resigned and at wit's end, his superiors would release the restraints of officialdom and give him again a free hand. By preference they would then place him in charge of dead-end cases, or they would assign him to small, meaningless thefts, or misdemeanors. DeKok never objected.

He knew that, sooner or later, they would recall him from this apparent purgatory. As soon as a really important case made no progress. When the rest of the force was in a quandary, they called for DeKok. That is why he took the liberty to stay home, not to appear in the office. It was Monday, and that seemed to be an excellent day to take his dog for a walk.

First he and his wife leisurely drank their coffee. They talked companionably about everything and nothing; they discussed the wedding present for Niece Clara, who, rather late and unexpectedly, had finally found a man and as such had become a frequent topic of conversation within the DeKok clan.

When that subject had been exhausted, at least for the moment, he called the City Registry and asked for particulars regarding the family connections of a man widely known as Father Matthias and about a woman, just as widely known as "Boobs" Barbara. He marked the supplied information in his notebook and comfortably sat down for his third cup of coffee.

"Who's Barbara?" inquired his wife curiously.

DeKok smiled like a sphinx.

"A darling little whore," he answered smirking.

His wife raised her eyebrows.

"Darling whores?" she queried with just a hint of suspicion, "do they exist?"

DeKok nodded emphatically.

"Barbara is one of them. The child doesn't belong in the Quarter at all, at all. I think she should be a nice little housewife with a brood of nice little children and a good husband. Perhaps a rough-and-ready, slightly uncouth character, but with a good heart."

"A man like you?"

67

DeKok looked sharply at his wife.

"Strange," he remarked, "that's exactly what *she* said."

His wife studied the expression of the beloved face across the table.

"Do you know her well?"

Reluctantly he shrugged his shoulders.

"Well . . . it depends on what you mean by that. I know she's from a small town. She finished high school and some years of college. After her schooling she wound up in an office. She had a relationship with one of her bosses, an older, married man, with daughters of his own. Daughters close to her age. When the relationship leaked out, there was a lot of talk. She was vilified. The man went back to his wife and asked forgiveness for his 'mistake'. He was welcomed back with love and open arms."

"And what about Barbara?"

DeKok stirred his coffee.

"People," he said pensively, "are sometimes cruel and unjust. Barbara was blamed for everything. Of course, so they said, she had seduced the respected and virtuous father and husband. It was a scandal. The nice little town was in an uproar. People cursed her as a slut and pointed at her in the street. After a while Barbara couldn't stand it any longer and moved to Amsterdam to make their accusations true. Partly from spite, I'm convinced, she became a prostitute."

"Was she guilty?"

He made a vague, apologetic gesture.

"Ach," he said, "what's guilt? Who talks about guilt? Such things happen. In a big city it's hardly noticeable. But in a small town there can be enormous consequences for the parties involved. Barbara was neither better, nor worse, than other girls of her age."

He sighed, peered into his empty coffee cup.

"It was just too bad that her love, her infatuation, was focused on an older man, a married man. Otherwise, I think, nothing much would have happened. By now she could be living in a small apartment, with clean curtains and her days would be occupied with the washing of diapers. She would be horrified by the mere mention of prostitution."

His wife smiled at him.

"Her interests," she said quietly, "seem to be channelled toward older men."

DeKok rubbed his face with his hands. He knew every intonation of her voice and he could taste the gentle hint about his age.

"I'm not all that old," he answered in a slightly petulant tone of voice. "Anyway . . . anyway, it doesn't mean a thing. I'm probably the only decent man to ever enter her room, these days. Besides . . ." he grinned, totally unaware how attractive that made him look, ". . . besides what woman could really be interested in my dog face?"

Laughing, she walked around the table.

"Me," she said, "you should know that."

He looked at her.

"Ach," he said, melancholy in his voice, "one can get used to everything."

Wearily he pushed himself away from the table and stood up. He kissed his wife on the forehead and took the dog's leash off the back of his chair. Flip was waiting attentively with raised head and wagging tail. DeKok patted the dog's flank gently and put the leash around its neck.

"Come on, pal," he said, "let's go for a walk."

He put his notebook in a pocket before leaving.

6

The funeral was a demonstration of grief.

Near the gate, a bit shyly, they were bunched together in mourning along the edge of the driveway; the rawboned pimps, strangely awkward in expensive suits, the fat brothel keepers laden down with gold and jewels and the wide variety of prostitutes with too much make-up. They stared with somber faces at the well kept grounds and the funeral attendants in formal clothes and top hats who walked to and fro with official self importance. It was busy at the cemetery. One cortege after another, consisting of black, gleaming limousines and flower-bedecked hearses moved with precise orchestration. Death is a business without recession.

DeKok had forced himself into a dark suit. His favorite outfit consisted of slacks without a crease and a shapeless coat of good tweed. But for Pale Goldie's funeral he had unearthed his dark suit from the moth balls. He considered the torture of the constriction caused by a cut that was just not generous enough, a small token of respect for the victim. But he had been unable to part with his old, felt hat. Despite the protests of his wife he had not left his faithful head gear at home. There were limits, he thought.

Vledder face was a study in amazement when he saw DeKok, dressed in his unusual attire, approach across the gravel of the driveway. He met him halfway.

"My, you look formal," he mocked.

DeKok looked at him.

"You made no special effort, I see."

"What do you mean?"

"You're dressed like always."

Vledder grinned. His grin was not as pleasant as that of DeKok.

"What did you expect?" he asked contemptuously, "Perhaps you think I should mourn about a whore?"

He shrugged his shoulders nonchalantly.

"I'm on duty. You told me never to miss the funeral of a victim. Well I'm here. What else do you want?"

DeKok's eyes flashed angrily.

He looked around to see if anybody would notice and then he placed his big hand in the middle of Vledder's chest and grabbed a handful of shirt. The shirt crackled in his grip. He pushed.

He had wanted to say something about living and dying, about death and eternity. But because he suddenly did not know how to voice his thoughts about that subject, how to express his feelings, he let go of the younger man and remained silent. He already regretted his loss of control and tried to smooth the wrinkles in the shirt with his rough hands.

"Sorry, my boy," he said hoarsely and ambled away.

The chapel filled slowly with visitors. Soft organ music accompanied the shuffling footsteps. The coffin was placed in the center, surrounded by wreaths and flowers. DeKok remained in the background, his crumpled hat forgotten in his hands. His gaze drifted from the pipes of the organ, along the murals to the somber faces of the onlookers.

Father Matthias stepped forward when the organ music faded into silence. He had combed his hair for the occasion and he had brushed his old, decrepit coat. His voice echoed against the walls. Again, he spoke of God's wrath and about Sodom and Gomorrah. His speech seemed a copy of the sermon in Little Lowee's bar.

DeKok listened intently. He did not allow the words to drift by him, but he absorbed them one by one and examined them. He listened carefully to the intonation and again he had the feeling that they meant something special. He looked at the graybeard, the expression on his face and his sinewy hands.

The end of Father Matthias' speech was mild. He spoke about Christ who loved sinners especially; Christ who had suffered so much to make forgiveness possible for all sins. His voice trembled with tenderness and a soft sobbing came from the audience.

The organ began again and the doors opened. Silent funeral attendants placed themselves next to the coffin. They lifted the coffin on their shoulders and carried it off. The mourners followed. Silently they shuffled out of the bleak Chapel into the bright sunlight.

DeKok followed slowly, by himself. From the corner of his eye he noticed Vledder unobtrusively walking among the crowd.

The procession followed a long route over the gravel among a forest of grave markers; "Here rests. . ." repeated a thousand times. The living had caused it to be carved with conviction into the patient stones.

"Here rests," murmured DeKok to himself. He was not at all sanguine about that.

Suddenly he noticed, diagonally in front of him, the figure of a young woman, elegantly dressed in a dark suit and a hat with veil. At first he just noticed her self-possessed demeanor, the supple line and the grace with which she moved. His critical glance moved up from the slender legs and he discovered Barbara's face behind the veil.

He was startled.

It was not so much her physical presence that surprised him pleasantly, as much as the complete transformation. He did not know her this way. The other women, despite efforts to hide it with their attire and attitude, were unable to totally remove the evidence of their profession.

But not Barbara.

Nobody would have guessed that she could be a prostitute. Not from the way she was dressed and not from the way she behaved. She walked slightly apart from the others. She walked alone, as if a stranger. DeKok increased his pace and walked beside her. She looked at him and smiled vaguely. DeKok leaned toward her and spoke softly:

"Wait for me," he whispered, "wait afterwards, near the exit."

She nodded. It was barely perceptible.

* * *

Meanwhile, the procession had arrived at the grave site. They formed into a wide circle. DeKok walked away from Barbara and shuffled toward the outskirts of the crowd. He stopped when he saw, a few backs removed, the figure of Father Matthias. He recognized the man next to Father Matthias by his posture. DeKok pressed himself a little closer until both backs were directly in front of him.

"You spoke beautifully, father," said the man.

Father Matthias shook his head.

"It wasn't me, Tobias," he said with a hint of reproach in his voice, "but God. I was merely the tool in His hands."

The man nodded.

"What do you think, father," he continued, "will God accept her with mercy?"

72

Father Matthias placed his hand on the arm of the man in a confidential gesture.

"God's mercy," he whispered, "is infinite."

The attendants removed their top hats and lowered the coffin.

* * *

When the mourners had left, DeKok remained alone next to the grave. As was his duty, he looked into the pit and observed that the coffin was still sealed. The seals were intact. The steel bands were clearly visible. He remained a little longer and murmured a few words in farewell. Then he turned abruptly, placed his hat back where it belonged and waddled down a side path, where Vledder waited for him.

"Well, how did it go, my boy," he asked, "did you notice anything in particular?"

Vledder shook his head, smiling at his mentor.

"No clandestine spectators," he said. "Just a young widow who seemed particularly interested in me."

DeKok grinned.

"Just you be careful," he admonished, "it wouldn't be the first time that a new romance begins at the grave site of a recently deceased husband."

Vledder laughed.

"It doesn't seem to be such an ideal spot for romance," he remarked.

"Don't be mistaken, my boy," answered DeKok. "There are plenty of contacts made at cemeteries and grave sites that result in eventual nuptials. It seems that mourning visitors are easily attracted to each other."

Vledder looked at him suspiciously.

"No kidding, you mean it?"

DeKok nodded.

"I don't think," he said, "that exact statistics are available, but the frequency would probably astound you."

"Not my cup of tea, though."

They strolled toward the exit. DeKok walked with his hands buried deep in his pockets. He had loosened his too tight vest and breathed more freely. In the Chapel, during the eulogy the tightness around his chest had particularly distressed him.

Somewhere, deep down in his thoughts, obscured by more recent memories, there had been an idea. A spark of insight. The beginning of an idea. DeKok had wanted to nurse it, feed it, until the tiny spark had increased sufficiently in strength to set off the larger mechanism of his brain, but the tightness in his chest had disturbed the smooth deduction process. The spark had died and did not return. Suddenly he halted and looked at Vledder in an absent-minded way.

"Do you have any ministers, or priests, among your acquaintances?" he asked.

Vledder frowned, taken aback.

"Priest, ministers?" he asked perplexed.

DeKok nodded impatiently.

"Priests or ministers," he repeated.

Vledder shrugged his shoulders with a gesture of total incomprehension.

"I . . . eh, I'm not very religious," he stammered.

"That's not what I asked you," retorted DeKok, irked by Vledder's hesitation.

Silently they walked on. Just before reaching the exit, DeKok stopped again. His face looked thoughtful.

Vledder looked at him searchingly.

"What's the matter? You're miles away. Is something bothering you?"

DeKok ignored him. It was one of his maddening characteristics, at times. He walked away from Vledder and approached Barbara who was waiting for him near the gate. Again he realized how beautiful she was, how attractive. The blonde hair which could not be contained by the hat, glistened in the sun like spun gold. A few funeral attendants gave her admiring looks as they passed.

"Hey," yelled Vledder, "I'm talking to you!"

DeKok looked at him, distracted.

"Oh, yes," he said hesitatingly, "I've got a job for you. Visit a priest, or a minister, this afternoon. Just pick one. I don't care who."

Vledder grinned suddenly.

74

"Why should I, for crying out loud. You don't want me to repent, do you?"

DeKok pushed his hat further back on his head.

"That is your own business," he said suddenly very serious. "I just want you to ask which town was destroyed for moral turpitude, *after* Sodom and Gomorrah. Priests and ministers ought to know that sort of thing."

Vledder's mouth fell open with utter astonishment. He had wanted to ask about the who, what and wherefore, but DeKok had already walked away.

Barbara smiled.

"You always make dates in the cemetery?"

DeKok shook his head.

"I just want to offer you a lift. My car is close by."

He took her arm and led her away in the direction of his car.

"You look extremely nice today," he said admiringly, "I almost didn't recognize you."

She smiled at him.

"Thank you," she answered. "as long as I've known you, this is the first time you gave me a compliment."

DeKok did not react. He unlocked the car and gallantly held the door for her. When he was seated next to her, he cocked his head at her.

"I plan to kidnap you," he said with a straight face. "I'm warning you in advance. If you don't want to be kidnapped, now's the time to get out."

She laughed.

"You don't really think," she said defiantly, "that I would leave after such a challenge. I love it! I've never been kidnapped."

She obviously enjoyed the situation. She placed her hat and veil on the rear seat and shook her hair loose. Her eyes shined. DeKok started the engine, but did not drive away.

"This is not a joke, Barbara," he said. "You can still leave."

She looked at him. In his eyes she saw again the look of tender affection. She knew that he loved her in his own, confused way, that he could put up with her, no matter what.

"Come on," she cried impatiently, "what are we waiting for?"

He shrugged his shoulders and sighed.

"So be it," he said resignedly and engaged the gears.

With consummate skill he manoeuvred the car through the busy traffic in the city. It took all his attention. Not until after he had reached the wide highway out of town, did he move his seat slightly further back and did he relax a little. The speedometer locked on fifty five.

"I'd never imagined," she said pleasantly, "that you'd do it."

"Do what?"

"Well, this."

She remained silent for several miles.

"Don't you have any regrets about your job? You're such an unique and born policeman."

DeKok sighed.

"I wouldn't worry about the future, if I were you," she continued soothingly. "I can make enough money. We just start over, somewhere else. In Rotterdam, or The Hague, for instance. Somewhere where they don't know us."

She moved closer to him.

"Or would you prefer," she asked in a sultry voice, "that I give it up, stop doing it?"

"That's it," he said calmly. "I want you to stop doing it."

She smiled tenderly.

"But it doesn't matter. That other means nothing. You know that, don't you? It's just business. You have to keep those things separate."

DeKok tightened his grip on the steering wheel. He did not have the courage to tell her the truth.

"We can also try," she continued cheerfully, "to get a girl to replace me in the District, we can 'rent' her my room. We don't have to skin her, but it would be nice to have the extra income. If you knew what I . . ."

DeKok could not contain himself any longer.

"Barbara . . ." he yelled angrily.

She placed a hand on his knee.

"Hush," she soothed, "if you're absolutely against it . . ."

DeKok's face was a mask. Only his nostrils quivered slightly in indignation. It was the only outward sign of his inner feelings. He knew what she wanted. He understood her meaning. No matter the utter immorality of her proposals, DeKok recognized the deep love that prompted them. He knew a lot about the thought processes of the women who engaged in prostitution. After a while they thought a certain way. And he knew how deeply disappointed she would be when she realized his true intent, when she understood what he really wanted.

It was deception. Only the previous day he had talked to her parents, found out that they would eagerly welcome her, with love and without recriminations. He had not needed to say much of anything. The old people looked forward to the reunion. But he had no wish to shock them.

Therefore he hoped that she would be more or less presentably dressed, during the funeral. Then he had shamelessly counted on the affection she so obviously had for him. He wanted her away from the Red Light District. At all costs, at any price. She had to go, she should not be allowed to remain. And not just from a strictly impersonal, business motive. DeKok was enough of a realist to know that the physical removal from Amsterdam was not designed to keep a person like Barbara from prostitution. On the contrary, such an action could very well result in her doing the exact opposite. To persist at all costs, at any price. He knew that, he understood that.

But she had to leave. It was imperative. There was a killer at large, a murderer who, DeKok was convinced, would kill again.

He could not evacuate the entire neighborhood because of one killer. That was both too silly and too impractical to contemplate. But Barbara . . . Suddenly he realized how much he cared for her. She, Barbara, was not going to be the next victim.

She had nestled closer to him. He felt the warmth of her body and smelled the sweet fragrance of her perfume. A slight shiver crawled over his skin and tingled in his finger tips. His reason was at war with his body, a body of whose strength and weaknesses he was fully aware. Next to him, nestled trustfully against him, was the possibility to change his life completely. What was immorality? His years of digging in the dirt, his life among the prostitutes and pimps, the continued confrontation with crime had blunted his personal limits somewhat. What was immorality?

He kept his eyes locked on the road. The tires hummed and next to him Barbara babbled about her plans for the future, *their* future.

DeKok, not for the first time, sighed.

What *was* his future? Another ten years, or so, and then a pension. And what could he look back on? What was the result of all his exertions? Crime prospered, even more so then when he started, some twenty years ago, full of illusions to do battle. What was immorality?

Suddenly it seemed as if something inside him snapped. What was he doing? What drove his brain on this tortuous path? Barbara? He inhaled the scent of her perfume and stole a guilty glance at her long, slender legs. A tight feeling came over him, a suffocating feeling, a feeling that restrained the fervent rhythm of his heart. The soft hand on his knee burned into his skin. Suddenly he knew where the feeling originated, he knew the source of his thoughts. It was a painful discovery. Fool, he cursed himself, old fool! He rubbed his eyes and laughed out loud. It was a short, cheerless laughter, echo of a strange sorrow.

"What's the matter?" she wondered.

He did not answer. But when the big, blue signs announced the approach of the small town, he reduced the speed and turned off the highway.

"Where are you taking me?" she asked anxiously.

DeKok sighed deeply

"Don't you recognize the area?"

She pushed herself away from him.

"Take me back!" she screamed. "I see it! I know! You're taking me home!"

DeKok nodded slowly, sadly.

"Your parents are waiting for you."

In a sudden explosion of fury, she belabored his arms and face with her fists. Tears streaked her face. All of her emotions, so long kept under strict control, discharged at the same time. She lashed out in a frenzy. DeKok did not try to defend himself against her attacks. He succumbed without protest, like a sinner convinced of a well deserved penance. He did not feel her fists. She was unable to hurt him physically. Calmly he drove on. Now and again, for just a moment, he closed his eyes tightly and swallowed his heartache.

7

"Moshe has a new cart."

DeKok was standing in front of the window of the detective room in his favorite position, legs straddled wide, hands on his back.

"Nice one. Business must be good. Five years ago he only had a bucket. You know, a white enamel bucket with a plank for cleaning the fish. He'd drop the guts, heads and scales anywhere."

He turned to Vledder.

"Just look at him now."

He laughed heartily.

"That Moshe! Smart fellow . . . even as a kid. In a few years he'll be able to rent the station as a warehouse."

He laughed again.

"He won't have to change much. It already stinks of fish."

Vledder came over and stood next to him.

"Nice cart," he commented admiringly.

Together they watched as Moshe handily manoeuvred his movable stall around the corner of the alley across the street. A little further on, grandma shook her dust rag out of a window. When Moshe had disappeared from sight, Vledder looked intently at DeKok. A faint smile played around the lips of the younger man.

"How did you get that scratch?" he asked.

"That scratch . . ." said DeKok, evading the issue. "That, oh, that . . . eh, I think I caught it shaving."

Vledder grinned maliciously.

"You shave that close to your eyes?"

DeKok looked in the mirror above the small sink.

"Is it that high?"

He feigned surprise.

Vledder followed him. DeKok saw his grinning face next to his own in the reflection.

"Yes, rather high, don't you think? To happen while shaving, I mean."

Grinning, DeKok faced him.

"You'll make a good detective, one of these days," he said. "Just stick with me for a few more years and I'll be able to take my pension with a clear conscience."

Vledder did not let himself be distracted.

"No kidding," he said, "did you get it from the lady?"

"What lady?"

"Well, the lady you left with, after the funeral."

DeKok looked at him seriously for several seconds.

"Yes," he admitted finally, "yes that scratch is from that lady. Her name, by the way, is Barbara. She's a prostitute from the neighborhood." He paused again, then added: "And just in case your imagination starts to run away with you, I took her back to her parents, because I'm afraid she may very well be the next victim. She scratched my face in gratitude."

Vledder made a vague gesture.

"The charity of the godless is cruel."

DeKok looked at him in astonishment.

"What is the connection?"

"I don't know," answered Vledder. "I read it somewhere. Can't remember where."

DeKok sighed.

"Perhaps at the minister's, yesterday."

"It wasn't a minister, it was a priest."

"What did he say?"

Vledder shrugged his shoulders carelessly.

"He would look it up. As soon as he knew, he would ring. I gave him your number." He snorted, then he said accusingly: "Reserve that sort of assignment for yourself, from now on. The priest looked at me as if I were crazy. He couldn't figure out why I would want to know."

"And you?"

"What do you mean?"

"Can you figure it out?"

Vledder shook his head.

"Is it for a crossword puzzle?"

For long moments DeKok looked pensively at his younger colleague.

"I do believe," he observed finally, "that I have to wait a little longer for my pension."

Vledder blushed.

DeKok poured himself a mug full of coffee and seated himself comfortably behind his desk. His thoughts went to Barbara whom he had left at the house of her parents. She had been furious. He wondered how long she would be able to stand it; how long it would be before she reappeared on the scene. He hoped she would give him a little time. At least enough time to unmask the stealthy strangler.

Vledder interrupted his train of thought.

"Do you know that Father Matthias is in the building?"

DeKok jumped up, spilling some coffee.

"What!?"

Vledder nodded.

"Oh yes, I saw him, he was with Bierens."

"Why is he here?"

Vledder shrugged.

"To file a complaint, or something."

Contrary to his normal habits, DeKok swore loudly and in detail. He ran out of the room and stormed into the office of Inspector Bierens. Much to his relief, he immediately noticed Father Matthias, quietly sitting on a chair next to the desk. He waited a moment to catch his breath and then approached Father Matthias with a friendly smile on his face and outstretched hand.

"What a surprise," he said cheerfully, "I could have imagined a number of people, but I would never have expected to see you inside a police station. Not you, Father Matthias."

The graybeard rose hesitantly.

"I . . . eh, I don't believe I have had the pleasure," he said formally.

DeKok laughed.

81

"I beg your pardon," he said apologetically. "My name is DeKok. I heard you speak in the Chapel, yesterday. I listened to you with considerable interest. I must say, you know how to mesmerize an audience. We were all very much impressed."

Father Matthias nodded absent mindedly.

DeKok's face became sympathetic.

"You're not in trouble, are you?"

"Yes, I think so," answered the oldster. "Yes, I must be."

DeKok took him gently by the arm and led the old man to his own room. Inspector Bierens suddenly realized what was happening and bolted upright in his chair. His mouth opened in utter surprise.

"But . . . ," he cried, completely taken aback, "I was . . ."

With a hefty poke in the side, DeKok silenced him.

"Father Matthias is entitled to the best service we can offer," he said jovially, "I'll personally take care of his problems."

Bierens' face was red with suppressed fury. But a tiny flicker in the back of DeKok's eyes prevented him from giving vocal vent to his vexation in the presence of Father Matthias. He sank back into his chair and with uncontrolled gesture ripped an incomplete report from his typewriter.

DeKok led the way courteously and Father Matthias followed him into the large detective room. DeKok placed a chair next to his desk and invited the old man to seat himself.

"Please sit down," he said graciously, "and tell me your troubles." While talking he placed himself behind his desk.

"I came to file a complaint", said the oldster.

"After all," said DeKok, nodding sympathetically, "authority has not been burdened with the Sword of Justice for frivolous purposes."

Father Matthias looked up.

"Are you religious?"

DeKok smiled.

"You could call me a lost sheep, a prodigal son," he said apologetically. "Over the years I have lost my way, so to speak."

"That is a shame," replied the graybeard. "People in your profession could benefit from God's help."

DeKok nodded agreement.

"You are right," he said seriously. "Policemen should study religion more." He gestured with a sigh. "In my early, younger days, I used to know the Bible quite well. I enjoyed reading God's word, in my youth. But as I said: I've strayed." His face assumed a pensive expression. "Only this week I became painfully aware of that. I remembered the first few words of a text. Eh . . . it starts like . . . eh, this: she's fallen, fallen something . . ." He grinned shyly and shook his shoulders. "The rest . . . I don't remember the rest."

Father Matthias smiled.

"*And there followed another angel, saying, Babylon is fallen, is fallen, that great city, because she made all nations drink of the wine of the wrath of her fornication.*" His reverberating voice resounded through the room.

DeKok's face cleared.

"That's *it!*" he cried happily. "I've been worrying about it all week. I even looked in my old Bible, but I couldn't find it. It nagged at me."

Father Matthias gave him a friendly look. His light, gray eyes looked at him sharply and a mysterious smile played around the thin lips.

"Revelations," he said, amused, "Revelations fourteen, verse eight."

DeKok nodded vaguely.

"Revelations," he repeated.

Father Matthias pulled his chair a little closer. He obviously enjoyed DeKok's ignorance.

"It is the last book of the New Testament," he explained. "A strange book." He raised an admonishing finger. "I would not advise you to study it too much, you'd get lost in it."

DeKok's eyebrows started one of their incredible dances. Vledder was always fascinated by the sight.

"Why is that, Father Matthias?"

"The Book of Revelations contains many secrets, hidden meanings, mysteries. It has often led to strange speculations. Most Bible students are at a loss. Revelations is a dark book."

DeKok bit on his lower lip.

"That seems a bit of a contradiction," he said after a long pause.

Father Matthias shook his head.

"Not really," he said grandly. "They are Revelations for those who seek the mystery."

Again DeKok nodded vaguely and let his gaze rest on the graybeard. His eyebrows quieted down a little and deep wrinkles appeared in his forehead. A painful expression formed around his mouth.

"Yes, that's it," he sighed. "Revelations-for-those-who-seek-the-mystery. That's it. You are a wise man, Father Matthias. It is a pity that even wise men sometimes listen and do not hear; look, but do not see."

The oldster studied the face of the Inspector.

"I don't know," he said slowly, searching for the words, "But ... I have an idea, a vague feeling, that you want to reveal something to *me*, that you are trying to clarify something for me." He moved restlessly on his chair. "Your knowledge of the Bible is not nearly as incomplete, as you want me to believe."

"No," admitted DeKok. "I've misled you."

The old man looked at him with considerable surprise. He seemed hurt, disappointed.

"But why," he asked, "Why would you want to mislead an old man, Inspector?"

DeKok swallowed.

"Yes," he said listlessly, "why?" He rubbed his hand over his face, as if trying to clear cobwebs from his brain. "We should be . . . we would . . . in this world we should be able to tell each other the truth, and nothing but the unvarnished truth. In the best of all possible worlds we should be able to meet our fellow man with an open mind and without suspicion. I mean, better than now. But . . ." He did not complete the sentence and rose slowly from his chair.

"This is a difficult interview for me," he continued seriously. "You must believe that. It's part of my job to interrogate people. It's my profession. I have never despised my opponents, but there have been precious few I admired. But you, Father Matthias, I *do* admire you. I admire your courage. I've always admired people who have the courage of their convictions and who try to live and act according to those convictions. That . . . that takes real courage. That's why I would like so very much to . . ."

He stopped abruptly. He looked at the finely chiseled features of the old man and discovered the mildness, the benevolence that radiated from the serene gray eyes. The discovery was painful. A feeling of sympathy came over him. He was suddenly gripped by pity and compassion. He walked away from behind his desk and stood in front of the window. Without seeing anything in particular, he stared in the distance. There was a veil in front of his eyes and his hands shook. For a long time he stood there, silently. Only after he had been able to bring himself again under control, did he turn around. He looked almost tenderly at the old man.

"People such as you, Father Matthias," he said with a quiver in his voice, "are often thought to be a bit peculiar." He shook his head. "That's not so bad, because usually it's just a matter of not being understood, of ignorance." He sighed. "But people such as you are also, sometimes, out of touch with the world. And that can be serious, because they have to live in this world. You too, Father Matthias. You don't have to look far to find the wickedness of the world. You don't have to seek it in the Red Light District. You don't have to seek it all, it will seek you out on its own."

Slowly he walked over to the old man and placed a brotherly hand on the bony shoulder.

"What else can I tell you?" he asked sadly. "Go home. This afternoon we'll come to investigate the theft of the money."

The graybeard rose laboriously and faltered toward the door. With the doorknob in his hands, he turned around and said:

"You speak in riddles."

It was a last attempt to take flight in ignorance.

DeKok smiled sadly.

"I thought," he said, "that I had been clear enough."

The old man looked at him for some time absent mindedly. Then he turned and walked out.

DeKok watched him go.

"So long, Father Matthias," he whispered.

The old man did not hear him.

* * *

Vledder emerged from the corner of the room where he had been listening unobtrusively. He had stayed quietly in the corner. He had not moved, or said anything during the visit of Father Matthias. He had listened and tried to find a line, a purpose to the conversation. He had felt the tension in the conversation and he understood that more, much more had been said than was obvious from a bare recital of the words that had been spoken. He seemed lost in a labyrinth, a labyrinth of thoughts and unspoken theories. No matter how hard he thought about it, time and again he would be stopped by an invisible wall that interrupted his own train of thought. There had to be an exit, a narrow, twisted path that would lead to a solution.

He looked at DeKok's face who, oblivious to his surroundings, seemed lost in thought in the middle of the room. Vledder suspected that DeKok already knew the answers, that the solution was locked behind the wrinkled forehead, the path was clearly delineated. He tried to read the face, but it was an even mask, without expression.

"Did Inspector Bierens tell you that Father Matthias came to report a theft?"

DeKok, interrupted in his thoughts, pressed his eyes closed for a moment, shook his head slightly, as if to clear it.

"Why do you ask?"

"I didn't hear Father Matthias mention it."

Confused, DeKok looked at his assistant.

"Didn't Father Matthias mention it?" he asked.

"No. Positively not! He didn't mention a thing about a theft."

Slowly DeKok shook his head.

"Bierens didn't tell me," he said.

Vledder looked at him in amazement.

"But . . . b-but," he stammered, "if neither Father Matthias, nor Inspector Bierens told you, then . . . t-then how did *you* know?"

DeKok grinned. His face was suddenly transformed to that of a mischievous boy.

"I'll tell you sometime. I'll explain later."

He looked at the disappointed face of his pupil and laughed.

"You've got to allow an old man his little secrets," he said. "Why don't you pour us another mug of coffee?"

Vledder did as he was asked. He walked to the percolator and poured the coffee. It bothered him that DeKok did not seem to trust him. Ever since he had teamed up with the old sleuth, he had the feeling that he did not "belong", that he was just a spectator, removed from the actual investigations.

DeKok did nothing underhanded, or secretly. He was allowed to be present all the time. He could strike out on his own, if he so desired. DeKok did not prohibit anything. On the contrary, he was jovial, friendly and allowed him complete freedom. But he did not share his thoughts. And he deplored that. It made him miserable. He wanted to learn something from the great detective about whom the strangest tales circulated among the detectives in Amsterdam, as well as in other jurisdictions. But he did not *learn* anything. At least, he did not understand what was happening. It irritated him. He picked up the mugs and placed them morosely on the desk.

DeKok looked at him intently.

"What's the matter, my boy?" he asked. "Something bothering you?"

Vledder sat down across from him. The sulky look on his face had not disappeared.

"Yes," he said moodily, "Something is bothering me. Oh, believe me, I consider it a privilege to work with you, to listen in on your interrogations, but because I don't know you, your thoughts, the sense of it escapes me. I can't follow you."

"And . . . that's my fault?"

"Yes . . . I, . . . eh, . . ."

DeKok leaned toward him.

"Listen to me, my young friend Vledder," he said seriously. "If I were to tell you exactly how to think, how to interpret certain happenings and words, there would be a real danger, a good chance, that you would start to lean on me, mentally, that is. And I don't want that. I've no intention of making you into a marionette, a puppet-on-a-string, a younger shadow of myself."

He paused to take a sip from his coffee.

"I want you to think for yourself," he continued. "I want you to develop your own ideas. Thinking, too, is a matter of practice. You know as much about these murders as do I. You've seen the same people and heard the same things. If you, therefore, suspect that I'm closer to a solution than you are yourself, then you should only see that as an incentive to take more trouble, to think harder. *Think*, my boy! Try to fit the pieces of the puzzle together. Use your brain. Use it!"

Vledder sighed despondently.

"You're not going to tell me a thing?"

DeKok shook his head.

"Not now," he answered. "Not now. Perhaps later . . . if we've caught the suspect."

Vledder grinned, strangely reassured.

"If . . . ," he laughed.

DeKok stood up and put his coat on.

"Come on, my friend," he said quietly, "we're going to Father Matthias. He should be home by now."

* * *

Together they stood on the stoop of the house near the Wester Market and Vledder rang the bell. Father Matthias opened the door himself. Silently he led them to a disorganized sitting room. The detectives started around with incredulity. It was obvious that the house had lacked a woman's influence for some time. The place looked neglected. Grubby wall paper hung down in shreds. Dirty plates and cups were scattered around the room and a thick layer of dust covered the sideboard. A few easy chairs that had seen better days, were placed in the middle of the room, in the center of a worn carpet. The chairs were more or less covered with a torn and discolored fabric. The total impression was desolate. A young, heavily built, muscular man was reading in one of the easy chairs. His big feet rested on a low table.

"This," introduced Father Matthias, "is my son, Tobias."

The young man placed his book on the table and stood up smiling.

"How do you do?" he asked pleasantly.

DeKok shook his hand.

"Thank you," he answered, "very well, thank you."

Tobias looked amused.

"You were at the funeral," he said, childishly excited. "I saw you in the Chapel." He shook his head sadly. "Poor Goldie." He remained silent and looked dreamily into the distance. "But God's mercy is infinite," he concluded.

DeKok nodded.

"Did you know her?" he asked.

The young man shook his head in a particular way, came to attention and recited, as if it had been learned by rote:

"Goldie, nicknamed Pale Goldie, place of birth Rotterdam, daughter of a police corporal, reformed protestant religion, unmarried, no children, eight years in prostitution, borrowed . . ."

Father Matthias lifted a restraining hand.

"That's enough," he said severely.

Tobias hung his head in shame.

Father Matthias placed a hand on his son's shoulder.

"Tobias is a dear boy," he said gently, "and a real support."

The boy's face cleared. It looked happy again.

"Go upstairs," said the graybeard, "go to your own room and take your book with you."

Tobias obeyed willingly. He took the book from the table, pressed it under one arm and left the room. DeKok's sharp eyes had noticed the book. It was an old Bible.

Vledder turned to Father Matthias.

"Where," he asked, "did Tobias learn all those facts about Goldie? He said things even I didn't know."

"From the files," smiled the old man.

"Files," asked Vledder, surprised by the answer.

The oldster nodded.

"Yes," he said, "the files. You see, I've been practicing evangelical work for years. In the beginning I could remember all the girls, and their names, easily. There were not that many I visited, then. But slowly the number increased. So I started a filing system, mostly three by five cards, and I noted the names and other particulars."

He smiled shyly.

"But I have a very bad handwriting. In the course of time, the notes became unreadable. Last year Tobias started a new filing system. He writes much more clearly than I. He also has a fantastic memory" He smiled again. "You could notice that yourself. He practically knows the entire file by heart."

"How did you gather the information?" asked Vledder.

Father Matthias made an indefinite gesture with his hands.

"From personal conversations," he said. "The girls tell me about their needs and I try to help. Sometimes I lend them money to help them out of some difficulty, or other. Sometimes I'm just a shoulder to cry on, an ear to listen."

Vledder nodded.

"May I see those files?" asked DeKok.

"But of course."

Father Matthias searched in an old, cluttered desk in a corner of the room and unearthed a big, rectangular book from one of the drawers. Letter tabs showed on the side.

"They're listed by christian name, that is, first name," he said, "The surnames don't interest me. I'm interested in the girl and in her soul."

DeKok nodded slowly.

"I understand." he said.

Together with Vledder he flipped through the pages and found a number of well known names and some remarkable particulars. It had all been written down in a typical, characterless handwriting. The writing of a thirteen year old. When they had finished scanning the pages, Vledder asked if Father Matthias would release the information to the police.

DeKok intervened hastily.

"No," he said quickly, "we can't expect that. The file and everything in it, is the property of Father Matthias. It's confidential information. It wasn't confided to us, but to Father Matthias. We're not entitled to it."

He gave Vledder a cautioning look and returned the book to the old man.

"To be honest, I would not like to part with it," said the oldster. "Some cases are noted where, with God's help, I've had some results, have been able to save girls from the evils of prostitution. There are not many, but those cases are precious to me. Whenever I'm tempted, out of weakness, to abandon my evangelical work, then those few cases reconcile me and give me the strength to carry on."

"That joy shall be in heaven," proclaimed DeKok, "over one sinner that repenteth, more than over ninety and nine just persons, which need no repentance."

Father Matthias looked at him, nodding his head.

"The Gospel according to Luke," he agreed, "Chapter fifteen, verse seven."

DeKok smiled.

"I don't know that so precisely. I'm more familiar with the Articles of the Law."

Father Matthias did not react. He replaced the book in the drawer.

DeKok came closer.

"Is this the desk from which the money was stolen?" he asked.

The old man nodded.

"Yes," he said, "from this drawer."

He pulled out the lowest drawer of the desk and took from there a large, yellow envelope.

"I always keep my money in this envelope," he said. "It's not my habit to count it every day, but I did so yesterday. You see, I had to make a payment and . . ."

"Yes, yes," interrupted DeKok, "And . . .?"

"I was short a hundred."

"Since when? I mean, when is the last time you counted the money, *before* yesterday?"

"Last week," answered the oldster, "yes, last week. I think it was a Saturday."

"Was there money missing, then?"

"Yes," answered the old man timidly. "A hundred again, that is, I think so." He made a contrite gesture. "You see, I'm rather careless . . . nonchalant. I'm not all that interested in money."

DeKok pressed his lips together.

"There are others," he said tersely, "who do have an abiding interest in money. You should have thought about that, Father Matthias. Your carelessness has created a lot of suffering."

The old man lowered his head.

"I . . . I did not think about it."

Again DeKok was gripped by pity and sympathy.

"At what time did you count the money?" he asked in a milder tone of voice.

The old man looked up in surprise.

"Yesterday, you mean?"

"No, last Saturday week."

"Oh, that was in the afternoon, about three o'clock, I think."

DeKok nodded to himself.

"Altogether, you're missing about two hundred guilders, then?"

"Yes," sighed the old man, "two hundred guilders."

DeKok rubbed his eyes. It was a gesture of utter physical exhaustion. But his mind worked clearly. In his mind's eye he saw every facet of the problem; the motives, and . . . at this time probably the most important, the proof.

"May I see the money?" he asked.

Father Matthias bent over and retrieved a large yellow envelope from the bottom drawer.

"You know how much is in here?"

The graybeard nodded.

DeKok walked to one of the easy chairs and sat down with his back to Father Matthias. Vledder, too, could not see what he did. He came back after a few minutes and placed the envelope on the desk.

"Please count it again," he said.

The old man did as he was asked.

"Is it accurate?"

"Yes," answered Father Matthias, "it's all there."

DeKok sighed.

"Now, please listen to me carefully," he said. "From now on, I want you to count the money every day. Let's say at eight o'clock every evening. Yes?"

"As you wish."

DeKok looked at him.

"That's how I want it," he said sternly.

The old man nodded slowly. He seemed a bit stunned. It seemed as if he did not understand what was happening.

DeKok raised a forefinger in the air.

"As soon as you notice," he continued, "that money has disappeared, you ring me immediately. I'll leave my number."

"I'll call you at once," replied the old man mechanically.

"Very good, Father Matthias," said DeKok. "I expect you to do so, without fail. It's the only way to catch the thief."

The oldster looked at him sadly.

"I really don't know," he said, "if we're really dealing with a thief. I told you before, I'm very careless with money. It's possible that there is nothing missing. That I was mistaken."

DeKok placed a hand on the slender shoulder of the graybeard. He felt the body shake beneath his hand.

"Father Matthias," said DeKok with emotion, "you don't want to burden you conscience any more, do you? You know there is a thief. You even know that he'll return to steal from you again. And . . . you know why he needs the money."

8

With his hands burrowed deep in the pockets of his raincoat, DeKok strolled through the streets of the old city. His face was somber. After the last handshake, he had turned around several times and looked at the old, lonely, slightly bent figure in the distance. Alone on the stoop of the neglected house. He had slowed his pace several times, fighting the impulse to turn back; back to Father Matthias, to say it differently, to give new instructions. But he had walked on, while he knew that every step took him a closer to a dramatic denouement.

He did not know, anymore, if the solution was something he wanted. Not now. He could still turn back. Of course, he could. He could tell the old man to leave the city, right now, at once, in any case, no later than Saturday. He shrugged his shoulders as he walked on. It was so senseless. It would be too silly to give in now, to give in a to a sentimental impulse. It was his duty to carry on.

Vledder walked silently next to him. He mused about the background, the reason for DeKok's sudden interest in a simple theft at the home of an inoffensive, harmless graybeard. He could not reconcile that with the strangulations, but he did understand that there had to be a connection. It was not DeKok's habit to waste time with inconsequential incidents, with trivialities, when engrossed in an important murder case. At least, Vledder did not think so.

When they reached the station, DeKok went straight into the room of the Commissaris. Vledder wanted to wait outside, but DeKok motioned him to follow.

Commissaris Roos, such a contrast to his successor, Commissaris Buitendam who would take over soon, immediately came from behind his desk. His face radiated pure friendliness. He shook hands with almost abundant joviality and gestured expansively to a group of easy chairs in a corner of the room.

"But please sit down, gentlemen," he said heartily. "Make yourselves comfortable. And tell me, how's the case. Any progress?"

Vledder and DeKok lowered themselves into a chair and accepted a generously offered cigar. Both placed them in their coat pockets. DeKok smoked seldom and Vledder did not smoke at all, but they were not about to offend the old man's hospitality. He so obviously wanted to put them at their ease, but understood that they would feel uncomfortable smoking in his presence.

"I'm talking daily to the Judge-Advocate about this case," began the Commissaris. "It's terrible. The strangler causes me sleepless nights." He sighed deeply. "And the press ... ," The friendly expression on his face changed to one of pure despair.

DeKok was amused. He knew the game that was being played. The gestures, the mimicry, the changing emotions, flowing from one into the other, without a pause, made a mighty impression on young Vledder. DeKok was not impressed. Not any more.

"I would like," he said businesslike, "to have three detectives and a female officer assigned to me next Saturday, from about ten at night, until further notice."

The Commissaris frowned. His cherubic face changed to wonder.

"A female officer?" he asked amazed. "A female officer? For an operation? In the District?"

DeKok nodded emphatically.

"Precisely."

The Commissaris seemed completely taken aback.

"B-b . . .b-but," he stuttered, "what could you possibly want her for?"

DeKok looked at him evenly.

"I want her to impersonate a prostitute."

Offended to the core of his puritanical soul, the Commissaris stood up.

"But DeKok," he said, raising his voice indignantly, "you can't be serious. But that's impossible. Colleague Van Dyke, who's in charge of the female personnel, will never allow it."

"Then the party is off," he said, shrugging his shoulders. "I don't dare use a real prostitute as bait. Besides, what girl from the Quarter would volunteer as a possible strangle victim?"

The Commissaris looked at him wide eyed.

"But you don't mind risking a female officer?"

DeKok nodded soberly.

"Yes," he answered, "a well-trained female officer, fully aware of what may happen and able to defend herself accordingly."

"You want," repeated the Commissaris suspiciously, "to set a trap for the killer?"

"More or less, yes."

The Commissaris sat down again. Apparently he had overcome his initial shock and he thought about it more carefully.

"What sort of trap?" he asked.

DeKok sighed.

"It isn't really a trap," he said. "The killer will come, regardless. But instead of an innocent little whore, he'll encounter a trained police officer. That's all."

The Commissaris drummed his fingers on the armrest.

"And how," he demanded, "how does Inspector DeKok *know* that the killer will come?"

DeKok grinned.

"Because I think I know how he thinks."

The Commissaris nodded slowly.

"Oh," he uttered with pursed lips, "that's how it is?"

He stood up again and paced around the office.

"In our part of the District alone," he muttered, "we've about a thousand rooms from which the ladies practice the world's oldest profession." He smiled thinly and turned to DeKok. "Are you sure you know exactly in which room you want our female colleague to perform?"

The continued sarcasm in the words did not escape DeKok.

"Yes, on the Rear Fort Canal," he answered calmly. "In the room of Babette."

The Commissaris stopped in front of him. His mocking eyes surveyed DeKok.

"And why in Babette's room? Why not the room of Mary, or Kitty, or Sally, or whatever?"

DeKok did not answer at once. Calmly he adjusted a trouser leg that needed no adjusting and down a little more comfortably.

"Because ... ," he said slowly, "the killer will come to Babette's room."

The Commissaris looked at him in genuine astonishment, shook his head and started to grin.

"It's amazing," he said ironically, "do you practice telepathy? Or do you have a crystal ball?"

DeKok ignored the remark. DeKok could ignore everybody and everything when he had a mind to do so. He looked at nothing in particular and remained silent. His face was a mask of steel. The Commissaris walked around him, looking at him from every angle.

"Listen, DeKok," he said finally, exasperated. "I've always had a great admiration for you, as a detective. I know about your many successes in the past." He sighed. "I'm really not a man who's

96

adverse to a reasonable proposal and I would . . . in your case, be willing to go a little bit further than what is reasonable . . . but this, this goes too far."

DeKok made a vague, irritating gesture.

"It's your decision," he said calmly. "I've told you my plans. As far as I'm concerned, this is the only way to catch the strangler in the act, so to speak. If you don't agree with my proposal, then you must accept the risk that next Sunday there *will* be a third victim. That's not my responsibility, but yours."

He stood up and walked toward the door. Vledder, unsure, remained seated. There was a dangerous light in the eyes of the old Commissaris.

"DeKok," he said vehemently, "if I so decide, *I* will terminate this interview, *not* you."

DeKok made a slight bow in submission.

"As you wish," he yielded. He resumed his seat. He looked at the apprehensive face of Vledder. He understood that the young inspector felt uncomfortable. To say the least, he had embroiled him into an unenviable position. But why was the old man being so sarcastic? It irritated him. He had not come to report fairy tales. He wanted three detectives and a female officer. He needed them to catch the killer. He knew what he was doing. There was nothing personal about it. In a way, he liked the killer, felt for him, understood him to a certain extent. But it had to be done and the time that he could be spurred on by ambition, or notoriety, was far behind him. It was just business.

The killer had to be apprehended. Society demanded it. Very well, if the Commissaris refused to cooperate, he would himself assume the role of a prostitute. He grinned silently to himself. He wondered how his heavy torso would look in a low-cut decollete and a stuffed bra. It would be a ridiculous sight, no doubt, but if it had to be . . .

The Commissaris had calmed down and sat down across from him. The expression on his face had changed yet again. It was more cooperative. He took a deep breath, trying to forget his looming retirement.

"You must have good reasons to believe that the killer will strike again."

"Yes."

"You even think you know the next victim?"

"Yes."

"The next victim, according to you, is Babette. And if I understand you correctly, you want a female police officer to take Babette's place?"

"Precisely."

"And when is this supposed to happen?"

"Next Saturday."

"Do you know what time to expect the killer?"

DeKok nodded.

"About half an hour past midnight. Maybe a little later."

The Commissaris leaned forward.

"But we must have adequate assurances regarding the safety of the female officer. Have you considered that?"

"Yes," answered DeKok, "I have considered that. I know Babette's room. I've been there a number of times. In the back of the room is a door that leads to an unused cellar. I plan to place two detectives there. We make a few peepholes in the door, so that they can follow everything in the room."

The Commissaris nodded reluctant approval.

"Do you mean," he said hesitatingly, "that you intend for the female officer to display herself in front of the window?"

"Absolutely."

The Commissaris thought about that.

"But," he continued, "if she gets any customers . . . You can hardly expect that our female colleague . . . eh, keeps to her . . . eh, role to that extent?"

DeKok grinned.

"No," he answered, "I'll instruct her thoroughly."

The Commissaris remained silent.

"All right," he said after a long pause. "You win. I'll ask Van Dyke to assign a female officer. Do you have any specific preferences regarding type, hair color, whatever?"

DeKok shrugged.

"It doesn't matter much. Just ask for a blonde, . . . eh, a good looking blonde."

"They're all good looking women," answered the Commissaris. "And what's more important, they are all excellent officers." He gave DeKok a penetrating look. His face was serious. "It's because it's you, DeKok," he said with particular emphasis, "otherwise I would never have given my permission."

Vledder and DeKok stood up.

"And another thing," the old man raised a threatening finger. "If something *does* go wrong, DeKok, I will hold you personally responsible."

DeKok shook his head.

"Nothing will go wrong."

"Famous last words," muttered Vledder inaudibly.

The Commissaris waved his hands in resignation.

"Tomorrow," he said formally, "Saturday, from ten o'clock on, you'll be assigned two extra detectives, you already have Vledder, and a female officer." A smile played briefly around his mouth. ". . . a good looking blonde," he concluded.

"Thank you," answered DeKok, "Thank you, for your trust."

The Commissaris resumed his seat behind the desk.

"Let me know," he remarked in farewell, "when you're ready. I want to be there."

DeKok nodded. A slight grin on his face.

"Yes," he acquiesced, "I expected nothing less."

* * *

DeKok stood straddle legged in front of the window of the large detective room. From the outside he looked impassive and phlegmatic, but on the inside he was taut with barely controlled tension. He had placed all his cards on the table. Tomorrow it would happen.

"You're pretty sure of yourself," said Vledder.

DeKok turned around, but did not answer.

Vledder scrutinized him carefully.

"*Are* you all that sure," he asked with some misgivings.

DeKok shook his head.

"No, my boy," he sighed, "I'm not sure at all, at all. But if I had shown the least little bit of hesitation in front of the Commissaris, he would never have agreed."

Vledder nodded.

"Yes, I understand," he said seriously. "But . . . you're not planning these theatrics without some reason, are you?"

"No, Vledder, I have my reasons. It would be too silly, otherwise. But, you see, I can't control all the events. There are a lot of ifs." He looked at Vledder, a bit dreamily. "Do you have children," he asked.

Vledder grinned at the non sequitur.

"I'm not even married."

With a tired gesture, DeKok rubbed his face.

"Sorry," he said absent mindedly, "I'd forgotten."

Vledder looked at him in astonishment. His gaze rested on the face that slowly, but surely, had become familiar and yes, precious. He saw the deep lines around the mouth and the dark shadows under the eyes.

"You're tired," he said.

DeKok nodded slowly.

"Yes," he said, "I'm tired. Let's go home."

He took his coat from the peg.

"Tomorrow night, at ten, be here."

With the coat over the arm, he left the room. Near the door, he turned briefly.

"See you tomorrow."

Vledder watched him leave.

"So long, DeKok," he whispered.

* * *

"So you're the girl who's risking her life, tonight?"

DeKok appraised the figure of the young woman in front of his desk. She was well built, athletic. But not at all mannish, on the contrary, she was extremely attractive. A gamin face and short, curly blonde hair. She looked lovely in her simple dress. Vledder looked at her with admiration. It was obvious that he was not indifferent to the charms of the female officer.

"Do you know what is expected of you?"

"Yes, sir."

DeKok gestured impatiently.

100

"I'm not a *sir*," he said. "My name is DeKok, with . . ."

". . . kay-oh-kay," completed Vledder smirking.

"That's right," said DeKok unperturbed, "with kay-oh-kay. And if the helpful Mr. Vledder will make himself scarce for a while, then I will give you some specific instructions."

Vledder disappeared with a doleful expression.

"Listen, miss . . . eh, . . ."

"Ans."

"Ans. I can't emphasize enough that you've got to be very, very careful."

He searched for something in an inside pocket and withdrew an envelope.

"Here," he continued pleasantly, "in this envelope are your instructions. Follow them to the letter. Don't be afraid and don't panic. Nothing is going to happen to you."

He stood up.

"Take the envelope with you. In the room next door you'll find some different clothes. They're Babette's clothes, the girl you'll be replacing. Babette is also next door. She'll explain how to behave like a prostitute." He smiled. "One lesson is probably not enough, but you only need enough for tonight. Read your instructions carefully. If, after that, you still have questions, let me know."

She gave him a sunny smile.

"All right . . . eh, . . . DeKok."

DeKok grinned, unaware that he thereby instantly won her heart.

"Excellent, really excellent," he said. "Vledder will take you to your work room in a little while, when you're ready."

He watched her leave as she walked away with dapper, firm steps. Then he called the others in. Bierens and Graaf were the newcomers. He looked at Bierens and said:

"Sorry about the intermezzo with that old man, yesterday. I hope you won't hold it against me."

Bierens smiled.

"It's forgotten already."

"Thank you. I really appreciate that," said DeKok with satisfaction. He handed them each a sheet of paper. "Here are your instructions," he said, pointing at the closely typed pages, "if there are any questions, or if there's something unclear, please let me know. Just let me emphasize one thing: there will be *no* shooting!"

Bierens and Graaf left.

"And what about me?" asked Vledder.

"You stay close to me and to the Commissaris. A car has been placed at the end of the quay. From the car we can watch the window. As soon as the killer is inside, we'll block his escape route."

Vledder looked at him in amazement.

"But do you know the killer?"

DeKok nodded.

"But . . . b-but," stammered Vledder, "Ans, that child, I mean, our female colleague, does *she* know the killer?"

Silently DeKok shook his head.

Totally taken aback, at a loss for words, Vledder gripped DeKok by the lapels of his coat.

"But how can she know . . .? She must be warned! She must be made aware, she should know."

Smiling, DeKok placed a fatherly hand on the young man's shoulder.

"Oh, you knight in shining armor," he mocked. "Nothing will happen to Ans. She'll know exactly when the killer has arrived. Don't worry about it."

Vledder looked at him suspiciously.

"If something happens to her," he threatened, "then . . . , then . . ."

"Well . . . ," challenged DeKok.

"Then I'll never work with you again."

* * *

By eleven thirty they were all at their posts. Bierens and Graaf in the cellar, at the other side of the door. Ans, dressed provocatively and almost unrecognizable under her make-up, self-conscious and with an apprehensive face, in front of the window under the pink lights. Vledder, DeKok and the silent Commissaris in the car on the canal. They watched men stroll along the lighted windows. Once in a while one of them stopped in front of the window and took a good look at the new face in the District.

Vledder was extremely nervous. His tongue continually licked his dry lips. The Commissaris gave forth with a deep sigh at regular intervals. DeKok's face did not show any emotion.

Suddenly a man stopped in front of Ans' window, looked around and entered through the door at the side.

Vledder was ready to get out of the car, but DeKok stopped him,

"Wait for the curtains to close," he said.

Vledder sank back in the seat. He watched with eagle eyes as Ans stood up and talked to her visitor. He saw her lips move. The man handed her something. Ans took it, looked at it for a moment and then handed it back, shaking her head. The man gestured. Ans shook her head persistently. A little later, they watched the man emerge from the house. Ans went back to her chair.

Vledder gave vent to a loud sigh; a sigh of relief.

Slowly the minutes passed by.

The same game was played out a number of times. Again and again they watched Ans shake her head negatively and then, moments later, saw a surly man re-appear in the street.

DeKok looked at his watch. It was just about thirty minutes past midnight. He became a bit anxious. It did not escape the sharp eyes of the Commissaris.

"What's the matter, DeKok?" he asked softly. "Afraid he won't come?"

DeKok nodded slowly.

"Perhaps," he said, "but he *has* to come. I received the call tonight. It should happen soon. Let's wait a little longer."

A man stopped in front of the door. A heavy, muscled man. DeKok sat up straight. But the distance was just a little too far to clearly discern any facial features in the shadows in front of the house. It was difficult to be certain about the identity. It could be him. But Ans again shook her head and the curtains remained open.

The tension increased and the very air in the car seemed charged with uncertainty. The windows fogged over. They rubbed peepholes in the condensation in order to see.

Again DeKok looked at his watch. It was almost one o'clock. A sudden, unreasonable fear overcame him. The killer should already have shown himself. Something had gone wrong. Something must have happened. Something on which he had not counted, had not taken into account. But what? In despair he racked his brain. Had he followed the wrong trail? Were his conclusions wrong? What had been overlooked? Where had he made a mistake?

In a sudden flash of insight he saw the solution: *Barbara!* His heart stuck in his throat and he had a nauseous feeling in his stomach. He threw the car door open and ran down the canal. Vledder raced after him.

"What's the matter with you?" he yelled. "Where the hell are you going?"

DeKok did not answer. He was unable to answer. Fear made him unable to speak.

He ran the hundred yards from the car to Barbara's house as fast as his heart and lungs allowed. Two, three steps at the time he flew up the stairs.

Vledder followed, still completely in the dark. He streaked after him into the small house where Barbara used to ply her trade. Suddenly he stood stock still. The blood in his veins seemed to turn to ice. Momentarily paralyzed by shock he looked.

In the bedroom, almost completely pressed into the mattress, he saw a naked woman.

On top of her, knees in her belly, a heavily muscled young man leaned over the voluptuous figure of the woman. His arms were stretched out in front. The face was disfigured by a horrible grin, a grimace of hate and loathing. His strong hands encircled the slender neck of the woman. Her body twisted and turned in an attempt to escape and her eyes seemed to protrude from the sockets. Vledder still seemed paralyzed. As in a trance he saw DeKok make a waving gesture and, as if from a distance, he heard the dull smack as the detective's fist hit the young man full on the side of the head.

Only then did his body again obey the will of his mind. He ran forward and, together with DeKok, they dragged the young man from the bed. DeKok's blow had momentarily stunned the attacker, but it lasted only a moment. The attacker struggled to his feet and tried to escape. Vledder jumped on top of him.

The fight that followed took all of Vledder's skill and strength. His opponent fought as one possessed, while uttering raw, incomprehensible noises. It was a horrifying sound. With the greatest of difficulty, Vledder was barely able to control the assailant and he was genuinely grateful when the Commissaris, assisted by Bierens and Graaf showed up. With the help of the two other detectives, they managed, not without another struggle to handcuff the husky figure.

Tobias roared like a wounded animal as he was led away to the hastily summoned paddy wagon.

Still panting from the exertion, Vledder looked at DeKok. He was seated on the edge of Barbara's bed, a sad expression on his face. Vledder, still a bit unsteady on his feet, walked closer and said:

"I'll call a doctor for her."

DeKok nodded.

"Thank you, my boy," he whispered.

Vledder turned and left the house. The car was waiting, the Commissaris next to the driver. Vledder got in and they followed the paddy wagon with Tobias, guarded by Bierens and Graaf. The Commissaris directed one extra stop to collect Ans.

* * *

DeKok had covered Barbara with a plaid blanket and he softly stroked her long blonde hair.

"Why," he said with a choking voice, "why *did* you have to come back. I thought I'd left you safely with your parents."

He looked at the pale face and the closed eyelids and shook his head. It pained him to see her like that. He leaned over and covered her a bit better.

"Silly goose," he murmured softly in her ear. "You silly goose, I was almost too late."

Slowly she opened her eyes and looked at him. The tender look in her eyes moved him.

She stroked his rough face with a soft hand.

"I'm so sorry," she whispered, so softly it was almost inaudible. "Really, DeKok, I'm sorry."

"All right, darling," he answered softly. "If the doctor agrees, I'll see you'll be taken home at once. Tonight. I just hope that you've now been cured permanently."

She nodded, her eyes closed.

DeKok rubbed her cheek softly with his large, rough hand. Then he walked slowly away and left her to herself.

9

About an hour later, they were all together in the office of the Commissaris. The old man had ordered coffee and had been generous with cigars. Ans had changed back to her normal clothes. Her own, simple dress looked much better on her than the provocative clothes she had borrowed from Babette.

"In a short, pre-interrogation, Tobias has admitted to the two previous strangulations," said the Commissaris in a formal tone of voice. "We can look back on an extremely successful evening." He paused a moment. "Although something almost went wrong," he added, gently chiding.

All eyes turned to DeKok who silently slurped his coffee in a corner of the room.

"Yes," said Vledder, still astonished at the possibility, "something almost went wrong."

It seemed the signal for a general discussion. Nobody could hear anybody, because everybody was talking at once. The Commissaris made a gesture, asking for quiet.

"I've known DeKok for years," he said calmly. "And I know that he sometimes arrives at the solution in unorthodox ways. When he asked my permission for this operation, yesterday, I didn't ask about the who and wherefore. But . . . I do believe that I'm entitled to an explanation at this time."

"Yes," agreed Vledder, "the Commissaris is right. You really owe all of us an explanation. In fact, you probably made us younger people look a bit ridiculous. It's no more than your duty to tell all, at this time. After all," he added with a grin, "we don't mind learning from your experience."

The others nodded in accord.

DeKok placed his coffee cup on a nearby table and smiled.

"Put yourself in the place of your opponent," he said, "and try to think the way he does. It's difficult, sometimes impossible, but . . . every once in a while it can be done."

He picked up his cup again and slurped loudly. A most uncivilized sound, that did not seem to bother him at all.

The others stared at him.

"And that's *it*?" asked Bierens finally.

DeKok nodded.

The Commissaris intervened.

"No, no, DeKok," he said hastily, "you don't get off that easily. Tell us everything. They're entitled."

DeKok sighed a long, weary sigh.

"All right, then," he answered. "I'll try. If I'm not clear enough for you, just ask questions."

He stood up and walked over to the desk of the Commissaris. He leaned his back against the desk and faced them.

"The thing that bothered me most," he began, "was the apparent lack of any connection between the two murders. Yet, from the start I suspected that both had been committed by the same perpetrator. In view of the profession of both victims, I thought at first that the killings had some sexual overtones, but that did not fit the circumstances at all, at all."

He paused and scratched the back of his neck. Then he went on in an even voice:

"The victims did not resemble each other. In the case of sexual murders, we generally find that all the victims have something in common in regard to type, figure, and so on, because a sexual maniac, as a rule, prefers a certain type, be that young, or old; fat, or skinny; blond, or brunette. Whatever. But there was no such similarity."

He paused and looked with longing at his empty coffee cup next to his chair.

"Anyway," he continued, "while I happened to be visiting Little Lowee's bar, Father Matthias suddenly entered. I'd never met him personally. I just knew him from the stories the girls told about him and I knew that he practiced some sort of evangelic work in the Quarter. There had never been any reason for me to seek him out. But in that bar, shortly after the second murder, Father Matthias began to preach. He spoke about the wrath of God and he talked about Sodom and Gomorrah, two cities that had been destroyed, because of moral turpitude and sexual excesses. Suddenly, in a flash, I saw the connection. The Sunday murders, God's wrath, Sodom and Gomorrah and sexual degeneration. The connection had to be found in a religious sense."

His audience hung on his every word. With a weary gesture he rubbed his face. he took a deep breath.

"I suddenly realized," he explained, "that Father Matthias had consciously taken the opportunity to make that connection, to compare the murders to the destruction of Sodom and Gomorrah. It must have seemed an ideal subject for a sermon. I've had a religious upbringing and it's one of the favorite practices among ministers and priests, to find everyday, current examples in our daily lives and to use them as a foundation for the discussion of God's word. It happens all the time. But I kept turning it over and over in my mind and suddenly I noticed, or rather, became aware of, a strange coincidence."

He looked almost apologetic as he explained:

"The murdered prostitutes were called Sonja and Goldie, respectively. When you take a close look at the first two letters of their names, you'll notice that they coincide with Sodom and Gomorrah. As you'll see, the S-O of Sonja for Sodom and the G-O of Goldie for Gomorrah."

"Really," cried Vledder enthused by the possibility.

"It could be, of course," continued DeKok, ignoring the interruption, "nothing more than pure coincidence. But somehow, it seemed too obvious to me and I felt, rather than knew, that I had to keep looking in that direction. After a while I was convinced that I was on the right trail."

He smiled briefly at Vledder.

"Therefore," he resumed, "I had to find a man with a religious bent, a religious conviction. Not a normal man, but a man with a sick mind, a fanatic, a man who, strengthened, or inspired, by the Bible, looked upon himself as the instrument of God's wrath, tasked to wipe out prostitution. For a while I considered Father Matthias. But Father Matthias was no fanatic. He turned out to be exactly what he seemed to be. An honest man, driven by a true Christian belief in the innate goodness of his fellow man. His aim was to save the ladies, especially the young girls, from the perils of prostitution. He was not the type I was looking for."

DeKok released a deep, sad sigh.

"But Father Matthias has a son. His name is Tobias. Later that night, after the sermon in Little Lowee's bar, I followed the old man to his house. Near the house on the Wester Market he was met by a large, muscled young man. The distance from which I was observing the encounter, was a little too great to be able to distinguish much detail. But his gorilla-like posture, the way in which he placed his feet, his general behavior, gave me the feeling that there was something wrong with the boy. I just couldn't put my finger on it. Next day, after some research, it appeared that my feelings had been right. Tobias is not quite normal. He's retarded and never grew past the mental age of a thirteen year old. I also found out that the boy was completely under the influence of his god-fearing father and that he was not allowed any literature other than the Bible."

DeKok shook his head, as if in wonder.

"I'm not a Bible scholar," he said seriously. "For that I lack both the gift and the conviction, belief if you will. I *do* know, however, that the Bible is an extremely difficult book. Father Matthias, in his simple goodness, made a tragic mistake. He believed that his son would be able to gain the same comfort, joy and happiness from the Bible, as he did himself. He was wrong."

Again he looked with longing at his empty coffee cup, but went on with his discourse.

"Father Matthias had some trouble with his son, in the past. The boy is as strong as an ox. There had been incidents of violence, perhaps battery. There were a number of such incidents, it's difficult to determine the cause, or identify the participants, at this late date. But that's why the old man kept the boy in the background, sheltered from real life. Tobias was almost never away from the house. He didn't work and never had any money."

DeKok looked at the serious faces of his audience.

"Although," he continued, "Tobias *did* fit the description of the type of person I had envisioned as the possible perpetrator, there was one additional difficulty."

He smiled faintly.

"I've been working in the Red Light District for more years than I care to remember and I'm thoroughly familiar with the habits and peculiarities of most of the girls in the District. As you know, both Sonja and Goldie were found nude, or nearly nude. From the way in which the clothing was folded, it could easily be determined that the women had undressed themselves, of their own free will. If a prostitute undresses completely, than it's considered a special favor, a favor which also has to be paid for. A sort of surcharge. I know a bit about the prices normally charged, the rate structure, so to speak. In addition, every prostitute *always* makes the customer pay in advance. From that we can be certain that the killer must have had money. And Tobias *never* had money. He never *owned* any money."

The Commissaris took pity on him and handed him a cup of coffee. Gratefully, DeKok took a sip. As if refreshed, he carried on:

"I thought and thought, but I couldn't figure out how Tobias could have had enough money to pay both girls enough to get them to undress. The only possibility was theft. He had to steal the money. But how and from whom?" He glanced at Vledder and Bierens. "Thus, when Father Matthias came to the station, I felt intuitively that he had come to report a theft of money. It was the only possibility."

Vledder nodded and said:

"All right, so far I understand your reasoning. But . . . what about tonight? How did you know that Tobias would try again?"

DeKok sighed.

"I didn't know for sure," he said, "but it was to be expected. Take a look at the calendar. It's Sunday. And another thing. For a new murder, performed the same way, Tobias would need money again. I had warned Father Matthias to count his money every day and to warn me immediately, the moment he found any of it missing. Well, earlier tonight he phoned me."

Vledder nodded pensively.

"But I still can't figure it out," he said. "the comedy with Babette and then the sudden run to Barbara's house . . . how . . . how do you explain that?"

DeKok smiled again. Drained his cup of coffee and placed it on the desk behind him.

"Just think carefully," he said. "The previous two victims were Sonja and Goldie, thus, Sodom and Gomorrah. We have to think like Tobias. Trying to think like him, I couldn't help but wonder if there were additional cities mentioned in the Bible that had been destroyed, had incurred God's wrath because of debauchery and sexual depravation. You'll remember that I sent you to a minister, or priest, with the same question. I'd been looking in the Bible myself and, according to my research, the only other city so designated was Babylon. You'll also remember that I mentioned the specific text in a conversation with Father Matthias. Father Matthias was familiar with the text. He knew it so well, that he immediately cited both chapter and verse. It was a safe bet to assume that Father Matthias had discussed Babylon with his son, at least once, maybe more often."

DeKok moved his body slightly, as if wanting to take a look at the empty coffee cup, now behind him on the desk. Manfully he controlled himself.

"Well, using Babylon as a starting point," he said, "the next victim would be a woman, a prostitute no doubt, with a name that started with B-A. I knew just two of them. Barbara and Babette. Both names were also listed in the files of Father Matthias; the source from which Tobias selected his victims. He knew the files by heart. As often happens with retarded people, he's a bit of an

111

idiot-savant, in any case, he has a near photographic memory. Anyway, in order to reduce the odds, I managed to take Barbara away and deliver her to her parents. Although she protested furiously, she was out of the way. That left Babette."

"Aha, so that's why you were so sure about Babette. She was the only B-A left in the District. The B-A from Babylon."

DeKok nodded in approval.

"Yes," he sighed, "but then Barbara reappeared suddenly. I should have thought about it, but I was certain she was safe, back in the bosom of her family. I never expected her to return so quickly. You see, I had, more or less, insulted her and our farewell was, to say the least, a bit rocky." He grinned softly. "In our profession, the woman is almost always the unknown factor, the uncertainty."

Ans looked at him searchingly. She felt there was more to the story involving Barbara.

"So she came back," she said.

Her tone of voice made DeKok look at her sharply.

"Yes," he said evenly. "Only after the killer did not show up at Babette's, did I suddenly think of Barbara." A sad grin played around his lips. "I was almost too late."

Thoughtfully, he remained silent, then he stretched out his hand and looked at the skinned knuckles of his hand.

"It's too bad I had to hit the boy that hard," he whispered.

The Commissaris placed a hand on his shoulder.

"You've done a fantastic job," he said. "It's a typical example of how experience and intuition can bring results, no matter how unorthodox the methods. But there's one more question to which I would like an answer.: How could Babette, I mean our Ans, *know* when the murderer showed himself? I just saw her shake her head. The curtains remained open. When would they have been closed?"

DeKok grinned mischievously.

"As soon as the killer was inside."

The Commissaris made an impatient gesture.

"I understand," he said, "but . . ."

DeKok winked at his female colleague.

"Of course," he said, "I had described the suspect as completely as possible. But that wasn't all. She had another way of identifying him. While Vledder and I visited Father Matthias, I marked his money. With the pin from my tie clip I pierced a number of holes in the corners of the bills. If Tobias had any money at all, it *had* to come from his father. It could only be money he stole from his father. Ans just had to look at the bills. He would have found it normal to be asked for payment in advance. As soon as she saw, or felt, the tiny perforations, she would be sure that Tobias was in the room with her."

Vledder shook his head despondently.

"Good grief," he said, "I really still have a lot to learn."

DeKok gave him an encouraging nod.

"You'll learn," he said, "just a few more murders and . . ."

He did not complete the sentence. In his typical, waddling gait, he walked to the door.

"I'm sorry I can't stay any longer," he said apologetically, "but I need to leave now."

The Commissaris nodded permission.

DeKok waved vaguely, turned slowly and left the room. For a moment Vledder stood, uncertain about what to do next. Then he ran from the room. He overtook the gray sleuth in the corridor.

"May I come with you?" he asked hopefully.

DeKok smiled faintly.

"But of course, my boy," he answered.

Vledder's face lit up with happy expectation.

"And where are we going?"

DeKok looked at him seriously.

"Change your face," he said severely, "we have a sad duty to perform."

"Duty?"

"Yes," he answered resignedly. "Somewhere there is an old father who has to know that his son is not coming home anymore. Think about that, my boy! You must never forget that sort of detail."

DeKok
and the
Corpse on Christmas Eve

by

BAANTJER

translated from the Dutch by H.G. Smittenaar

INTERCONTINENTAL PUBLISHING

Printing History:
   1st Dutch printing: 1975
   2nd Dutch printing: 1978
   3rd Dutch printing: 1980
   4th Dutch printing: 1983
   5th Dutch printing: 1986
   6th Dutch printing: 1987
   7th Dutch printing: 1990
   8th Dutch printing: 1991
   9th Dutch printing: 1992

   1st American edition: 1993

1

The constable doing his rounds on Christmas Eve, was a devout catholic. His religious conviction is not pertinent to the events of that night, but it explains why he looked with a certain amount of envy at the people, who, after High Mass, hastened home; hands deep in their pockets, heads covered by scarfs and hats, collars of coats and jackets turned up. Because it was cold on that Christmas Eve in Amsterdam, bitter, bone chilling cold.

The constable would have loved to have attended Mass and then, just like everyone else, gone home, to Marie, his wife, not beautiful, not exceptional, but like a little stove in bed.

He looked at his watch and figured with a deep sigh that he had at least six more hours to go to the end of his tour. Six hours of cold.

Shivering at the thought, he turned left from the Haarlem Street and walked past the former bastion of the Dutch West India Company to the Gentlemen's Market. If he had been more alert he would have noticed Handy Henkie slinking along the facades of the houses on the opposite side of the Brewer's Canal.

Across the bridge over the Brewer's Canal he walked along in the typical step of a constable on patrol, he crossed toward the even numbered side of the Gentleman's Canal and hummed silently to himself: 'Silent Night, Holy Night'.

It was meant neither bitter, nor mocking. He just felt a bit lost, alone, on the silent canal quay. The footsteps of the latest churchgoers had long since echoed away. Silence remained. The crackling silence of a clear, freezing night. A lonesome rat scurried away from the sound of his approaching footsteps.

Suddenly he stopped. He heard a noise across the canal. The authority figure in him reasserted itself, the protector of life and property, the personification of the Law. His mind, pregnant with official language and the stilted style of law books, ruminated momentarily on the text of his forthcoming report: 'Theft, by means of unlawful breaking and entering, during the time normally reserved for sleep'.

Carefully and softly he stepped off the sidewalk and approached the edge of the canal. There was a gap between two parked cars. From the shadow of a tree he peered, through the gap, toward the opposite side of the canal. He noticed a security guard shuffling along the houses across the canal, testing doors as he went, making sure all were locked and secure. The constable grinned ruefully and growled in disappointment. False alarm.

He remained where he was for a few more minutes, unearthed a peppermint from the depths of his pockets and put it in his mouth. Almost immediately he spit it out again. The peppermint tasted like tobacco. Cursing himself for not cleaning his pockets after giving up cigarettes, he stared at the widening ripples caused by the peppermint as it broke the mirrored surface of the water.

That is when he discovered the corpse. It floated face down in the water, close to the shore. The coat billowed out from the back, aiding in flotation. Long strands of blond hair encircled the head like seaweed. For an infinitesimal moment the constable paused, undecided. Then he sprang into action.

* * *

Young Inspector Vledder was not happy. Shivering in a thick overcoat he watched from the side of the quay. The report had shocked him. A corpse on Christmas Eve was the last thing he had expected.

The paramedics of the special Drown Unit of the Amsterdam Municipal Medical Service manipulated a net and manoeuvred with ropes. It was not easy. Perversely, the water was not deep enough. The net was constantly snared by the rubbish at the bottom of the canal. Amsterdammers have a habit of disposing of used bicycles, and other non-perishable items by throwing them in the nearest canal. The constable ran toward the bridge and returned with a boat hook. Carefully he pulled the body into the net. The paramedics hoisted the catch up against the brick wall of the canal.

The constable came over and stood next to Vledder, the wet hook still in his hand.

"I heard a noise across the canal", he said, "but it was nothing, just a watchman checking doors. I was standing right here. I just wanted to go on my way, when I saw the corpse."

Vledder nodded absent mindedly. He did not feel good. As a police detective he had a natural aversion to corpses. He was also still too young to remain unemotional in their presence. And anything could happen once a corpse was found. The worst cases always started with a corpse. Under normal circumstances he would have been able to handle it, it would not have been so bad. Normally, there was always DeKok to fall back on, to depend on. DeKok his old partner, mentor and friend, for whom he had an inordinate amount of respect and admiration. But DeKok was not here. Was not available. He would have to tackle this problem on his own.

The paramedics lifted the dripping corpse from the net and placed it on a stretcher.

"Still a young chick," remarked one.

"And I thought," remarked the other sarcastically, "that the swimming season was over."

Vledder did not appreciate the coarse humor, but lacked the courage to remark upon it. He knew that the paramedics let off steam this way. Unless one was able to feign a hard, pitiless shell, the work would be heartrending in the extreme. Especially young people and children would bring out the most heartless remarks. It was that, or cry. Although every Dutch citizen learned to swim in Grade School, drownings were still an everyday occurrence. Especially in Amsterdam with its many canals and waterways. In fact, mused Vledder, wondering where the thought came from, Amsterdam has more canals and bridges than Venice.

Reluctantly he stepped closer. The light of a police car illuminated the pale face of the victim. A red scarf was knotted around the neck and covered part of the chin. A light make-up --some rouge on the cheeks and pale lipstick on the lips -- could not hide the mask of death.

The paramedics lifted the stretcher and pushed it into the ambulance. They also took the net. They were in a hurry. They slammed the door and drove off. Vledder stepped into the cruiser.

"Make your report to the desk sergeant," he told the constable, "and tell him that I'll be there shortly."

Vledder started his car and followed the ambulance. On the way he wondered whether he should alert DeKok. But why? It would probably be a common suicide. It was not unusual that a person ended her, or his, life in the water. Especially during the Holidays it seemed to be prevalent. Loneliness, no doubt, he thought, they even had a new word for it, Holiday Suicide Syndrome, or something. Loneliness, or despair, seemed to take on an extra significance during feast days. Anyway, for a simple suicide he did not need DeKok. Some basic research and the family could take care of the funeral. Still, too bad, such a young woman. If she were that lonely, he would have been happy to comfort here during the Holidays. She could have kept him company during his off hours. She had not been that bad looking.

Not bad at all . . . that is. Scandalized by his own thoughts, he stopped his musings. The ambulance passed through the gate of the Wilhelmina Hospital and stopped in front of the morgue. The paramedics carried the stretcher inside.

The doctor on duty showed up after a few minutes. He rubbed the sleep from his eyes, nodded toward the paramedics and looked a question at Vledder.

"I'm Inspector Vledder, Warmoes Street," said Vledder. "This young lady has been fished from the Gentlemen's Canal."

"Suicide?"

Vledder shrugged his shoulders.

"I . . . I'm not sure," he said hesitatingly. "I don't even have an identification, yet."

The doctor walked toward the stretcher and opened the eyes of the girl. Then he undid the scarf around the neck. Vledder watched attentively. Carefully the doctor pulled the scarf away and bent the head of the victim slightly backward. Vledder was shocked. The breath stuck in his throat. He leaned forward in order to see better. There was no doubt. There were red marks in the neck; unmistakable traces of strangulation.

He lifted his head and looked at the doctor, confused.

"B-but . . . ," he stammered, "t-that . . . that's murder."

The doctor nodded slowly.

"Indeed, Inspector, strangulation."

The unflappable paramedics remained silent.

* * *

Vledder, still somewhat shaken, was in the white tiled basement of the Pathology Department of the Wilhelmina Hospital. He held the receiver of the telephone to his ear. He had already heard the phone ring three times and he wondered how long it would be before DeKok finally woke up.

He was within six feet of the gurney. The corpse of the young woman had been placed on it, the red scarf draped over her breasts. Dirty canal water dripped from the slips of her coat as they hung down on both sides of the gurney. He could clearly hear the steady dripping on the tile floor. The sound was louder, more penetrating, than the ringing of the phone in his ear.

"DeKok."

It sounded sleepy.

Vledder changed his stance.

"Yes, well, DeKok," he said, "Vledder here. Sorry to have to wake you."

"I'm not awake yet." It sounded peevish.

Vledder swallowed.

"Listen, DeKok. I'm in the basement of the Wilhelmina. In the morgue, the Pathology Lab, that is. We fished a young woman from the Gentlemen's Canal and . . ."

"You have to wake me for that?"

"No, yes, just listen a moment, will you?" called Vledder hastily, afraid DeKok would break the connection. "It's not a normal drowning. She's been strangled."

It remained quiet on the other side of the line.

"Do you have a name?" came after a pause.

"No, no, I don't know anything, yet. I . . ."

Vledder heard a deep sigh.

"Very well, my boy, all right. I'll come. I'll be there in about ten minutes. Did you call anybody else? Dactyloscopy? Photographer?"

"No."

"Then do so. I want pictures and fingerprints of the corpse."

"All right, DeKok, I'll do that. I'll call them immediately. And, you know . . . thanks!"

He heard a growl.

"Yes, well, thanks and a quarter doesn't even buy me a cup of coffee."

Vledder smiled.

"You never know," he said, "maybe if you save enough of them."

He listened to a few more indistinguishable sounds and then he heard the click of a broken connection. With a deep sigh, partly of relief, Vledder replaced the receiver.

He was sorry to have to wake his partner. He really did not like to do it. He would have preferred to leave him be, but he was afraid to tackle this case on his own. It was, after all, murder. And if he botched it . . .

He imagined how DeKok at this moment was trying to force his ever painful feet into his shoes, meanwhile cursing Vledder, who had alerted him, thereby spoiling his Christmas leave.

He had so looked forward to his days off. Away from duty, away from crime and away from the old, renowned police station at the Warmoes Street where he had been assigned for more than twenty years of almost uninterrupted duty as part of the Homicide detail.

Vledder banished DeKok from his thoughts and stared at the girl on the gurney. The tableau made a strong impression on him; the closed eyes, the half-open mouth, the pale face. Again he was struck by the sound of the dripping water. It echoed against the bare walls of the basement. He also noticed the puddle on the other side of the stretcher. The drops fell in turn.

2

He was there before Kruger, the fingerprint expert and Bram, the photographer. With his peculiar, waddling gait, dressed in an old fashioned raincoat he entered the stark basement. His old, much loved, but decrepit little hat pushed back on his head.

Vledder met him halfway.

"I'm sorry, DeKok," he said, "I would have liked to let you sleep, but you see . . ."

DeKok made a vague gesture.

"It's all right, my boy, where's she?"

Vledder pointed at the gurney.

"I didn't let them undress her, yet. She's just as we found her, except for the scarf, that was wound around her neck."

DeKok shuffled over to the gurney and leaned over the body of the young woman. He looked carefully at the marks left by the strangulation. They were almost horizontal. Just beneath the chin was a bruise, indicating a subcutaneous bleeding, probably caused by the knot of the scarf as it was tightened around her neck.

DeKok straightened up. His face was serious, almost grim. His gaze explored the soft lines of the dead girl's face. He liked the face. He did not know why. Perhaps because the face, even in death, looked mild and unassuming. Perhaps because it reminded him of someone, a long forgotten love, a girl friend, years ago. He did not know. He was hardly conscious of it. DeKok knew so many faces: beautiful, ugly, sly, naive, cruel, suspicious, cunning and brute faces, encountered during his long career. But he liked this face.

Sometimes it is difficult to find the reasons for inner, subconscious decisions. No matter what intellectual reasons may be cited, intuition is mainly a matter of feeling, a hunch, that has nothing to do with reason. At least ninety percent of all decisions are based on instinct, based on emotional rationalization. DeKok was not an emotional person, at least, not in the normal context of the word. He had learned control. But the sight of the soulless body of the young girl awakened something in him. A feeling of bitterness, mingled with hate. He decided then and there that he would find the perpetrator of this cowardly and cruel crime. He would bring the killer to justice, no matter what.

Kruger dropped his heavy case on the tiles and stood next to him.

"Is that her?" he asked.

"Yes."

"Good looking child."

"Yes."

"Strangled?"

"Yes."

"You're not very talkative."

"No."

Kruger shrugged his shoulders.

"If you think," he said, "that I'm here for fun, you're wrong." His voice sounded offended, hurt.

DeKok turned slowly toward him.

"Neither am I," he said slowly. "Neither am I." His tone turned sarcastic. "But there is one big difference," he continued, "when you've taken her fingerprints, you're through. Don't have to concern yourself any further. But I don't have that luxury. If I want to find the perpetrator, I'll have to dig in her past. People will tell me how she was, how she thought. And before long she'll come alive for me. She'll become somebody, a person, with everything that entails, love and hate, joy and sorrow. For you she'll never be more than a few lines on a plate. *That's* the difference, Kruger. And please excuse me for not being very talkative."

He turned abruptly and picked up a yard stick and a tongue depressor.

"Are you about ready?"

124

Vledder, who had remained in the background with Bram, the photographer, hastily picked up his note book and found a pen in one of his pockets. Kruger unpacked his paraphernalia silently. His face was red.

DeKok went to the gurney.

"Write it down," he yelled. "Description: Female, approximately eighteen to twenty years of age, average height, about five foot five, slender figure, white skin, oval face, symmetric, long, blonde hair, not tinted, high forehead, eyebrows: bow type, not shaved or plucked, light blue eyes, straight, narrow nose with slight upturn at tip, full lips, corners of mouth turned up."

He sighed.

"You got that?"

"Yes," called Vledder, "I got that."

DeKok placed the tongue depressor into the half open mouth and lifted the upper lip.

"Healthy, regular teeth, no stains, no fillings."

He put the tongue depressor away and pushed the hair slightly aside.

"Small oval ears, pierced earlobes."

Then he lifted the arms, one by one.

"Small hands, wide back. Right index finger and right middle finger show slight nicotine stains. No jewelry. Faint mark of ring on the left ring finger. As far as can be determined, no dirt under the nails. Polished nails. Nail polish color . . ."

He hesitated momentarily.

"Vledder . . . come here a moment."

Vledder approached reluctantly.

"What kind of color is that nail polish?"

"That's cerise."

"What!?"

"Cerise."

DeKok snorted.

"All right, write that down, cerise."

He lifted the cold hands of the victim and rubbed his finger tips along the inside of the hands.

"She's been working hard at something, not too long ago. Traces of callouses. Hands otherwise well cared for."

He looked up.

"You got that, too?"

Vledder nodded.

"Splendid. Then friend Kruger can now take her fingers and friend Bram can make his pictures. After the attendants have undressed her, we can take another look at the outside of the body. Dr. Rusteloos will look at the inside, later."

Vledder always shuddered a bit at the sound of the common expression among police officers for taking fingerprints. Sometimes he imagined Kruger walking around with a case full of severed fingers.

"Autopsy?" he asked in response to DeKok's mention of the pathologist.

DeKok nodded.

"Certainly. I'll call the Commissaris myself. He can roust out Dr. Rusteloos."

He ambled toward the telephone and Kruger started his work. Muttering to himself about DeKok's words, he used a curved holder in which he placed a new piece of card stock as he passed each finger in turn through the process, recording the unvarying patterns of the finger tip swirls. Fingerprints, the only reliable means of identification.

Then Bram took his shots.

"What's the matter with DeKok?" he whispered to Vledder in between changing plates and focal lengths. "Nervous?" He snorted, then answered his own questions: "That's hardly like him. How many murder cases has he solved, already? Dozens, maybe hundreds. He'd be the last to get uptight about another murder."

Vledder shrugged his shoulders.

"I called him out of bed. He was off for the Holidays. First time in more than ten years, I think. Perhaps that's what's bothering him."

Bram sighed.

"Yes, it's a rotten job," he admitted.

He made a few more exposures and began to pack his equipment slowly.

"Of course, you didn't dare tackle it on your own, I bet. You thought: come, let's call DeKok out of bed. The old man will take care of it, right? You thought: Why should I take a chance on messing it up, when I can lean on the old man. Isn't that so? That's what you thought, right?"

Vledder looked at him searchingly. Was that a reproach? Did it sound as a reproach? He did not know. The expression on the face of the experienced photographer was unreadable. Should he have taken care of things himself? Is that what Bram meant? Should he not have called DeKok and should he, perhaps, have welcomed this opportunity to show that he was capable of acting on his own?

Bram prepared to leave and the attendants undressed the corpse, quickly and routinely.

Vledder collected the wet clothes in a plastic bag. DeKok returned from his telephone and looked at the naked body. His experienced eyes searched for the least little deviation from the norm. He had attended scores of autopsies and knew what to look for. He remained thoughtfully silent. Then he turned to one of the attendants.

"What do you think," he said, "the lower belly seems slightly swollen. Could she be pregnant?"

The attendant pursed his lower lip forward.

"Hard to say," he answered.

DeKok rubbed his thick fingers through his hair.

"Anyway," he sighed, "we'll let Dr. Rusteloos find out. The body needs to be delivered to the Police Lab. The autopsy is set for nine o'clock. You'll have everything ready?"

The attendants nodded in unison.

"Excellent, then we'll go."

He glanced once more at the corpse and walked away. Vledder rushed after him. The sack with wet clothes hanging from one hand.

"When do you want the pictures?" asked Bram.

DeKok turned slightly toward him.

"In about two hours," he said.

Bram protested.

"But," he said, despair in his voice, "it's Christmas."

DeKok nodded agreement.

"I know," he said resignedly, "Happy Christmas."

It sounded like a dissonant.

* * *

Vledder sighed deeply.

"It's not going to be easy," he said. "I looked over everything very carefully. The clothes give us no clues. No exclusive models, no special labels. No laundry marks. On the whole the clothes are neat, above average quality, but subdued. Only the brassiere could perhaps be termed a bit frivolous." A wan smile showed briefly on his face. "A black piece of frill, with a lot of lace," he concluded.

DeKok sat comfortably, almost lazily, behind his desk and looked at the photographs Bram had made of the girl.

"Shall I go over the list of missing persons again?" asked Vledder.

DeKok shook his head.

"That's not much use," he said. "I think she has been dead for no more than hours. If she's missing, it would not yet have been reported. It's simply too soon for her to be on the list."

He drummed his fingers on the desk.

"Obviously the murderer did not realize that most Amsterdam canals are rather shallow near the edges. Normally a corpse will remain underwater for several days. That's probably what the murderer counted on. Otherwise he would hardly have had to throw her in the water. Apparently he wanted to delay the discovery for a few days. I'm glad that constable discovered the corpse so quickly. It can work to our advantage. It's just too bad that we don't know who she is, yet." He sighed. "In any case, transmit a telex to all posts and give as clear a description as possible. Perhaps a worried father, or husband, will report in."

Vledder nodded and left the detective room in order to execute his orders.

Thoughtfully, DeKok leaned over the photographs. Bram had done his work well. Clear exposures of details and sharp close-ups.

DeKok looked carefully at the face. Again he realized that he liked the face. It seldom happened, had not happened for years. But this face. This ... sweet face, touched him somehow. It penetrated the steel mask of indifference that he carried as an insulation, as a protection, that had carefully been built up over the years. A protective layer of self-preservation that shielded him from all the sorrow he was forced to confront in his job. Idly he shuffled the photos through his hand.

"Poor child," he murmured to himself. "How did you wind up in the cold waters of a canal, especially on Christmas Eve? Why did someone seek your death? Who'd have anything to gain from your death?"

He pressed his lips together and shook his head. Just an ordinary, sweet girl. Nothing spectacular, nothing special. Not a vamp, not a seductress. Just an ordinary girl. Quiet . . . quietly dead. Quite dead. The play on words struck him and set the inner working of his meditative mind in a spin. The religious basis of his upbringing, half forgotten admonitions from his youth, parts of Bible texts, later experiences; they all sought a place in a wild kaleidoscope of thoughts.

Suddenly he stood up and started to pace through the room.

"Fool," he cursed himself, "All those thoughts, just because of a sweet face? The sweet face of an unknown corpse? Or was there something else? Is there something to it?"

He halted in front of the mirror above the small sink. He looked at a face, marked by the deep creases of a boxer. He tried to smile at his own reflection, but it went no further than a grimace.

"Peace on Earth," he murmured, "and good-will toward men . . ."

He strolled toward the window and looked out. The morning gray announced the first day of Christmas.*

* * *

Vledder came enthusiastically into the detective room. He showed a white lady's handbag in his outstretched hand. His face beamed.

"Look at this, DeKok," he called excitedly. "Just as I was downstairs, to send the telex, a man reported to the desk sergeant

---

* In the Netherlands, as in most European countries, Christmas is a two-day celebration. In England the second day of Christmas is commonly referred to as "Boxing Day".

with this handbag. He'd found it, he said, in the portico of a house on the Brewer's Canal. He was walking his dog, when he saw it sitting there."

"When?"

"This morning, just now, perhaps half an hour ago."

"Have you looked inside?"

"Not yet. I came upstairs at once. Perhaps it belongs to the girl. The Brewer's Canal is not too far from where we found the corpse. A few hundred yards, maybe, as the crow flies."

Vledder placed the bag on the desk. There was not much to see on the outside. A cheap plastic handbag, closed with a simple clasp.

"These are a dime a dozen," remarked DeKok. "It's rather strange, however, that the bag is dry, bone dry. Apparently it has not been fished out of the water."

He took a large piece of paper from a drawer and shook the contents of the bag out on the paper. A small bottle of nail polish almost rolled off the desk. Vledder caught it and looked at the label.

"You see," he said, "cerise!"

DeKok smiled at him.

"Since when," he asked with a hint of suspicion, "are you so well informed about women's colors. Have you been taking lessons?"

Vledder grinned at him in a friendly way.

They searched through the contents of the handbag. For the most part there were just items that could be found in any woman's handbag: a mirror, a comb, a powder puff, a bottle of perfume, lipstick, emery board, a key ring. There was also an identity card, complete with photograph. That was the first thing DeKok reached for. His face cleared when he saw the photograph.

"I could be mistaken," he said carefully, "but I do believe that this is her."

Vledder looked over his shoulder.

"Yes, you're right," he cried enthusiastically, "that's *her*. No question about it."

They compared the photo on the identity card with the pictures of the dead girl, made by Bram. There was no question. It was the same girl.

DeKok took a sheet of paper and copied the details from the identity card: *Helena Maria Vries, nineteen years of age, address at 213 Hudson Street, Amsterdam.*

"We'll have some blow-ups and copies made of the identity picture, perhaps they'll be of use."

Vledder sorted the contents of the bag by apparent importance. There was an unused train ticket, one way, coach, to Gouda, dated December 24; a multiple trip ticket from the Amsterdam Municipal Transport Authority with three trips marked, all for Line 1 at 08:15, 13:15 and 18:15 respectively. Also an envelope containing a love letter from one Tom Weick, showing a military address in La Courtine, France. The letter was dated October 5. There was no money in the bag, but there was a plain gold ring with an inscription: *Ellen, May 1, 19..* The thing that surprised Vledder most of all, however, was a black, leather, man's wallet, containing a number of papers, identifying the owner as a certain Joost Hofman from Alkmaar, the cheese market.

He held the wallet up to DeKok.

"How did this wind up in her handbag?" he speculated.

DeKok took the wallet and sniffed.

"It's got a different smell," he said, "a different smell from the other items in her bag."

Vledder held Tom's letter close to his nose.

"This smells of powder and perfume."

DeKok nodded.

"She carried the letter around all the time. But the wallet doesn't belong. In any case, it hasn't been there long enough to be penetrated with the overall scent of her handbag. It certainly is one indication that the wallet hasn't been in the bag for long."

"But," exclaimed Vledder, a bit impatient, "How did she come by it? How did she get a hold of a wallet belonging to Mr. Hofman from Alkmaar? Stolen?"

DeKok shook is head.

"I don't think so. First of all, she doesn't seem the type. Secondly, we have found no money, neither in the handbag, nor in the wallet. It seems much more likely that *she* has been robbed."

"By the killer?"

DeKok rubbed his hands through his hair.

"One *could* come to that conclusion," he said. "It would be a reasonable explanation for the fact that her bag was still dry when found in the portico on the Brewer's Canal. While she was found floating in the water of the Gentlemen's Canal."

"In what way?"

"Well, let's suppose that the killer was after her handbag. An ordinary purse snatching, so to speak. But as he tries to take it away, she starts to scream. At first, he just claps a hand over her mouth, but then he uses her scarf to strangle her. He takes the purse and throws the body in the water. He walks off and on the way removes the money from the purse. As he passes the Brewer's Canal he throws the bag into an empty portico. That's one way in which the bag could be found dry, but empty of all money."

Vledder nodded.

"It sounds simple enough," he said, "but it still doesn't explain Hofman's wallet."

DeKok shook his head.

"No, it doesn't. But there are a number of additional questions. For instance: How did she get to that Canal? What was she looking for? Most canals are pretty deserted at night, especially during the days just before Christmas. In addition, she had never planned to be there."

"What do you mean?"

"Look at the train ticket. She wanted to go to Gouda. Possibly she planned to spend the Holidays there."

Vledder sat down, sighed wearily, and again looked over the contents of the handbag.

"Silent witnesses," he murmured, "if they could only talk, they might explain a lot."

"But they do," said DeKok.

"Perhaps, but not enough."

He poked through the sparse possessions of the drowned girl and picked up the ring, weighed it in his hand.

"What do you think of this?"

DeKok shrugged his shoulders.

"A broken engagement."

"Engagement?"

"Yes, you young people do it different now, I think. But it wasn't so long ago that it was customary to buy a wedding ring for an engagement, for both parties. You would then inscribe the day of the engagement and wear it on the right hand. Just before the wedding, the date of the wedding would be added to the inscription and the ring would be moved to the other hand. It's a custom that lasted for centuries. Our frugal ancestors never believed in what they called a lot of useless jewelry. They placed their faith in trade, ships and cold, hard cash."

"Thanks for the history lesson, but then, who's 'Ellen'? You read the inscription . . ."

DeKok smiled.

"She, or her fiancee, may have been old-fashioned enough for a traditional ring ceremony, but I think that our blond Helena called herself 'Ellen'. It could have been Lena, or even Elena, but both are considered a bit old-fashioned, these days, not American enough. Thus: Ellen."

Vledder looked at the ring in his hand.

"Why does one break off an engagement?" he mused.

DeKok grinned. It was his most attractive feature. The coarse face with the look of a good natured boxer, would light up and take on something boyish. It was impossible not to like DeKok when he grinned.

"Ach," he said, "there are dozens of answers for that. Infidelity, for instance."

Vledder nodded slowly and tried the ring on his own fingers. The ring was much too large.

"It had to be a man with thick fingers," he mumbled, "thick, strong fingers." He looked at DeKok. "Would . . . eh, would a broken engagement, could it be, . . .eh, a motive for murder?"

DeKok smiled indulgently.

"Have you formed a theory?"

Vledder threw the ring back into the handbag.

"Well, no," he sighed. "But I was just thinking. Somebody must have had a reason, or thought they had a reason, to kill that poor child. That's not something you do on the spur of the moment, is it?"

DeKok nodded.

"Of course, my boy. Somebody had a motive. But it's much too soon to worry about that. We still don't know enough." He looked at his watch. "Come on," he continued, "get your coat. It's almost nine o'clock and we shouldn't keep Dr. Rusteloos waiting."

3

DeKok pulled the shades up. The still hesitant light of the dawn crept slowly over the window sill and did battle with the mysterious twilight in the corners of the autopsy room. The naked body of the victim had been prepped and reclined under a harsh overhead light on the cold, marble slab of the cutting table.

DeKok greeted Dr. Rusteloos.

"I'm sorry," he called.

Dr. Rusteloos made a bowing motion in DeKok's direction.

"I'm sorry," repeated DeKok, louder this time, "I would have liked to leave you out of it, what with Christmas, and all."

The slightly deaf doctor smiled.

"It isn't your fault," he said soothingly. "We can seldom get away from it all. I regret it more for my wife's sake."

DeKok nodded emphatically. He thought about his own wife, about the Christmas present he had bought her and hidden away: the dressing gown with which he had hoped to surprise her.

Dr. Rusteloos prepared himself for the autopsy. He looked impressive in a long, white coat. His ubiquitous assistant placed the dissecting instruments in the right order. DeKok thought about home. He thought about the Christmas breakfast, the goose and all other special things his wife had bought and prepared and felt his stomach growl.

"You stay here," he told Vledder. "I'm sure that the good doctor will go as fast as he can. I'll be back around eleven. By that time it should all be over, I think."

"Where are you going?"

DeKok grinned broadly.

"I'm going home, to my wife, to wish her a Happy Christmas."

Vledder could almost taste the bitterness. He knew that DeKok, despite his expertise, did not like murder cases. He had paid his dues, over and over again. He felt, rightly so, thought Vledder, that it was time for the younger generation of detectives to pay *their* dues, to start taking over, to lighten his load. He would assist them, of course, and allow them to benefit from his long and varied experience, but he preferred to remain in the background, if at all possible. He had gained enough successes and recognition,. He did not crave any more, did not need it. Vledder looked at him searchingly, while these thoughts went through his mind.

"You'll be back, won't you?" It sounded a bit anxious.

DeKok looked up.

"But of course, my boy. What else?"

Vledder bit his lower lip and made a sad gesture.

"Ach," he said unhappily, "never mind. I wouldn't blame you if you pulled on your slippers and stayed home."

DeKok rippled his eyebrows. It was a most amazing sight. DeKok was able to make his eyebrows do things, that seemed impossible. Many people were convinced that DeKok's eyebrows lived a life on their own.

"Are you sorry?" DeKok asked. "Do you regret having shared the case with me?"

Vledder released a deep sigh.

"Believe me, DeKok," he said timidly, "I would have loved to leave you out of it. Please don't think that I enjoyed disturbing you. You had more than earned those few days off, really, I know that. But, you see, I don't think I'm ready, that is, I . . . I lack the experience. I'm still too unsure of myself. I . . ."

DeKok smiled.

"You're making noises like a schoolboy. Of course, I'll be back. I wouldn't leave you now. I'll stick by you."

Vledder swallowed and said:

"In any case, give my best to your wife and wish her a Happy Christmas for me, too."

He turned abruptly and walked to the cutting table. Dr. Rusteloos had already made the first cut.

* * *

Two hours later Vledder walked up and down in front of the Lab. Dr. Rusteloos had finished and he and his assistant had left. Vledder watched their car leave with mixed feeling. Head bent, he resumed his pacing.

The autopsy had shaken him. He wasn't hard enough, callous enough. Not yet. He was still too squeamish. He had shivered while he watched Dr. Rusteloos at his gruesome job. His stomach had protested and only by iron determination had he been able to watch the autopsy to its bitter end.

He took a deep breath. The cold, clear air seemed to revive him. He looked at his watch. It was just about eleven.

DeKok drove up almost on the dot of eleven o'clock. He parked near the sidewalk and opened the passenger door.

"Come on, my boy," he called cheerfully.

He looked fresh and rested. While at home, he had taken a quick shower, shaved and had taken a bite to eat. And he had admired his wife in her new dressing gown.

"How was the autopsy?"

"Terrible, as always," growled Vledder.

DeKok pushed a paper bag his way.

"My wife sent this for you," he said. "Some Christmas bread, or something."

Vledder pulled a face.

"Sorry, DeKok, really. It's very nice of your wife, but I couldn't swallow a bite."

DeKok shrugged his shoulders and drove on.

"What did the good doctor say about the cause of death?"

"A clear case of strangulation. More than likely with the scarf."

136

"What else?"

Vledder looked at him from aside.

"You were right," he said.

"What about?"

"She *was* pregnant."

DeKok whistled softly between his teeth.

"So, so," he said.

Vledder nodded.

"Dr. Rusteloos removed the fetus. It would have been a boy." Suddenly he hid his faces in his hands. "It was terrible," he sighed, "just terrible. You can be glad you weren't there. It was not a pretty sight."

DeKok manoeuvred handily through the traffic and parked on a side street.

"At least she had a painless delivery," he remarked evenly.

Vledder turned toward him abruptly.

"What sort of remark is that," he hissed. "What kind of rotten remark is that? How can you say something like that. You're really too cynical, sometimes."

DeKok switched off the ignition.

"I'm not being cynical," he answered calmly. "And I don't mean to be cynical. I just stated a fact. You see, we still don't know enough about our little Ellen. But I suspect that she looked with fear and trepidation toward the delivery of her child." He made a vague gesture with his hand. "Fear is a terrible pain, my boy. At least she's been spared *that* pain."

Vledder's face assumed a stubborn look. He pressed his lips together.

"Goddamn murderers," he hissed, full of venom. "Bastards! They should be forced to watch the autopsy of their victims, as part of their punishment." He slammed the dashboard with his fist. "I would force them to lean over, press their noses into the gore. Then they could see, experience, then they . . ." His voice broke. "Then . . ."

DeKok let him be. Allowed him to let off steam, relieve his overwhelmed emotions.

"How large was the fetus?" he asked after a while.

"About three and a half inches, nine centimeters. Dr. Rusteloos measured it. A partially developed fetus of three and a half inches."

"Nine centimeters," repeated DeKok, "nine centimeters, that is . . ."

Vledder looked absent mindedly at his surroundings.

"What . . . what are we doing here, anyway?"

DeKok pointed through the windshield.

"Hudson Street," he said, smiling. "You remember? The address on the identity card."

Vledder looked at the monotonous facades on the nondescript street.

"What somber housing," he murmured, as they walked toward the house. "I wouldn't live here for the world." He nudged DeKok. "Did you see? The curtains! Everybody is watching us."

DeKok grinned

"Free entertainment."

He dipped into his pocket and took out a bunch of keys. One by one he tried them on the front door. Vledder watched intently.

"The keys from her bag?"

"Yes, I thought they might help."

One of the keys fit and DeKok pushed against the door. They faced a narrow staircase, covered with a cocos runner and gleaming, brass rods as fasteners. A few colorful prints covered the whitewashed walls.

"What floor?" asked Vledder.

"Let's start at the top," answered DeKok. "I'm almost sure it will be an attic room."

Carefully they pulled themselves up along the bannister. DeKok panted. He had gained some weight, over the last few years. Climbing stairs took a lot more out of him than it used to do. The stairs creaked under their feet.

On the second floor a door opened and the head of a curious woman appeared. The smell of a stuffy room wafted into the corridor.

"Where are you gentlemen going?" she asked.

"Miss Vries."

The rest of the woman appeared in the door opening.

"Oh," she said, "that's all the way at the top. Shall I go with you?"

DeKok made a declining gesture.

"No, no," he said, "thank you. We'll find our way."

He didn't need an audience.

The woman withdrew sullenly.

Vledder and DeKok climbed higher.

The attic floor had been divided into five, or six, little rooms, separated by improvised partitions of lattice and plywood. There were no names on the doors. Undecided Vledder and DeKok looked around. They did not have a clue about the right door and they did not want to alert everybody on the floor. Much to their relief, they did discover a narrow door at the end of the dark corridor with the word 'Vries' written in pencil on the unpainted wood of the door.

DeKok again produced his bunch of keys and tried several keys on the padlock which closed the door. After a few moments they were inside a chilly, unheated attic room. The only light was provided by a small skylight between the rafters of a slanted wall. To the right of the door was a single bed with a bookshelf mounted above it. A framed picture stood on the book shelf. It was a photograph of Helena.

DeKok sat down on the edge of the bed and looked around the small room. A rattan chair, an electric stove, an old dresser and a night stand. It was a mixture of old, discarded furniture and a few fresh, modern pieces, probably obtained by Helena herself, over the years.

Vledder snorted.

"So, this is where she lived."

DeKok nodded slowly.

"Not exactly cozy, or comfortable, if you ask me. What could have possessed the child to move to Amsterdam? I think she probably had a much better room with her parents. Anyway, let's look around. Perhaps we'll find something that will be of help. Notes, letters, papers. Everything that seems the least little bit useful. Look for addresses, especially."

Vledder nodded and started with the dresser.

He had just spread the contents on the floor when suddenly, without knocking, a young woman entered the room. She looked at both men with wide, surprised eyes.

"W-what . . . what are you doing?" she stammered. "W-why are you here? Who . . . who are you?"

DeKok was still on the edge of the bed. He pushed his hat slightly back on his head and appraised the young woman. About twenty five, he estimated.

She looked like the type one associated with a clever executive secretary. Not exactly good looking, but handsome, very handsome in a strange way. His gaze rested on her face. Intelligent, he decided. A pair of bright eyes sparkled behind a heavy pair of horn rimmed glasses. He gave her one of his most winning smiles.

"Those," he said laconically, "were three questions in a row."

Slowly he rose and approached her.

"To answer your last question first," he said in a friendly tone of voice, "my name is DeKok. DeKok with . . .eh, kay-oh-kay. This is my colleague, Vledder. We're detectives, attached to the Warmoes Street station."

She looked at both men with suspicion.

"Inspectors?"

DeKok nodded.

"Police Inspectors."

It took several seconds before his words penetrated.

"Police, police," she repeated. "But, what's the matter. What are you looking for, here?"

DeKok gestured vaguely.

"Before I answer your questions," he said calmly, "I would very much like to know who you are. With whom do I have the pleasure?"

She stroked her hand through her black, glossy hair.

"Yes, yes," she sighed. "Of course, you're right. I was a bit shocked, you know. So unexpected." She sighed again. "Ellen is a friend of mine. We work in the same office."

"And your name?"

"Femmy, Femmy Weingarten. I live here, on the same attic. I helped Ellen find this room."

"How long did Ellen live here?"

She suddenly looked at him sharply. A deep crease appeared in her forehead. She was thinking hard. DeKok knew he had made a mistake. He had formulated his question incorrectly.

"You . . . said . . . *did* live?"

DeKok nodded slowly.

"You listen carefully," he said seriously.

She gripped her head with both hands. A wild gesture of despair.

"W-what . . . w-what happened?"

DeKok took her by the arm and led her to one of the rattan chairs. He saw the scared, terrified look in her eyes.

"Ellen," he said softly, "Ellen is dead."

4

"Ellen's death has raised a number of questions. Pertinent questions. It's part of our job to find the right answers to these questions. You could help us a great deal with that task."

She had cried for a while. The glasses in her lap. Big tears still dribbled down her cheeks. DeKok took a clean handkerchief from his pocket and wiped the tears away. Without the big, headstrong glasses she looked a lot different. Softer, nicer, not quite as competent, less self-assured.

"What happened?"

DeKok sighed.

"Last night we found her body in the canal."

"Did she . . . did she jump?"

DeKok did not answer. He sat down opposite her and offered her a cigarette. She accepted greedily, with shaking hands.

"Were you good friends?" he asked, lighting her cigarette. "I mean, did she tell you things?"

She inhaled deeply and let the smoke escape slowly. It seemed to steady her. The way in which she smoked indicated a studied effect. A calculated routine that did not seem to fit with the rest of her behavior. DeKok wondered if her tears had been real. If she had been truly grieving.

"Did she discuss things openly, with you?" he repeated.

"Oh, yes," she said, a bit hesitant, "yes, she talked."

"So, she kept things from you," he concluded.

She made an impatient gesture.

"Well, yes, you see," she said, a bit irritated, "we were not *close* friends. Of course, she didn't tell me everything. What woman will?"

DeKok grinned at that remark. He had his own thoughts on the subject. But he kept those to himself.

"Was she engaged? Engaged to be married?"

"No longer. It was over. She still wore her engagement ring, but it was camouflage. I knew that she had broken the engagement."

"When?"

"Oh, shortly after she came to work in our office. Let's see, she started after the summer vacations, on September 1. About two months later, or so, she broke off the engagement."

"Any particular reason?"

She shrugged her shoulders.

"Not as far as I know."

DeKok leaned backward.

"So, she *did* wear her ring?"

She nodded.

"Yes, she never took it off. She was still wearing it yesterday. She used to say that the ring protected her from insistent admirers." She smiled weakly. "Ellen was the sort of girl that men found attractive."

"Did you ever meet her fiancee?"

She shook her head.

"No, I never met him. I've seen him, though. One day he waited for her outside the office. He's in the service. Big, blond stud, son of a wholesaler in Gouda. She was from Gouda, you see. Her parents have a grocery store there, a super market, actually.

Before Ellen started in the office with us, she used to work in the store in Gouda."

"Why did she come to Amsterdam?"

She gave him a bitter smile.

"She wanted a change."

DeKok nodded pensively. He thought about the answer. It sounded cynical, he thought.

"How did she get a job in your office?" he asked. "Did she apply for the job? Was there an opening?"

For the first time he noticed a sincere reaction from her. An involuntary, short hesitation in her answer.

"That ... eh, I don't know that," she said, "I really don't know. It was never discussed."

DeKok knew she lied.

"Was she a good worker?"

Her lips formed a smile.

"Well, not really," she said, sympathy in her voice. "Actually, Ellen really wasn't up to the work. I had to help her a lot and often. She just didn't have any experience with office work."

"But she was kept on?"

Again the slight hesitation.

"Yes."

"But her unsuitability must have been noticed?"

"Yes."

He looked at her sharply.

"Well ... and?"

She avoided his eyes.

DeKok rubbed his face with a weary hand. He did not like Femmy Weingarten's reactions. It was almost like talking to a wall, as if she hid behind the walls of a fortress, a fortress he could not penetrate. She hid her true face and showed him a mask. She was constantly alert. Afraid to say too much, or the wrong thing. Afraid of saying something she wanted to hide. As if she had a deep, dark secret that could not be discussed.

DeKok sighed.

"Apart from her fiancee, did she associate with any other men?"

143

"I don't know," she answered petulantly. "Anyway, it was none of my business."

"Come, come," said DeKok, "after all, she was your friend. Did she ever receive men in her room?"

"No, the landlady doesn't allow that."

"Did she ever stay out, overnight?"

She moved restlessly in her chair, worried the hem of her skirt with nervous fingers, but did not answer.

"Miss Weingarten," said DeKok in a friendly tone, "I asked you a question."

She nodded slowly.

"I heard you," she said calmly.

"Well?"

"Sometimes . . . she didn't come home, at night."

"Where would she be, in that case?"

She shrugged her shoulders, releasing a deep sigh.

"That, I don't know. I've asked sometimes, in a round about way, you know, female curiosity."

"And?"

"She always avoided my questions and smiled mysteriously. I never did find out."

"But you had a suspicion?"

She pulled a minuscule handkerchief from the pocket of her skirt and started to clean her glasses. Obviously it was a way to delay an answer, give herself time to think.

"No, eh, . . . I had no idea."

DeKok listened carefully to the tone of voice, to the intonation. There was a slight vibration in her voice that warned him. He just did not know, yet, what the warning was about.

"No idea?" he repeated.

"No . . . no."

He looked at her searchingly for a long time, one hand under his chin. You do have an idea, he thought. Of course, you have an idea. When she was not here, when you did not find her in her room, when you found her bed undisturbed, then you knew exactly where she was spending the night. He pressed his eyes half closed. Why, he wondered, why do you not give me his name?

Slowly he rose from his chair.

"Where do you work?"

"For Dolman and Fleet on the Emperor's Canal. I've been there for five years."

He shuffled slowly around the room. Diagonally behind her he halted and watched for her reactions.

"Did you know," he asked nonchalantly, "that she was pregnant?"

He saw a shock go through her body. She turned abruptly and faced him. There was confusion in her eyes.

"Pregnant?"

"Yes, Miss Weingarten, Ellen was pregnant."

She put her hands in front of her eyes and started to cry again. Softly, without sobs.

DeKok let her be for a moment, then he asked:

"You didn't know?"

Slowly she hook her head.

"No, I didn't know. The poor child. She was so often sick, lately. I used to think how bad she looked. But ... but I never thought ... it never occurred to me that ..., I mean, pregnant?" She looked at him with teary eyes. "By whom?"

DeKok's eyebrows rippled.

"You don't know? You really don't know?"

She perceived the question as a threat. Her eyes narrowed. Suddenly she was again alert and suspicious.

"How should I know?" she asked pointedly, "She didn't invite me to watch!"

DeKok grinned.

"No," he admitted, "that's not usually the custom. But I thought that you would be able to help me. After all, you *were* her friend."

She did not seem to listen. She stared in front of her. Her lips pressed together into a straight, thin line.

"Bastards," she yelled suddenly, "bastards! Of course they left her. That's what it is. The poor child just didn't know where to turn, anymore. They left her holding the bag, as always. They ..."

DeKok interrupted her.

"Tell me about yesterday," he said. "Was she in the office?"

She wiped her eyes with the sleeve of her sweater and nodded.

"Until one. We all worked until one, yesterday. We closed early because of Christmas Eve."

"Exactly. Did you leave together?"

"No, she had to go to the railroad station first. She wanted to get a train ticket in advance. She thought it might be very busy, later. That's why. She was planning to spend Christmas with her parents, in Gouda."

"Did she come home, from the station?"

"Yes, she packed a suitcase."

"What time did she leave?"

"Around six."

"With her suitcase?"

"Yes."

"Was she planning to go directly to the station?"

"No, she still had an appointment."

"An appointment?"

"Yes."

"With whom?"

"I don't know exactly. She said she still had a stop to make. I think she was meeting her fiancee."

"But the engagement was off?"

"Yes, but she did maintain contact with him. He used to call her often. Yesterday, too. You see, I sit directly opposite her, in the office. Subconsciously you listen, you hear things."

"So, she made a date for later that evening?"

She nodded.

"At least, that's what I thought I understood from the conversation."

"Why? I mean, why a date?"

"He wanted to talk to her once more, I think."

"How did the conversation go."

"Oh, very friendly. She even laughed a few times. Perhaps because of something he said. Of course, I could not hear *him*."

DeKok walked over to the window and looked at the somber houses across the street. His brain worked at top capacity, but he could not find a connection. There was no line to follow. It was all still too dark, so mysterious, incomprehensible.

Slowly he turned and looked at Femmy Weingarten, Ellen's friend. She had put her glasses back on. The tears had disappeared. A black smudge showed near her left eyebrow, caused by the sleeve of the sweater as she dried her tears. It was the only sign that indicated that she had been crying. She reposed calmly, hands in her lap. DeKok looked at the clothing, the high collared sweater, the stiff skirt, the black stockings and the low, utilitarian shoes. Sober, respectable, almost too respectable for a young woman.

A strange type, he thought, difficult to evaluate. He did not understand her at all. He felt that she kept something back, hid something. But what? Did it have anything to do with Ellen? Or was it something else?

"You're not married?" he asked hesitantly.

"No, I am single."

"No . . .eh, no friends?"

In a sharp, bitter movement she threw her head back and snorted. Her long hair whipped backward.

"Men," she said contemptuously, "men are bums, arrogant, puffed up, bums. Men aplenty, as long as you allow them their pleasures. But don't ask for more," she grinned broadly, "or they give you the brush-off."

DeKok looked at her searchingly for a long while. Her spirited reaction had not surprised him. He had expected it, more or less.

"How old is your child by now?" he asked sympathetically.

His question seemed like a shot in the dark, but it was the logical conclusion after her reaction. He saw a tic develop near one corner of her mouth and he knew he had made the right guess.

"My little Hans," she said, "Hansie is two years old." She fiddled with the hem of her sweater. "I'm an unwed mother. You see, they left me in the lurch, too. That's why I can understand so well what Ellen went through. Men are bastards! Believe me, all men are bastards!"

DeKok scratched the back of his neck. It was not the first time that he had heard such a passionate denunciation of his sex. He had met plenty of women who had vengeful feelings about men. Often with very good reasons.

"I used to warn Ellen," she continued. "I told her what happened to me. I told her to be careful." She shrugged her shoulders in a careless gesture. "But, you know, she just wouldn't listen."

DeKok gave her a bitter smile.

"Did *you* listen, at the time?" he asked softly. "We generally don't like to listen, when we're young."

He sat down again, in the chair opposite her.

"Where is Hansie now?"

She sighed.

"With my parents, in Hoorn. I can't keep him here. He's still too small. Also . . . I have to work."

A long silence reigned after her words. DeKok looked at Vledder, who had quietly continued his investigation of the room. He was now finished and leaned against a wall, waiting.

Femmy looked thoughtfully in the distance.

"Poor Ellen," she sighed, "she looked so forward to Christmas. She told me what she had planned to do in Gouda. She would take long walks with her younger brothers. She was going to visit an elderly aunt, where she used to spent a lot of time as a child. She was . . ."

She stopped abruptly. Her face became pensive. It was as if she suddenly became aware of a thought, a horrible thought, a horrible thought that slowly took form. Confused, she looked up.

"Ellen . . . ," she said, thoroughly shaken, "Ellen didn't seem the type. She didn't give any signs, I mean, it seems incredible. She . . . she never planned to commit suicide."

DeKok sighed.

"But who," he asked softly, "who said anything about suicide?"

Her eyes became wide and scared.

"Then it wasn't . . .?"

DeKok shook his head.

"Ellen was murdered."

5

Lazily, almost horizontal, DeKok lolled in his chair. The heels of his shoes rested on the desk. He was not at all happy with the way things were developing. He combed his thick fingers through his hair.

"I don't know," he said, irritated. "There was something about her I didn't like. She was too closed, too self-contained. At times. Especially about Ellen's relationships with men."

"Perhaps Ellen *had* no relationships with men?"

DeKok grinned.

"Oh, come on! Just think about the broken engagement and the nights she spent away from home. No, no, Vledder, apart from her fiancee, there were other men who played a part in Ellen's life. And Femmy knows more than she's willing to tell us. When I told her that Ellen had been murdered, I could almost feel her think. It was as if she *knew* who'd done it."

Vledder shrugged his shoulders unconcernedly.

"I didn't notice anything particular about her. She was shocked. But what do you expect? That would be a normal reaction. After all, it was her friend."

DeKok stared at his fingernails.

"Maybe you're right," he said after a pause. "It could have been my imagination. Women are difficult, if not impossible, to read. But, yet ... you see, I have a deep respect for female intuition. Women can come to the right conclusions with the skimpiest facts to support them. They are much more perceptive than we, than men. In addition she has the advantage of having known Ellen during her lifetime. We haven't. That's one of the worst things about a murder case. You always start with the corpse of an unknown. A man, or woman, who's a complete stranger to you. We're totally dependent on what others say about the deceased. And you never get an objective report. For instance, what do we really know about Ellen? We've seen her body. A good looking girl, at least on the outside. Dr. Rusteloos may add that her insides, too, were not bad, not bad at all, at all. But otherwise . . .?"

The ringing of the telephone interrupted his discourse. Vledder picked up the receiver and listened. He looked up after a few seconds, covering the mouthpiece with his hand.

"It's the desk-sergeant." He sounded surprised. "Tom Weick is downstairs . . . escorted by two MPs."

DeKok nodded.

"Tell them to come up."

Vledder relayed the order and replaced the receiver.

"How," he wondered, "did Tom Weick get here?"

DeKok grinned mischievously.

"While you were at the autopsy, this morning, I called the Military Police and asked them to bring him in. Very simple. Just a question of organization. I also arranged to have friend Hofman, from Alkmaar, picked up. I guess he'll appear in the course of the afternoon. I'm curious to find out how he'll explain the presence of his wallet in Ellen's handbag."

Despondently, Vledder shook his head.

"I should have thought of that," he said softly, "after all, it's supposed to be my case."

DeKok laughed at him in a friendly, almost fatherly way.

"Don't break your head over it. You'll learn. You're still allowing yourself too much to be influenced by events. You should guard against that."

Vledder sighed.

"Easy for you to say. It's just routine for you. But not for me. When I discovered, last night, that the poor thing had been strangled, I shook in my boots. I'm still upset about it. You'll have to excuse me, DeKok, but it was difficult for me to think straight, after that discovery. The girl dominated my thoughts. It really seems as if it made me lose the ability to think clearly, to make cool and objective decisions."

Wearily DeKok removed his legs from the desk and rose slowly. He looked calmly at Vledder, digging his hands deep in his pockets. His face was expressionless. Vledder started to get nervous. The corners of his mouth developed a tic. He was uneasy under that scrutinizing look.

"Yes, yes," he yelled, uncontrolled. "I know what you're going to say. I know! But I can't do it. Not me, you see. I'm not a machine."

DeKok's eyebrows vibrated dangerously. They actually bristled.

"Am I?" It sounded sharp. "Listen carefully to what I'm going to tell you, my friend. Don't become a doctor if you faint at the sight of blood. In other words, if you're going to cry over every corpse, you're no good for police work. Somewhere there's a guy who has killed. Who strangled Ellen, murdered her. And he's still walking around free. Concentrate your energies on that! If you ever want to catch him, you'll need all your faculties."

There was a knock on the door.

DeKok ambled toward the other end of the room and opened the door. He was confronted by two husky MPs. Between them was a young man in uniform, without any insignia, or indication of rank.

"We picked him up in the barracks and brought him over as soon as possible. Do you need a report on our findings?"

DeKok gave them a friendly smile.

"No, not for the moment. In any case, my sincere thanks. I'll take care of our young friend from here on."

The MPs saluted correctly, did an about face and marched off.

DeKok stood in front of the young man for a few moments. His gaze traveled from the face to the hands. It did not take long. A fleeting impression. Then he stretched out his hand.

"My name is DeKok," he said cheerfully, "DeKok, with . . .eh, kay-oh-kay. And you're Tom Weick?"

The young man nodded.

"Welcome, Tom. Please come in."

He led the way and pointed to a chair next to his desk.

"Please sit down and make yourself comfortable."

A bit reluctantly, the young man sat down. He looked from Vledder to DeKok and from DeKok to Vledder. He felt unsure. His face was red. The fingers plucked nervously at the beret in his lap.

DeKok leaned toward him and brought his face closer. He saw his own face mirrored in the blue eyes of the young man. He noticed a blue vein near the forehead pulsing in an agitated rhythm.

"No need to be frightened," whispered DeKok. "Just tell the truth. No more. It's useless to lie, anyway. Especially now. The case is too serious for that."

"B-bu . . . b-but . . . ," stammered the young man, "I . . ."

DeKok straightened up and pointed at Vledder.

"This is my colleague, Vledder. He wants to ask you some questions."

Without another word, he turned around, ambled toward the window and looked outside, his back to the room. The presence of the young military man seemed to be a matter of sublime indifference to him.

Vledder was startled. This had never happened before. DeKok always led the interrogations himself. He *never* left it to others. As long as Vledder had known him, he had never known DeKok to relinquish the initiative. He stared at DeKok's back. His silhouette was sharply delineated against the gray light from the windows. Suddenly he grasped DeKok's intention. The old man was forcing him to devote his full, undivided attention to the investigation.

A bit apprehensive, Vledder placed himself in DeKok's chair and looked at the soldier. He did not know quite how to start. What sort of questions to ask? Was he confronting the killer? Did he strangle his fiancee? The motive? Vledder felt himself sweat. His back itched. He took a handkerchief from a pocket and wiped his forehead.

"Where," he started, "were you last night, after six?"

Tom Weick studied Vledder's face.

"I don't really understand what you want from me," he said. "What am I doing here? Without a word of explanation I am lifted from my bunk and transported here. What's the meaning of all this?" He grinned a bit shyly. "You're from Homicide, aren't you?"

Vledder nodded.

The young man gestured.

"Well, I have done nothing."

"We'll see about that."

The young man moved in his chair.

152

"We'll see about that," he repeated, irritated. "We'll see about that. What sort of nonsense is this? I should know if I've done something, or not, yes or no?"

Vledder leaned forward.

"Where," he repeated, "were you last night, after six?"

The young man grimaced.

"In the barracks, where else?"

Vledder shrugged his shoulders.

"You didn't have leave, or a pass?"

"No, they're not all that generous."

"You're engaged to be married?"

"I *was* engaged."

"With whom?"

"Ellen, Ellen Vries."

"How long were you two engaged?"

"A few months."

"Did you, . . .eh, have you had carnal knowledge of her?"

The young man looked astonished.

"What are you saying?"

Vledder swallowed. He was a bit embarrassed.

"It's not a dirty word, you know," a bit sharper than intended. "It's in all the law books. The Bible, too."

The young man just stared at him.

Vledder bit his lower lip. It was an icky subject, he thought. But he needed it for his investigation. It seemed pertinent.

"I don't ask," he said apologetically, "from prurient interest. I just ask because I want to know, need to know. Did you have carnal knowledge of her, yes or no?"

The young soldier nodded.

"Yes," he said softly, "it happened, from time to time."

Vledder swallowed again, steeling himself.

"And . . . and did you use a condom on those occasions, eh, . . . a prophylactic, a rubber, or whatever they're called these days?"

Tom shook his head.

"No, we just did it."

"Were there never any consequences?"

"What do you mean?"

Vledder sighed.

"Did she get pregnant?"

"Pregnant?"

"Yes, was she expecting a child?"

The young man grinned a bashful grin.

"No," he answered, "no, not as far as I know. I never heard that. I mean, she never told me." He grinned again. "A child." The thought seemed strange to him.

Vledder looked at him for a long time. He could not quite make up his mind about the young soldier. Was he play acting? Was it an elaborate comedy? Did he really *not* know that Ellen was pregnant? It seemed obvious that he would be the first to know. That she would tell him first, before anybody else.

"So, the engagement was broken off?" he confirmed.

"Yes."

"When?"

"As soon as I came back from La Courtine."

"How long were you there?"

"The entire month of October."

"Why was the engagement called off?"

"I don't know. She didn't want to go through with it."

"What did you think about that?"

"What I thought about it? I thought it was terrible, just terrible. I was upset for days. Later, I became angry. She had no right . . . there was no reason. I . . . ."

He stopped abruptly. It was as if a change came over him. He looked at Vledder through narrowed eyes.

"Why . . . why all these questions? What business of yours is my private life? You don't have the right to ask me such questions. That's private. It's none of your business."

Vledder sighed.

"When did you see Ellen last?"

Agitated, the soldier stood up. There was a stubborn look on his face.

"I'm not answering any more questions until you tell me what this is all about."

"Ellen has been murdered."

Tom Weick paled. His mouth fell open. Slowly he sank back in his chair and stared as if stunned.

"M-m . . . m-mu . . . murdered," he stammered. He seemed unable to absorb the news. "Ellen has been murdered?"

Vledder stood up.

"Yes," he said pointedly, "Ellen has been murdered." He stretched out an accusing arm toward the young soldier. "And that's on your conscience. You were angry, because she broke off your engagement. Last night you made a date with her. You wanted to force her to keep the engagement going, to stay with you. When she refused, you became furious, grabbed her and you strangled her." His voice became hard. He seemed to mean what he said.

Tom Weick looked at him with wide eyes. He looked scared and in desperation he shook his head wildly.

"No," he screamed, "No! It isn't true! Not me! I didn't kill Ellen, I couldn't have . . ."

Vledder's face became red. His lips curled in a combination of anger and contempt.

"Yes," he yelled. "You strangled her and threw her body in the canal."

Abruptly the young man stood up. His chair clattered against the floor behind him.

"You're lying," he roared. "Me, *me* . . . kill Ellen? You're crazy, stark raving mad!"

Vledder could not control himself any longer. His blood boiled. From across the desk he grabbed Tom by the front of his uniform jacket.

"Yes," he barked at the soldier. "With your thick fingers you tightened the scarf around her neck. I've *seen* the marks in her neck. You, you BASTARD!"

The vision of the dead girl dominated his thoughts. In an uncontrollable rage he tightened his grip on the young man and practically dragged him across the desk. His hands shook with the exertion. All his emotions, all his hidden anger at the cowardly killing, discharged all at once. He had excited himself into believing, whipped himself into a rage with the firm conviction that he was facing the murderer. And he could kill him right now, out of pure revenge, without remorse, without pity.

"Vledder!"

With large, quick steps, DeKok left the window. He had listened closely to the development of the interrogation and listened even more closely to the intonations, the hidden undertones. He knew a little about human emotions, about human frailty, and he was well aware of the dangers inherent in an uncontrolled interrogation.

"Let him go," he roared, "and get out." His eyes flickered dangerously, angrily.

Vledder nodded slowly. For just a moment he stood there, subdued and undecided. He looked at his opponent. "Sorry," he murmured, beaten, "sorry." Then he left the detective room with bowed head.

DeKok watched him leave and sighed. He liked the boy. He had seen his successor in him, but sometimes he doubted his choice. Too emotional. Too much feeling.

Slowly he turned to the totally devastated soldier.

"I warned you," he said. "It's your own fault. You should have told the truth."

He went to the little sink and poured a glass of water.

"Here," he said consolingly, "drink some water. And straighten your uniform. You look a bit wrinkled."

The young man was visibly upset. His teeth rattled against the glass. His hands shook.

DeKok sat down opposite him and waited patiently until the soldier had more or less recovered.

It did not take long. Some color came back in his cheeks. He sighed deeply, several times, placed the glass on the desk and pulled his blouse straight. DeKok looked at the young face of the soldier. Tom Weick was a handsome man. Even, regular features, blond hair and sparkling blue eyes. He and Ellen, thought DeKok, would have made a good looking couple. A nice couple. But Ellen was dead.

"Why didn't you tell the truth?"

DeKok leaned forward and rested his elbows on the desk.

"Come a little closer," he invited. "I want to talk to you confidentially. I don't dislike you. Vledder doesn't dislike you either. He's still a bit young, just like you. And young people sometimes lose their heads." He smiled. "It's part of youth, part of growing up."

Tom scooted his chair closer to the desk. The good natured, craggy face in front of him invited trust. It allayed his suspicions.

"Why didn't you tell the truth?" repeated DeKok in a fatherly tone of voice. "You started with a lie. You weren't in barracks, last night."

The young man lowered his head a little.

"Is . . . , is Ellen really dead?" he asked softly.

DeKok nodded.

"We found her in the canal."

Tom's eyes filled with tears.

"I don't understand it," he said, shaking his head. "She was . . . she was . . . Who would do something like that?" he rubbed his eyes. "Could I . . .could I see her, once more?"

"It's not usual. It's also not a pretty sight. Buy I could arrange it. If you really want it."

The young man sighed.

"Yes, please, sir. I . . . I . . ."

"Yes?"

The young soldier swallowed.

"You see, I really loved Ellen. Loved her a lot. She broke off our engagement, but I never believed she meant it. She knew I was crazy about her and . . . she used to tease me about that, sometimes."

"But breaking off an engagement is rather a serious sort of tease, isn't it?"

"Yes, you're right. But still . . .you see, it was just an impulse. She met Mr. Dolman last summer. Or rather, she had known him for some time. The Dolman family spent their vacations in Gouda, every year. They rent a villa. Ellen used to deliver the groceries. Her parents have a grocery store in Gouda."

"A supermarket."

"Well, yes, but that's recent. They used to have just a regular grocery store, rather small. But last year they started to remodel,

157

to expand. My father and old man Vries, Ellen's father, have been doing business for years. We have a wholesale operation, coffee, tea, spices, whatever. I used to deliver to them. That's how I met Ellen, got to know her."

"You mentioned an impulse?"

Tom Weick sighed.

"Yes," he said, "you could call it that. Last summer she suddenly got it into her head to start working in Amsterdam. That Dolman had made her crazy. He has a business on the Emperor's Canal and he promised her a job in his office."

"You didn't like that?"

"No, I didn't like it at all. I would have preferred for her to stay in Gouda. A girl, alone in the big city, that's no good. I told her so, straight out. But she laughed at me and asked if I was afraid of something. I told you, she liked to tease me."

"So she went?"

"Yes, she started last September. Oh, well, I'd reconciled myself to it. We were going to get married anyway, next year. As soon as I came out of the service. In October my unit was sent to La Courtine, in France, for maneuvers." He grinned a bitter grin. "I wasn't there for more than two weeks, when she sent me a 'Dear John' letter, telling me the engagement was off. Just like that."

"Suddenly?"

"Yes, suddenly. Nothing had happened."

"Tell me again, how long were you in La Courtine?"

"All of October."

"Of course, I can check that, Tom. I mean, if you were really there, all month."

The young man looked at him, surprised.

"Yes, of course. That's real easy."

DeKok nodded thoughtfully.

"And last night you tried to make it up between you and Ellen?" It was more a statement than a question.

The young man stiffened.

"You think I killed her?"

DeKok ignored the question. He could be infuriating that way. Many people believed that he could literally switch his ears

158

off, when he so desired. There was never any way to make sure he had seen, or heard something, if he did not want to react to it.

"You called her yesterday, at the office," continued DeKok as if Tom's question had never been spoken. "You made a date with her. Did she keep the date?"

The expression on Tom's face changed.

"You suspect me of murder," he answered bitterly. "You think I killed Ellen because she broke our engagement." He shook his head. "No, sir, I didn't kill Ellen. I didn't call her yesterday and I didn't have a date with her."

DeKok sighed.

"Tom, Tom, this way we're getting nowhere," he said resignedly. Then, in a commanding tone of voice: "Stand at attention and empty your pockets."

"Why?"

"Because I'm telling you."

Sullenly the young man stood up and stood more or less at attention. Slowly he emptied his pockets and placed the items on the desk: a comb, a handkerchief, a small notebook, some change. He placed it all in front of DeKok.

"Is that all?"

"That's all."

DeKok looked at him evenly.

"Tom, my boy," he said in a friendly way, "you don't want to be searched, do you? You don't want me to search you, do you? I *know* you have it with you. She still had it last night."

"I don't know what you mean."

It was an awkward attempt. A weak excuse.

DeKok shrugged his shoulders.

"You asked for it," he said wearily and prepared to rise from his chair.

The young man looked at him for a moment and then he reached into a breast pocket and threw the ring at DeKok.

DeKok caught it and read the inscription: *Tom, May 1, 19..*

6

"Do you understand clearly?"

"Yes, Mr. DeKok."

"Not a word about having been here and not a word about what we discussed."

"Yes, Mr. DeKok, it's all my own idea."

"Exactly. You have heard from the police that Ellen has been killed. That's all. Then you went out to investigate, to find out what happened."

Tom Weick nodded.

"I'll do my best. If something turns up, I'll call you."

DeKok smiled.

"Excellent, really excellent. On your way, then."

As soon as Tom had closed the door of the detective room behind him, DeKok grabbed the telephone and called the desk-sergeant.

"There's a soldier on the way down. You know, the one who was brought in by the MPs. I would like you to provide him with an escort. He'll tell them where to go. Please instruct them to let him out of the car when he says so."

"Nothing else?"

"No, that's all. Also, you don't need to mention him in your daily report. For the time being he's just a witness."

"I'll take care of it."

"Oh, yes, send Vledder back up."

With a sluggish gesture he replaced the receiver. and started to slowly pace up and down the detective room. He stopped before the window, straddle legged, in his favorite position, hands behind his back, slowly rocking up and down on the balls of his feet.

He looked at the maze of rooftops at the other side of the old Warmoes Street. He was familiar with the view, every hour of the day, every day of the week, every month of the year. How many hours had he stood here? Lost in thought, trying to find an exit from the labyrinth of human passion, emotions. He had become

160

gray in the job and the lines in his face had become deeper with the passing years. He did not reflect on it with bitterness, but calm and sober, as was his habit when viewing life in all its manifestations.

He had served the Law for more than twenty years. The Law in which he did not really believe. He didn't really work for the Law, but for his fellow man. A simple concept of 'love thy neighbor', without frills. He had never thought about it consciously, but had just lived it, because he discovered something of himself in every person he met. There was little difference, he thought, between a murderer, a thief and himself. The difference was negligible. They were all people with everything that entailed. But some could control themselves less easily. That was the only difference. That's why he stood here, on the first day of Christmas, while his wife moped at home and worried about the goose and the braised hare that had been such an effort to get and prepare, just because he happened to love braised hare.

Vledder stormed into the room.

"You sent him away, you let him go!"

DeKok turned slowly to face him.

"Yes," he answered calmly, "I let him go."

Vledder looked astonished.

"B-but . . . ," he stammered, not understanding. "But he had a date with her on the night of the killing, last night. We know because Femmy told us."

DeKok nodded.

"It checks. He admitted it. He had a date with her for seven o'clock in the hall of the Central Station. They went to the restaurant on the first platform. There they talked. It was a rather vehement conversation, laced with many cups of coffee. Ellen told him that she wasn't going to change her mind. It was impossible, she said, to continue the engagement. She also told him, that no matter what, she would always love him. Anyway, it was a dramatic scene. They parted around nine o'clock."

"And you believe that?"

"What?"

"That he left her at nine."

"Why not?"

"But . . . DeKok," Vledder cried out, totally baffled. "Tom was the last person to see her alive. He could have killed her. Perhaps his story won't check out. Neither the Gentlemen's Canal, nor the Brewers Canal are far from the railroad station. Maybe five minutes on foot. He could have taken her for a walk. Also, he has an acceptable motive. He even admits that they quarreled."

DeKok nodded.

"You're right," he said calmly, "Tom could have killed his fiancee. He did have the time. He didn't check back into the barracks until after midnight."

Vledder was getting more and more excited.

"But you let him go!?"

DeKok sank lazily back into his chair and yawned. He thought to himself that he had not had enough sleep. He opened a desk drawer and took a roll of peppermints out. Slowly he selected one. He held the roll out to Vledder. "Want one?" he invited.

Vledder's face resembled a thunder cloud.

"You let him go, DeKok. You even laid on a police car to take him where he wanted to go. Why?"

DeKok grinned.

"Because Tom Weick was in La Courtine, all through October."

Vledder grinned back, unable to resist the charm DeKok exuded when he grinned.

"What's that got to do with anything?"

"Enough, so that he's not our only suspect."

"What!?"

DeKok sighed.

"Don't I speak clearly enough for you, my boy? Let me repeat it for you: Tom - Weick - is - not - our - only - suspect. There's got to be someone else."

"Someone else?"

DeKok looked at his young partner, shaking his head.

"You're too restless, today," he said, a slight reproach in his voice. "That interrogation was also less than an overwhelming success." He gestured toward the chair next to his desk. "Sit down, take a load off your feet, and I'll teach you some basic mathematics. Can you muster the patience to listen to me?"

Vledder felt the rebuke, the admonition, however gentle. He was very well aware that his behavior, to say the least, had been less than calm. DeKok was right, he *was* too impatient, tending to go off half cocked, almost from the moment that Ellen's corpse had been fished from the canal. And he knew why. Deep down, he knew what the reason was. It was mostly a feeling of inadequacy, fear, lack of confidence in himself, a feeling that had made him reluctant to tackle the case by himself. DeKok made it all look so simple, so self-evident, so natural, that he could only blame himself, afterwards, for not having been able to find the solution on his own. It had happened more times than he cared to remember. That was part of the reason he tried to impress his old mentor with words, gestures, even histrionics, but he felt, no, knew, that he would never be another DeKok.

Sighing he rubbed his face and realized suddenly that it was one of the many 'DeKok' gestures that he had involuntarily made his own.

"Mathematics?" he asked absent mindedly.

DeKok nodded.

"There is," he began, "a rather interesting formula that can be used to determine the length of pregnancy, based on the length of the fetus. If pregnancy is of one month's duration, the fetus will be one times one equals one centimeter long. After two months, the fetus will be two times two, thus four centimeters long. Three months: three times three equals nine centimeters. And so on, until the fifth month. Starting with the fifth month it is enough to multiply by five. A fetus of eight month's duration is, eight times five, equals forty centimeters long. Understand?"

Vledder nodded.

"For this formula one uses the first day of the last menses as a starting point and the months are not figured as calendar months, but as so-called moon months, or menstrual cycles, of twenty eight days."

Vledder took a sheet of paper and industriously made some notes.

"You got that?"

"Yes."

"Let us therefore examine the pregnancy of Ellen Vries," continued DeKok in his best lecturing voice. Dr. Rusteloos measured the fetus during the autopsy and gave us a length of exactly nine centimeters. Therefore, based on our calculations, at the time of her death, Ellen had been pregnant for three months of twenty eight days each. Can you follow that, or is it getting too complicated for you?"

Vledder smiled.

"It's rather simple."

DeKok rubbed the bridge of his nose with an outstretched index finger.

"So," he went on, "since we know that Ellen died on the twenty fifth of December, that is, the first day of Christmas, we count back eighty four days and we arrive at the second of October. Keeping in mind that a woman's menstrual cycle is roughly twenty eight days, what would then be the ultimate conclusion?"

Vledder looked at his notes.

"That . . .eh, roughly, she conceived between the second and thirtieth day of October."

DeKok nodded agreement.

"Very good! Thus we know that our beautiful Ellen did have, as you so delicately expressed it, carnal knowledge of a man between those dates."

Vledder looked at him pensively.

"But, if . . ."

DeKok nodded encouragement.

"Yes," he remarked, "go on."

"But if she became pregnant in October, it wasn't her fiancee."

"Exactly my boy," grinned DeKok, "exactly, because he was in France during the entire month of October. In La Courtine and that's just a little too far to keep an assignation. Anyway, I checked it."

Vledder sighed.

"So, there's another man involved."

DeKok nodded.

"Yes, another man. A man about whom we don't know a thing, yet. An unknown." He pushed his lower lip forward. Rubbed his chin. "And because the relationship was as intimate as we have been able to deduce from our calculations, I would very much like to make his acquaintance."

"Personally," smirked Vledder.

"Yes, personally."

At that moment the phone rang. DeKok lifted the receiver. "Yes?"

It was the desk-sergeant.

"I've got Joost Hofman down here, from Alkmaar."

7

Femmy Weingarten knew.

Her knowledge could not be documented in a report, could not be put down in official documentation. It was too subtle for that. Not a single prosecutor would have dared mention it in an eventual court case. He would be ridiculed, because judges consider intuition no more than a nebulous phenomenon, something that could not be allowed in a court of law. Their inclination was to consider facts, just facts and clear-cut evidence. And evidence is what Femmy lacked. But she knew. She was absolutely certain. Intuitively.

Almost at the same moment when the detective had told her that Ellen had been killed, she knew the murderer. Like a flash, a sudden vision, made out of a kaleidoscopic swirl of colors and images, dripping colors and bright red and somber dark dots, like a surrealistic painting, of which only she knew the meaning. It had shaken her. It had shaken her deeply.

She had noticed the pensive, questioning look in the eyes of the older detective and she had known that he could not read her, did not understand her. But she had not dared to say more, afraid he would ask more, more evidence, concrete evidence. And that she did not have. But she knew him, the man who murdered Ellen. She had noticed the hidden glances, the vague expressions, the veiled hints. It was carved into her memory.

She sat down on the small stool in front of her make-up table and looked at her face from three sides. She was pale and she shivered. Instinctively she pulled the collar of her sweater higher and tighter around her neck. The mirror reflected fear.

Of course, she felt sorrow for Ellen's death, but that was not uppermost in her mind, no matter how abhorrent she found the thought. All that faded away, faded away when she thought about the man who had been capable of doing something so horrible, so reprehensible. It frightened her. For several reasons.

She suddenly realized that she had always been aware of the latent possibility. Subconsciously she had always known and she remembered a gray, rainy evening in August, now several years ago.

At his insistence and without anybody knowing about it, she had rented a small cottage for a month, in Seadike. It was bad weather that night and it had grown dark much earlier than usual. Black clouds raced along the skies and a heavy downpour lashed against the windows. She had proposed that they stay home, cozy, warm, enjoying each other's company, but he had insisted on an evening walk along the beach. She had complied, as she complied with everything, because she loved him. On the way he had looked at her, a strange look, a look she did not know. The sad desolation of the beach, the lonely beach, the rain, the ear shattering drumming of the surf; everything stood out in her memory in stark, detailed reality. It had been just a segment of a thought, a sudden flash of insight, a black spot on the surrealistic painting. She could still feel his strong hands around her neck and the nervous, exploring fingers on her scarf.

Again a cold shiver went through her.

She had called out, not for help -- nobody would have heard in the storm -- but a lie: *Mother knows, she knows I'm here with you!* She had cried it out, fearful, louder than the thundering of the surf.

The muscles in his arms had slackened and the exploring fingers had withdrawn, slowly, hesitantly, with a reluctant gesture.

Later she had thought about it. Why the lie? Mother did not know at all, did not know a thing. The exploring, touching fingers at her scarf. It could have meant nothing. It could have been a caress, the beginning of an embrace.

She nodded at her mirror image.

The lie had saved her life at the time. She knew. This time with a certainty that was as clear and cool as crystal.

Suddenly, abruptly, she turned around. Somebody was knocking at her door. Softly at first and then a little louder. She did not answer. The knocking repeated, became more compelling. Then it stopped. Paralyzed with fear she remained seated and looked at the doorknob. Slowly it moved She was unable to utter a sound. Slowly the door opened.

A young man stood in the door opening. A shy smile played around his lips.

"Femmy?"

* * *

"Have you checked the incoming reports?"

"Yes."

"Anything about a suitcase?"

"Suitcase?"

DeKok sighed.

"Where are your brains, today? Ellen left her room with a suitcase. That suitcase must have wound up somewhere. I would very much like to know what happened to it. It could be a clue. Send a bulletin to all stations and ask if it has been turned into Lost and Found. Call the luggage department at the railroad station. Perhaps she checked it in, temporarily. Don't forget the luggage lockers at the station. According to Tom she still had the suitcase when he left her at nine o'clock."

"Did she still have her handbag?"

DeKok raised his arms, as if doubting the evidence of his ears.

"When *will* you start to use your brain?" he asked, a note of despair in his voice. "Of course, she still had her handbag. Otherwise, how could we possible have found the engagement ring. That was in her bag, remember?"

Abashed, Vledder nodded.

"You're right," he conceded timidly. "They had exchanged rings, that is, they had given each other their rings back. Stupid. I had completely forgotten that." He sighed. "And what about Hofman? He's still waiting for us, downstairs."

DeKok nodded with a glum face.

"Take care of the suitcase and send Hofman up. I'll wait for him here."

* * *

DeKok waited in the open door of the detective room, at the end of the long corridor, and looked at the man who approached him from the head of the stairs. His eyes, under the bushy eyebrows, noticed every detail of his visitor. It did not take long. A single glance was enough. Short, energetic, angry steps; unhealthy, red color of the face; small, heavy set, almost round; loud tie; suede shoes. DeKok knew what type of man was visiting him and he adjusted his behavior accordingly.

Mr. Hofman attacked even before he had reached the door.

"You're Inspector DeKok?" it sounded like a challenge.

"Yes, I'm Inspector DeKok, DeKok with . . . eh, kay-oh-kay. That's just in case you want to file a complaint against me. I'd appreciate it if you would spell my name correctly."

For a moment Mr. Hofman seemed unsure of himself.

"Yes, yes," he said, "a complaint. Precisely, a complaint."

"I suspected as much," DeKok answered listlessly. "But do come in. Perhaps I can give you additional reasons for a complaint."

He offered the chair in front of his desk.

Panting, the man sat down. The answer had confused him. In addition, the climb up the stairs had interfered with his breathing.

"Why . . . ," he puffed, "why am I summoned here on Christmas? Why did you have me picked up. And such manners. Such methods. I wasn't even allowed to get properly dressed. 'Immediately,' they said. Immediately! As if I'd committed a murder."

DeKok pursed his lips.

168

"And, Mr. Hofman, haven't you?"

"What!?"

DeKok grinned in a friendly way.

"Haven't you committed murder? Don't you have a murder on your conscience?"

For several seconds Mr. Hofman was unable to utter a sound; then he burst loose as if the floodgates had been opened.

Resigned, with an expression of polite interest on his face, DeKok listened to the avalanche of words and waited patiently until the man had vented his fury.

"I can understand your anger," he answered calmly, "but I didn't ask you here for nothing. I asked you here for a reason. To be precise and concise: I suspect you of the murder of a nineteen year old girl."

Mr. Hofman could only stare at him. All color and the least spark of intelligence had been drained from his face. He looked pale and grinned idiotically.

"T-that . . . t-that's absurd," he choked. "It's just plain absurd."

DeKok rubbed his chin.

"Possibly," he retorted calmly. "Possibly it sounds absurd to you. But now you know my opinion and you also know why I had you picked up. Consider yourself a suspect."

The laconic, almost disinterested way in which DeKok tossed off those remarks, had their effect. Hofman pulled out a handkerchief and wiped the sweat off his brow.

"I didn't kill any girl."

DeKok looked at him. There was little left of the arrogant, dapper little man who had stepped so aggressively down the corridor, scant minutes ago. A little, fat man, puffing for air. DeKok regretted that he had been forced to reduce him so quickly to a quivering mass of fear, but he needed the truth, the naked truth. After all, thought DeKok, this involves murder. Also, he admitted to himself, he was in a hurry. He had no intention of wasting all of his Christmas Holiday on this case.

"So, you deny it?" asked DcKok.

Hofman nodded vehemently.

"Of course, I deny it. I have NOT killed anybody."

DeKok sighed.

"Excellent," he said, "I'm happy to hear it. But you really can't expect me to believe that, just on your say so. You'll have to have stronger arguments than that. You'll have to convince me before I change my opinion. For the time being I'm holding you for the murder of Ellen Vries."

"Ellen Vries? Never heard of her!"

DeKok's eyebrows rippled briefly across his forehead.

"Isn't that weird," he said laconically. "That's extremely strange. Then how do you explain that *your* wallet was found in *her* handbag?"

"What?"

DeKok nodded. He pulled a drawer open and took the black wallet from it. Carefully, as if handling a precious religious relic, he placed it on the desk.

Hofman's mouth fell open in utter astonishment. Almost automatically he reached out for his wallet. But just before he would have touched it, he pulled his hand back, as if afraid to burn himself. As if it was glowing piece of hot metal that actually had singed his fingers when he came near.

"Your wallet?"

Joost Hofman swallowed. His adam's apple bobbed up and down.

"Yes," he said hoarsely. "Yes, that's my wallet."

"Excellent," answered DeKok.

He leaned toward the drawer and took out Ellen's handbag. He lifted it by the strap.

"And this is the handbag of the murdered girl. Your wallet was found inside." He took a deep breath, almost a sigh. "So you see, Mr. Hofman, you really *do* owe me an explanation."

Hofman bounced on his chair.

"My wallet?" he cried, incredulity in his voice. "My wallet? In that bag? But . . . that's impossible. I've never seen that handbag. T-that . . . that's impossible. I've never even been out with a girl. I mean, I'm a married man. I've a wife and three children. I work hard . . . I've no time. I . . . would, I . . ."

Agitated, he stood up and stood behind his chair. His sausage-like fingers turned white with the force of his grip on the back of the chair. It was as if he was looking for a support, something solid, something to cling to in the bare detective room. Everything seemed to spin around him, he felt as if he was caught up in the center of a merry-go-round gone wild. His only frames of reference were the back of the chair in his hands and the cool, business-like face that spoke the most horrifying accusations in an amused tone of voice.

"I can't explain it," he finally said. "I can't explain how my wallet came to be in that handbag. I don't know. I can only speculate that I lost my wallet, somehow, last night."

"Where?"

"I don't know that, either. I think my pockets must have been picked. Or maybe I lost it. I don't know."

DeKok sighed.

"Your Christmas shopping must have put a considerable dent in your financial resources. There was no money in the wallet."

"But that's impossible. There had to be money in it. At least two hundred, maybe more."

DeKok took the time to think calmly about what had been said. He rubbed his hand along his chin and thought about the possibilities.

"Please, sit down again, Mr. Hofman," he said after a long interval. His tone was more friendly. "We'll have to discuss this calmly."

The telephone rang. DeKok lifted the receiver.

"Vledder here," came an excited voice over the line. "It's getting crazier and crazier. I just got an answer to my bulletin. A suitcase, full of female clothing has been turned in at the police station in Amstelveen, in the suburbs. And guess where they found it? In the Amsterdam Woods!"

"That's quite a distance from the Gentlemen's Canal."

"Yes, isn't that weird?"

DeKok sighed.

"Yes, for us. But get there as fast as possible. Look at that suitcase. Try to make sure that it's indeed Ellen's suitcase. Then you contact the finder and let him explain, as carefully as possible, exactly *where* the suitcase was found. Look for tire tracks, or other traces. Take a photographer with you. Perhaps our colleagues in the suburbs have one they can lend you."

"OK."

"And another thing. If you do find any clues, don't try to go after them on your own, but come here first. Understood?"

"Yes."

"All right, do your best."

DeKok replaced the receiver and looked at Hofman.

"Where were we?" he asked. He closed is eyes momentarily to help him concentrate, then he said: "Oh, yes, we were going to discuss your wallet, calmly and in detail."

Hofman nodded. The short interruption of the telephone had given him time to control himself. He was less pale and his eyes were clearer.

"I've been thinking about it," he said. "I must have lost my wallet here, in Amsterdam."

"How's that?"

"Yesterday I was in Amsterdam almost all day. Late in the afternoon I had a business conference. It ended late, much later than I had planned. It must have been close to nine thirty when I finally left. Along the way I noticed that I was almost out of gas and I stopped at a service station on the Main Fort Way. The heater in my car is somewhat erratic, at times. I told the attendant about it, while he was filling my tank. He said he knew what to do about it. It was just a simple repair, he said, that he could fix in about half an hour. Since I was late anyway, I had him fix the heating. I asked him how much it would be and I paid in advance, and added a fat tip."

"You still had your wallet, then?"

"Yes, I took the money from my wallet. I don't remember the exact amount, but the guy at the station should know."

"And then?"

"It was a bit cold and I didn't feel like waiting around the station. I decided to have a drink. I walked to the New Dike through some alley and picked a bar at random. I wasn't there very long, maybe twenty minutes. Then I went back to my car."

DeKok nodded.

"And you paid for your drinks in the bar."

A smile transformed the round face of Mr. Hofman.

"No, I didn't pay."

"You didn't pay?"

"No, you see, there was a man at the bar and we started a conversation." He smiled again. "A very drunk man. Oh, a nice guy, mind you, but very sentimental. He sat next to me and told me the sad story of his mother, who had died on Christmas Eve. He was actually crying. I didn't say much. I just listened. When I got up to leave and wanted to pay, he insisted that he should pay for my drinks. I was against it, but he wouldn't take 'no' for an answer. He said that he had never met as sympathetic a person before. What could I do? I finally left without paying. He even walked me to the door and waved good bye."

DeKok nodded pensively.

"That man," he said, "That man in the bar, he had short, bristly hair, a flat-top?"

"Yes."

"And every once in a while he would put his hand on your arm, real friendly like?"

Hofman looked at him, surprised.

"Indeed."

DeKok grinned.

"Do you know why he insisted on paying?"

"He liked me."

DeKok shook his head.

"No, Mr. Hofman, if you had tried to pay, you would have noticed at once that your wallet was missing. That's why."

"That man . . .?"

"Yes, my friend, Handy Henkie, ex-burglar, but lately specializing in picking pockets and purse snatching. He must have had at least three hundred and sixty five mothers."

DeKok grimaced.

"Yes, every day of the year, one of them died. He always uses the same story to get close to his victims. Always, just that day, his mother died and he's busy drowning his sorrow." DeKok sighed. "He should change his spiel. It's becoming monotonous."

"So, Henkie rolled my wallet?"

"Yes, I would bet on it."

173

"But, then, how did my wallet get into the handbag?"
DeKok ambled to the peg on the wall to get his coat.
"We'll go ask him that, together."
"Together?"
DeKok struggled into his top coat.
"Indeed, Mr. Hofman, together."

8

"Can you stand the loss of about two hundred?"
"It won't break me, if that's what you mean."
"That's what I mean."
His old, decrepit little hat pushed back on his head, hands deep inside his pockets, DeKok strolled through the infamous Red Light District of Amsterdam. Apparently unaccustomed to his surroundings, Joost Hofman kept pace with him, although he had to take almost three steps for every two taken by DeKok.
"Really, Mr. DeKok, the two hundred guilders don't interest me that much. I can live without it. I just hope you can solve the mystery of my wallet. I think that's much more important."
DeKok nodded agreement.
"Feel like a drink?" he asked.
Hofman grinned.
"Yes, to get over the shock. Dear me, you really had me going there, for a while. I really believed you meant it when you accused me of murder."
DeKok looked at him sideways.
"I'm not changing my mind, for the moment."
Hofman, taken aback, remained silent.
At the corner of the Barn Alley, DeKok slipped into a bar. Hofman followed him reluctantly.

With a movement that showed a lot of experience, DeKok hoisted his heavy body on top of a barstool.

It was quiet in the bar. In the back a few of the regulars played cards. To the left of the bar, mainly supported by the table over which he was sprawled out, a drunk was sleeping it off. Otherwise, there was nobody. Even the underworld celebrated Christmas.

Little Lowee took the bottle of fine French Cognac from under the counter, a bottle he kept specifically for DeKok.

"The usual?"

Little Lowee poured and threw a questioning glance in Hofman's direction.

"A stranger. New in the neighborhood?"

DeKok looked at the small barkeeper.

"A colleague of mine," he lied, "from The Hague. You should have seen that at once, just look how he's dressed."

Lowee took a step back and closely scrutinized Hofman.

"A bit small," he said suspiciously, "for a detective, I mean."

DeKok grinned.

"The police in The Hague doesn't mind that at all, at all. You know, with the government and all those embassies, they only worry about how you're dressed."

"Yeah, yeah," growled Little Lowee, still not convinced. "I'm sure." He looked dubiously at Hofman and said: "What's your poison, sir?"

"I think I'll have a sherry," answered Hofman with an unmistakable Alkmaar accent, so typical of those who live in and around the cheese trading capital of Europe.

The accent did not escape Lowee. He grabbed the required bottle and snorted.

"The Hague, he says, listen to him, I can smell the cheese from here."

DeKok laughed heartily.

"Listen, Lowee," he said, "I'm looking for Handy Henkie."

Lowee's face became glum.

"Oh, no," he said.

"Most assuredly."

"Ach, Mr. DeKok, leave that boy be," he asked, almost begging. "Give him a break. He just done a year. He just got out.

175

You gotta let him catch his breath, so to speak." He stopped talking and looked at Hofman. "I bet it's about the wallet of this gentleman, ain't it?"

DeKok did not answer.

Little Lowee now turned to Hofman.

"You shouldn't do it," he said, reproachfully. "Really you shouldn't. I don't know how much you got in the wallet. A coupla tenners, maybe. Now then, whatsa coupla tenners to you. Nuttin'! But for that guy it's lotsa money. Come one, sir," he cajoled, "give the poor bastard a break. Give him another chance. Cancel the complaint. After all, it's Christmas, ain't it? You know, peace on earth and . . . and all that . . ."

DeKok intervened.

"A wonderful summation, Lowee," he said admiringly. "You should have been a lawyer. And so straight from the heart, so sincere. I tell you, I've got tears in my eyes."

Little Lowee shrugged his narrow shoulders.

"Don't hurt to try, do it?" He sounded hurt.

"Of course not," agreed Dekok. "I even agree with you, up to a point. But there's nothing for it. I *must* talk to Henkie. There's simply no other way."

Again Lowee shrugged his shoulders.

"I don't know where he is."

"That's too bad," sighed DeKok. "I had looked forward to your cooperation. Especially after all the good things I've been saying about you." He leaned closer to the small barkeeper. "Would you believe what they've been saying about you? I mean, really, I've heard that some people accuse you of trading in stolen goods. Yessir, that's what they say. If you want to get rid of some hot stuff, they whisper, go see Little Lowee. He'll know what to do." DeKok made a gesture, encompassing the small bar. "Of course, I immediately denied it." Pure indignation could be heard in his voice. "I said: don't you come carrying those kind of tales to me. There's just no way I'd believe it. I *know* Lowee, I said. Lowee doesn't do that sort of thing. You see, that's what *I* said."

Lowee grinned.

"Oh, you can say it so nicely," he smirked, "butter wouldn't melt in your mouth."

DeKok shrugged his shoulders.

"Ach, I wouldn't start anything on my own. You know I like you, but . . . if I received orders, if I *had* to take official notice, then . . ."

He smiled for a long time at Little Lowee.

"Is, eh, . . . is Henkie staying with Red Bert," he asked slowly, "or is . . . eh, is he still with Crooked Cora?"

Lowee was obviously caught on the horns of a dilemma. But not for long.

"Cora," he said.

DeKok drained his glass and slid off the barstool.

"You're a real good boy," he said.

Lowee grimaced, a sweet and sour expression on his face.

"That don't buy me none."

* * *

"Perhaps you wondered, Mr. Hofman, why I wanted you to come along? Well I have a good reason for that. You must help me."

"Help you?"

"Yes, Mr. Hofman. You see, I don't feel like having to give Henkie long sermons, no matter how pleasant that may have been in the past. I don't have the time for that. Henkie has to break quickly. And you can help me with that."

"How?"

"Oh, that's real simple. In a while, at Henkie's, you just answer my questions. Don't worry about a thing. Believe me, I'll give you leading questions. Of course, what I propose isn't exactly legal, but I've no choice. As soon as possible Henkie has to realize there's no way out. And I don't mean the pick pocketing, you'll understand that. I want Ellen's killer. That's what I promised myself. As a Christmas present."

Hofman nodded his understanding.

"I'll help you," he said seriously. "After all, it's also in my own best interest."

Handy Henkie looked up when DeKok entered unannounced, followed by Hofman. For just a moment he was speechless, then his face changed into a strange grin.

"Forget the chicken," he called toward the kitchen. "My appetite is spoiled, sudden like."

A young whore emerged from the back, a fork in her hand. She wore little more than an apron, which gave a comical impression. When she saw DeKok, she said: "O." There was more expression and meaning in that single letter, than in a sonnet by Shakespeare. Amused, DeKok looked at the couple.

The whore approached him.

"Couldn't you have waited until after the New Year? she asked, irritated. "Goddammit, it's Christmas for us too, you know."

Henkie quickly stood up.

"Shut your mouth," he hissed. "Mr. DeKok just stopped by to wish us a Happy Christmas." His tone changed, became ingratiating. "Ain't that right, Mr. DeKok? Ain't it so?"

DeKok laughed inside himself, but his expression did not change. His face remained even, severe.

"I'm afraid," he said, "that you have made a mistake. I came to introduce you to Mr. Hofman."

He turned to Hofman.

"Do you recognize this man?"

"Yes."

"You met him, last night, on the New Dike?"

"Yes."

"Before you met him, you still had your wallet?"

"Yes."

"You carried it in an inside pocket?"

"Yes."

"And you felt how this man grabbed your coat and lifted your wallet?"

"Yes."

"And you were afraid to mention it, because you wanted to avoid a scene in the bar, where you were unknown?"

"Yes."

"But you are absolutely certain that this man rolled your wallet?"

"Yes."

"You are prepared to swear to that in a court of law?"

"Yes."

Handy Henkie listened to this rather one-sided conversation with mounting astonishment.

"Hey, hey," he called, taken aback. "What's the matter with you? Hey, DeKok, you can't play them games with me. It's against the law! It ain't legal! You can't do it. It's . . ."

DeKok looked at him with a poker face.

"What's the matter," he asked innocently. "You've picked this man's pockets. That's all."

Henkie looked at him suspiciously. He had known DeKok for many, many years. This was by no means the first time that their paths had crossed. His brain worked at top capacity. He had not earned the nickname 'Handy' just for his light fingered skills.

He felt that DeKok wanted something. There had never been anybody who had felt him lift a wallet. He knew his job. That guy was lying. You could see it. That's why DeKok only let him say 'yes' and no more. Henkie's eyes narrowed to mere slits.

"And iffen I deny it?" he asked.

DeKok made a vague gesture.

"Then you go to jail. Here and now. Christmas or no Christmas."

Henkie paused for thought.

"And . . ." he asked after a while, "if I confess?"

DeKok gave him a friendly grin.

"Then . . . then we could possibly talk about it."

Henkie looked with cunning eyes from DeKok to Hofman and back again.

"There ain't nothing to talk about," he said. "I didn't take this man's wallet." He gauged the effect of his words.

DeKok sighed.

"Too bad about the chicken," he said. "I wouldn't have minded a drum stick. I haven't eaten a thing since this morning and Mr. Hofman, too, wants to go home again. But now I'll first have to write a report and then the processing . . . it's going to be late."

Henkie could taste the hint. He was fully cognizant of the police and their methods. He knew what DeKok meant. Mr. Hofman had not yet filed an official complaint.

"There ain't much left," Henkie ventured, "of that two hundred." A broad grin appeared on his face. "Some of it is in the kitchen. Can you smell it?"

DeKok nodded.

"I think we understand each other," he said. "What happened to the wallet?"

"Threw it away."

"Just like that?"

"Yep, after I'd taken the bread out, of course."

"I understand that. But did you just throw the wallet away? Wasn't there something else?"

Henkie looked glum.

"Times are bad, Mr. DeKok. I just got outta stir. I ain't had a chance to make some bread . . . And what with Christmas and all."

"So, you stole something else?"

Henkie did not answer.

"Get some chicken for the gentlemen," he told the girl. "Didn't you hear? Mister DeKok ain't had nothing to eat since morning."

The woman hastened toward the kitchen, thereby showing her bare backside, only covered by the string of her apron.

"But sit down, gentlemen," invited Henkie. "Sit down, already. Service is on the way."

DeKok sat down at the table. Hofman followed his example.

"You still haven't answered my question." DeKok said evenly.

Henkie pulled a disgusted face.

"You gotta dig, don't you? Don't I got enough trouble, already?"

DeKok rubbed his face. He knew he had to be patient with Henkie. There was no use in forcing the issue. If Henkie became scared, he would become stubborn, would not say another word. And that would be no help to anybody.

"Listen, Henkie," he said in a friendly way, "I am not out to get you into jail. Mr. Hofman, as well, has no objection to you eating chicken from his money. But in exchange I expect full cooperation from you. How did you come by the lady's bag?"

Henkie sighed. He gave up.

"You found the bag and the wallet together, of course. I get it. And now you wants to know about the bag."

"Exactly."

"Took it from a car, easy!"

"Where?"

"On the Emperor's Canal." He sighed again. "Lookit, Mr. DeKok, after I done rolled the wallet I went to see my old ma. She lives behind the Gentlemen Street."

"And I thought you mother had died, at least a hundred times."

Henkie made an impatient gesture.

"Ach, Mr. DeKok, that's business. Ain't nothing but business. No kidding. I'm crazy about my old ma and I'm glad she's still around. Sir's wallet had about two hundred innit. Not too bad. So I thought, come, let the old lady have some for Christmas. So, that's what I did. I was there for a while, a coupla hours, at least. On the way home, on the Emperor's Canal, I kinda took a gander at the cars. You never know, ain't it the truth? Anyways, in one of them cars I spotted the handbag. All by its lonesome on the back seat. I tried the car door. It weren't even locked. So, what could I do? I couldn't leave it there! Now, could I?"

"All right, and then?"

"Now, I took the money from the bag, of course. It weren't much. A few guilders, is all. I still had the wallet. I put it in the bag and threw the whole kittakaboodle in a portico. I figured, they'd find it. Why should I throw the junk in a canal? Sometimes, people need the papers, they ain't no use to me."

"How noble," grinned DeKok.

"Well, yes," sulked Henkie. "it *is* so. What for should I make it more difficult for them people. I got the bread. That's all I need."

DeKok thought briefly.

"Can you show me where the car was parked?"

"What car?"

"The one from which you lifted the bag!"

"Oh, of course, I knows exactly."

"Excellent, really excellent. We'll go there in a while."

At that moment the young woman returned from the kitchen. She carried a big round platter heaped with beautiful, browned Cornish hens.

"Just put it down, girl," cried Henkie cheerfully. "My appetite's come back sudden like."

It turned into an animated meal with a strange setting; the small room on the third floor of the decrepit house where Crooked Cora, the retired Madam, rented rooms to whores and people just released from prison.

A standing lamp threw a bright light on the wobbly table and painted distorted shadows on the walls. There was no cutlery. Just the large platter with the hens. A transparent piece of plastic served as communal plate. Henkie smacked his lips with enjoyment.

The little whore, her bare back turned toward a pot bellied stove in the corner, picked the white flesh from the bones with purple polished nails. DeKok praised her culinary accomplishments.

"You should stick to cooking," he said. "You're good at it."

Henkie grinned with his mouth full. His greasy hand reached under the apron that barely covered her.

"She's good in everything," he said with glistening eyes.

Mr. Hofman blushed and the young prostitute laughed.

DeKok reflected that he was actually committing a crime. He was eating Cornish hens from stolen money. It did not bother his conscience. It seemed to amuse him.

9

DeKok and Hofman waited by the door. The young whore took the platter back to the kitchen and cleared away the gnawed bones. Henkie delayed. He paced nervously up and down, could not get his tie knotted right and broke his shoe laces. It was all too clumsy, much to clumsy for someone called Handy Henkie.

DeKok noticed it.

"Get a move on," he admonished.

Henkie refrained from his stumbling activities and approached hesitantly. He cocked his head to one side. His chin still gleamed with the fat from the chickens.

"I'd just as soon not go with you now," He said. "I'd just as soon come on my own. I'll see you at the station, in a bit."

DeKok expressed a question with his eyebrows.

Henkie laughed bashfully.

"You see," he said apologetically. "I don't wanna be seen with you, iffen I can help it. Not in this neighborhood. You gotta believe me, Mr. DeKok, it ain't nothing against you, no, it ain't that. And I'll show you where the car is. No problem. But . . ." He hesitated. "You see, he continued, "I ain't been out all that long, and iffen they see us together, there'll be talk. They think I've been caught again, already." He pulled a sad face. "That . . . that's just too much, you know. It'll make me look bad. I've gotta think of me reputation, ain't that right?"

"I understand," answered DeKok gravely. "Why don't you come in a little while. I'll expect you in about half an hour."

Henkie laughed, relieved.

"You can count on me."

"I know," said DeKok. "I know I can count on you."

He politely said goodbye to the young whore and together with Hofman, he descended down the dark stairs of the old building. Outside, they parted.

"I've never in my life had a Christmas such as this," laughed Hofman. "What an experience. Would you believe it's worth every cent of that two hundred guilders?" His eyes sparkled with glee. "But I would like to know how your investigations develop. I'm just curious. Can I be of further assistance?"

DeKok smiled.

"Why don't you just go home, to your wife and children. You'll read all about it in the newspapers. In any case, much obliged for your help. I'll keep your wallet, for the time being. You may pick it up in a few days. I'll let you know."

Mr. Joost Hofman of Alkmaar, shook hands with Inspector DeKok of the Amsterdam Municipal Police, Homicide. It was as if two worlds had met.

"It was a pleasure to make your acquaintance," Hofman said formally. Then he walked away with short, dapper steps.

DeKok watched him disappear around the corner of the narrow alley.

"Not a bad guy, after all," he murmured to himself. Then he turned around and strolled toward the Warmoes Street. It was beginning to get dark.

Sergeant Wensdorp, the old watch commander who also served as desk-sergeant on this Holiday night, looked up from his desk as DeKok entered the police station.

"Well, well," he marveled, "still in harness?"

DeKok pushed his hat backward.

"What else can I do?" he asked rhetorically, spreading his hands in despair. "I can't just stop in the middle of things, now, can I?"

Wensdorp and DeKok had both become gray on the job. Now the old policeman looked searchingly at his plain clothed colleague. He grinned, then he said:

"I don't think there's any way you'll let go of this case. Not now, Not at this time."

DeKok shrugged his shoulders.

"It's murder. Otherwise I would have packed it in, long ago. But I can't let that boy muddle through on his own. He's still so young, so inexperienced."

"Who? Vledder?"

DeKok nodded.

"Have you heard from him?"

"No, not yet. But you have had two calls. Same guy. Somebody called Tom Weick wanted to talk to you. I asked him if I could take a message, but he said he'd call back."

"Fine," answered DeKok absent mindedly, "most helpful." Then, more brisk, he added: "Well, we'll wait for him to call again. By the way, do you have a spare detective for me?"

The watch commander checked his roster.

"Yes, Jan Klaassen is available. You want him?"

DeKok nodded.

"He'll do. Send him upstairs. Oh, by the way, when Handy Henkie shows up, please let him pass. No problems, just send him up. I need him for something."

He left old Wensdorp to his contemplations and, a bit laboriously, climbed the stone stairs to the third floor. Upstairs, in the detective room, he put on the lights, threw his hat on the desk and stripped his coat off. He felt lethargic. At home he usually dozed in his chair, after a meal. But he could not afford to do so at this time. He had to carry on and he reflected that it had been more than fifteen hours, already, since Vledder woke him up with that first phone call. All this time, almost without a break, he had been working on the case. He had worked himself through a number of witnesses and had made no progress worth mentioning.

He dropped into his chair and hoisted his legs onto the top of the desk. He felt his feet. It was bad sign. When he was making progress, when he was getting close to a solution, he would not feel his feet. But when there was no progress, if the case was going badly, if the solution seemed far and away, if his thoughts could not discover a single clue, when he seemed lost in a labyrinth of conflicting evidence and contradicting witnesses, his feet would come painfully to his attention. They would hurt.

Jan Klaassen came in. A friendly smile on his face and a mug of coffee in his hand. He served the coffee to DeKok with a flourish.

"For the great, gray sleuth," he mocked, "as a small token of respect from a silent admirer." He raised a finger in the air. "And I, my dear sir, am that admirer," he concluded.

DeKok looked at the grinning face and laughed. Jan Klaassen was known as a joker, who took little, if anything, very seriously. Perhaps that is why he was such a good officer. An officer who cajoled and jollied the public with his witticisms. Most superiors had little use for his jokes. That's why he was banished to the Warmoes Street, the Amsterdam equivalent of Hill Street. That is why, despite his seniority, he was on duty during Christmas. His promotion was problematical. Would probably never happen.

"The great sleuth," ridiculed DeKok right back, "is working on a near insoluble puzzle."

"Tell me all about it," cried Klaassen enthusiastically. "I love puzzles!"

For a brief moment DeKok almost forgot he had feet.

"What do you think," he stated, "about a corpse in the Gentlemen's Canal, a handbag in a portico on the Brewers Canal, a car on the Emperor's Canal and a suitcase in the Amsterdam Woods?"

"Scavenger Hunt!" declared Klaassen promptly.

DeKok laughed spontaneously.

"Yes," he said, "you're right. It seems that way. But it's winter and these are modern times. Scavenger hunts belong to summers in the twenties and thirties. But, to be serious for a moment, let me tell you what I want you to do."

"OK, boss," said Klaassen with a poker face, knowing full well that DeKok hated that expression. DeKok did not like to be called 'boss' and that, combined with 'OK' was enough to get him very upset, to say the least. But this time DeKok ignored the expression. He even smiled.

"Very good," he said. "very good1. I want you to go to the Central Station and I want you to find the waiter, or waitress, who was on duty in the restaurant on the first platform. Sometime between six and nine, last night." He pulled a desk drawer open and took out Ellen's photo. "Ask," he continued, "if he, or she, can remember this girl. If they can, they should be able to remember that she was accompanied by a good looking soldier. Perhaps the waiter, or waitress, caught part of the conversation. Try to find out when the girl and her soldier left, if they left together, or separately. Anyway, everything you can find about the girl and her boy friend."

"That's all?"

"No, there's something else. After you finish at the railroad station, I want you to go to a service station on the Main Fort Way. Try to get a hold of the mechanic who was on duty last night, around nine, or ten. Last night, around that time, he fixed the heater of a car. Ask him what he remembers about the driver, if he wrote a repair ticket and how the driver paid. For instance, did he take out his wallet, or did he have the money in his pocket. Have you got all that?"

"Absolutely."

"Then you come back here. If I'm not here, wait for me. Perhaps I'll need you again."

"OK, boss."

Again DeKok decided to ignore the hateful remark.

"And . . . thanks for the coffee."

Grinning, Klaassen departed.

He had barely left when the phone rang. DeKok lifted the receiver. He recognized the voice at once. It was Tom Weick.

"I did what you told me," he began. "I went to see Miss Weingarten. I was with her for several hours."

"And?"

"It was hard going. She didn't much feel like talking. She said she knew nothing about Ellen's men. But I insisted. I kept on and I said that Ellen wouldn't have broken off our engagement for nothing. There had to be a reason."

"Yes, well?"

"Finally, after some time, she told me a long story about herself. How she had come to Amsterdam as a young, naive girl, without experience. How she got an office job. How she got to know men. How she met men who pretended to love her. How she . . ."

"Yes, yes," interrupted DeKok impatiently. "But what was the point? How did it end?"

There was a silence on the other end of the line.

"Did you know," said Tom after a lengthy pause, "that Femmy has a child?"

"Yes, I know that."

"But do you know by whom?"

"No."

Again there was short pause.

"From Mr. Dolman."

"What!?" With a sudden jerk DeKok took his feet off the desk.

"Yes, by Mr. Dolman. She used to date him. On the sly, of course, because Dolman is married and has a bunch of kids."

"What did she say about Ellen?"

"Nothing."

"Did Ellen date Dolman?"

"She didn't say so."

"Did you ask?"

"Yes."

"And?"

"She . . . she said that I knew enough already."

DeKok bit his lower lip. The gears in his brains started to turn. The old machinery suddenly creaked into top speed. All lethargy fell away from him. He felt refreshed, revitalized.

"Where are you now?" he asked.

"In a bar, near Hudson Street."

"How long ago did you leave her?"

"About half an hour ago. I've called you several times, but you weren't there."

"Yes, yes," answered DeKok and reflected for a moment. Then he said: "Listen, Tom, go back to Femmy. At once! I hope she's still at home. If she *is* home, you stay there. You stay with her, until one of us shows up."

"And if she's not home?"

"Then you call right back. Understood?"

"Yes, Mr. DeKok."

He broke the connection and rubbed his face. It had been a good idea, he thought, to send the boy over to Femmy. A very good idea. He had felt from the beginning that Miss Weingarten held something back. Was hiding something. She was too closed mouthed. Actually, he knew precious little, even now. He would have to talk to her again, in depth. But here. Next time he would talk to her here, in the detective room, in his own surroundings, on his own ground. And he would be anything but gentle. What did she think, that little Missy? He had no time for games. He could not afford to play hide-and-seek. It was murder.

The ringing of the telephone broke into his thoughts. Wensdorp, downstairs, was on the line.

"Henkie is on his way up."

"All right. Has Klaassen left yet?"

"No, he's still here, putting on his coat."

"Hold him! I'll be downstairs directly."

188

He threw the phone down, put his hat on and grabbed his coat in passing. In the corridor he almost ran over Henkie.

"In a hurry?"

DeKok grinned.

"I can't wait to see that car of yours."

Henkie shrugged his shoulders.

"There was nothing special about it."

10

DeKok manoeuvred the small car through the narrow streets and alleys of the inner city. Progress was slow, because the core of Amsterdam was, still, more geared to fast handcarts and an occasional stage coach. Since time immemorial, the bulk of Amsterdam's traffic had moved by water. And although the quays along some of the canals had been widened, the extra space was soon absorbed by parked cars.

DeKok played with the high beams, stabbing holes into the darkness. Henkie sat next to him and studied the knobs, dials and switches of the communication gear. He showed a childish interest and concentration,.

"You know," he said, "I ain't never been in the front seat of a police car. Always in the back, with them things around me wrists."

DeKok smiled.

"You're making progress, then," he mocked.

At the corner of the St. Olof Alley DeKok stopped and waited resignedly for a lonesome drunk to clear the road. Then he drove on again.

"I wonder," DeKok said, "when you'll be ready to look for some normal work."

Henkie grinned.

"I've got two left hands when it comes to work."

DeKok shrugged.

"I seem to remember," he said, "that you are a tool-and-die maker by profession. There's plenty of work for someone like you. Good salary, paid vacations and other benefits. Find a nice woman and start a family. When your old mother dies, and that cannot be far in the future, you're going to be all alone."

Henkie grinned again, a bit sadly this time.

"Ach, Mr. DeKok," he said in a melancholy tone of voice, "you should know, that ain't nothing for me. I've gotta have adventure."

"Adventure?" smirked DeKok. "In jail, out of jail. And in between scratching for a living and shacking up with a second hand woman in what's no better than a slum."

Henkie looked offended.

"Come, come, Mr. DeKok," he said, tossing his head. "You seen her yourself. She ain't all that bad." He snorted. "And you calls that second hand . . ."

DeKok grinned.

"Well, you can hardly maintain," he said, "that she's still a virgin, can you?"

Henkie was getting excited.

"So, . . . and what's that supposed to mean? There's plenty of times you don't even think about that."

DeKok did not react. He had started a new train of thought. He wondered if he had covered all the bases. He had told Jan Klaassen to forget the waiter and the mechanic, for the moment. That could wait. First he had to call the police in Amstelveen and tell Vledder to pick up the soldier on his way back to the police station. He had asked Klaassen to contact the police in Hoorn. Perhaps they knew something about the background of the Weingarten family. You never knew. Femmy seemed to be the key to the solution, he thought.

DeKok parked the car on the Emperor's Canal, not too far from the Gentlemen's Canal. They stepped out of the car. It was quiet.

DeKok took the flashlight from the car and locked the doors. Henkie walked ahead. About a hundred yards from the Gentle-

190

men Street he stopped and pointed at a spot near the water's edge, under the trees.

"Here it was," he said. "That's where it were parked when I took the bag out. I thinks it was an American car."

DeKok bent over and played the light of the flashlight on the ground in the indicated spot. Tire marks were visible under the trees, delineated in a frozen porridge of rotted leaves. But it was a very indistinct mish-mash. DeKok noted at least six different sets of tracks and he knew that it would yield little, if any, concrete evidence. Slowly he straightened out and looked up at the facades of the houses. Between the bare branches he could just discern the fronts of the stately brownstones and imposing canal houses. Nobody lived in the houses anymore. They had all been converted to office space. It was too bad, but who, these days, was able to afford such a house as a single family residence?

Henkie lit a cigarette.

"Well," he asked, bored. "So what is we waiting for, already? You seen it. Let's go." He grinned broadly, "My second hand Rose is waiting for me." Obviously he was still bothered by DeKok's earlier remark. "Come on, there ain't nothing else to see. What else is there, around here?"

DeKok sighed. He had an instinctive feeling that he should not leave. Not yet. Something kept him here. He looked up and was struck by the intricate patterns, as if woven by a demented lace maker, formed by the contrast of the bare tree branches against the gray sky above.

"You found the handbag on the back seat, right?"

"Yep, all by its lonesome."

DeKok envisioned the scene. Henkie slinking from one car to another, peering through windows, looking for loot.

"Was the car still warm?"

Henkie showed a deep crease in his forehead and rubbed his stubbly hair with his hands.

"Well, yes, now that you mention it. Yes, the windows weren't fogged over, or nothing. I remembers now, at first I thought there might be a couple in there, you know, fooling around. But when I gets closer, there weren't nobody there. Just the bag."

DeKok nodded and gestured toward the houses.

"Was there a light on, in any of the houses?"

"That . . .eh, I didn't look for that. I ain't seen it, I mean. I took the bag and took a powder."

"Did you see anybody else in the street?"

Henkie snorted.

"I ain't that fond of witnesses."

"So, there was nobody in sight?"

"Nope."

DeKok ambled toward the sidewalk. The light of the flashlight moved along the imposing fronts and the distinguished, brass name plates next to the doors. He did not know the exact number, but he knew he had to be near. Suddenly he caught the name in the oval bundle of light. *Dolman and Fleet, Insurance Underwriters* in black, elegant script, engraved on a shiny, brass plate.

Handy Henkie had followed him and now stood next to him. DeKok was still illuminating the brass plate.

"Nice place," admired Henkie. "You'd think you gets a nice little haul from a place like that. But, nossir. It's mostly nebbish. When you just start out . . . you sometimes think it might be a good hit. Underwriters, you think, they got bread. Nebbish, just nebbish. They've got bread alright . . . but it's in the bank." He flicked his cigarette away and stomped on the butt. "Oncet," he carried on, "I seen just such a plate. Just as fancy. 'Cash' it said. Just like that, C-A-S-H! So from the outside, it didn't look all that tough. So I says to meself: give it a whirl. Let's see iffen they got more cash than me." He snorted contemptuously. "And whadda you think? Not a red cent. Not a goddamn penny! Nothing. Well, since then . . ."

DeKok listened to Henkie's experiences. He listened with half an ear, because his thoughts were with Ellen. He wondered what she had done, the last hours of her life. How did her handbag wind up on the back seat of a car? And so close to the place where she worked? There had to be a connection. He doubted that she owned a key to the office. She had not been employed long enough. But, taking the handbag into consideration, she must have been here, must have been inside the office. Who had let her in? What secrets were hidden behind the respectable, solid front of the old canal house?

Henkie talked up a storm. His experiences as a burglar were many and varied. He told them with relish.

DeKok looked at him.

"Would you . . . eh, could you," he interrupted the stream of anecdotes. "Could you open this door, without damage, without leaving a trace?"

Handy Henkie gazed at the door with an experienced eye. He nodded vaguely. His lips were pursed.

"Yes," he said slowly. "Yes, no problem. Iffen I had me tools with me, it coulda been done like *that*." He snapped his fingers. "Like a sardine can. Just take a coupla minutes, that's all."

DeKok thoughtfully rubbed a hand along his chin.

"Where are your tools?"

Henkie suddenly regretted his openness. He realized he had said too much. After all, DeKok was a cop. And his experience with cops . . . One way, or the other, you could not trust a cop. Should not trust a cop, thought Henkie. Suspicion reared its ugly head. Misgivings shined in his eyes.

"I don't use me tools no more, Mr. DeKok," he defended himself as if he was under interrogation. "Really. I done stored them away. My old ma's attic. Greased and everything. After that last breakie, you know, I ain't used them since. Honest."

With difficulty DeKok swallowed a complete stack of official directives, managed to forget them. He sighed. To hell with the rules, he thought.

"Would you get them out of the grease for me, just one more time?"

"What!?"

DeKok sighed again.

"Just this once. I want to get inside."

Henkie grinned sheepishly.

"You mean . . .?"

DeKok nodded. His face was serious.

"Yes, that's what I mean," he admitted.

Henkie laughed again, a strange, nervous laugh. He could not understand it. The idea was absurd. He had never heard such a thing. He scrutinized DeKok's face with his sharp eyes. He knew that face. He had become familiar with that face in the course of many interrogations. The deep creases in the forehead, the strange eyebrows, with a life of their own, the friendly, gray eyes, the deep markings around the mouth . . . it was all there. Only, the half amused look, the vague smile around the lips, was missing. DeKok was serious.

"You really wants to get inside?"

"Yes."

"And . . . eh, I's gonna be in the clear?"

DeKok grinned suddenly. It was impossible to resist a grinning DeKok.

"In case of trouble, I take full responsibility."

Henkie nodded thoughtfully. His lower lip was pushed forward. A slight tic developed in one cheek. Obviously he was of two minds. But not for long. He pulled his lip back in and a friendly smile appeared on his face. Even his eyes laughed.

"After all," he said, "you used to treat me pretty fair, all the time."

It sounded like the ultimate conclusion of a long deliberation. He glanced once more at the door and windows of the house, estimated his needs. Then he turned and walked away to get his tools.

11

Handy Henkie worked fast and soundless. Completely absorbed by the "job", he wore gloves and handled his tools with the expertise of a master.

DeKok watched from a distance, spellbound by Henkie's manipulations. He was supposed to be the lookout, but did such a poor job that they were almost surprised by a lone pedestrian. Happily the man was not paying any attention. Without noticing them, he passed within feet of Henkie. As soon as the passer-by had disappeared and was out of earshot, Henkie cursed.

"You stupid bas . . ." He remembered, in the nick of time, that he had a rather unusual partner on this job. "I'm sorry," he said apologetically. "He scared the shit outta me."

DeKok nodded understanding.

"Never mind," he said, "it was my fault."

Henkie went back to work. Within a few more moments he had opened the door. A professional job, the door was hardly damaged. It would have taken a careful examination to discover any traces of the illegal entry.

DeKok patted him on the shoulder and praised him.

"Come inside with me," he said, "there may be additional obstacles."

They closed the door behind them and began their search of the premises. DeKok did not know what he was looking for. He was following an impulse, totally intuitive. But Ellen had probably been here, the night she was killed. He was looking for the why and wherefore and he hoped to discover something that would supply him the answers.

With Henkie following close behind, he walked through the long, marble corridors, into one office and out another. The light of his flashlight danced along the steel file cabinets and typewriters under covers. Every once in a while it was reflected from the screen of a computer terminal.

Henkie nudged him

"You see, I tole you so. Nothing. The typewriters ain't worth a dime, all marked and numbered. The computers the same. The fence would laugh at you. And iffen you try somewheres else, you gets caught in no time."

DeKok smiled at the lecture.

"I'm not here to steal anything," he said.

Henkie stopped suddenly.

"Well, hey," he whispered, "so why did you have to get in, then?"

DeKok sighed.

"Because a girl has been murdered."

"Where? Here?" Henkie sounded scared.

"That . . . ," DeKok said, "is what I aim to find out."

Anxiously, Henkie's glance darted around.

"Damn," he said timidly, "you shoulda tole me."

Henkie let his flashlight wander around, lit up a painting on the wall and discovered a little plaster angel on the ceiling. Henkie studied the little angel.

"How old was she?" he asked.

DeKok had moved on.

"Nineteen," he called. "Why?"

Henkie lowered his flashlight and shuffled after DeKok.

"Nothing," he said somberly, "it'll pass."

DeKok discovered the private office on the second floor. It received his special attention. He saw that the heavy drapes were closed and ventured to switch on the lights.

"Stay outside the door," he told Henkie, "and don't touch a thing."

Henkie obeyed with blinking eyes.

DeKok put his hands in his pockets and looked around. The room was soberly furnished: a desk of dark wood and unusual proportions, heavy, black leather chairs, dark oak wainscoting and trim. It breathed an air of solid dependability. DeKok absorbed the atmosphere and looked for a dissonant, a disturbance of the surface serenity. He had a sharp eye for that sort of thing, a love for detail. It was a natural trait, sharpened and honed by experience. Suddenly he discovered a dull, almost white discolored spot on the shining parquet floor. The demarcation formed an irregular line that disappeared behind one of the heavy chairs. Immediately, DeKok was interested. He dropped to his knees and aimed his flashlight under the chair. He noticed how the line continued under the chair and finally closed to form a circle.

Henkie watched with bated breath.

"Somebody spilled something," he said.

DeKok rose and straightened out. His face had a pensive, engrossed expression.

"What do you do when you spill something?" he asked.

Henkie grinned.

"You gotta mop it up."

DeKok nodded slowly.

196

"Exactly," he repeated, "you have to mop it up."

He rubbed his hands over his face and stood deep in thought. Then he walked out of the room. Henkie followed him. In the corridor DeKok opened a door. It was a deep cupboard. He saw some dusty files and closed the door again. The next door gave him what he was looking for. The janitor's closet.

There were a few brooms, a vacuum cleaner, a duster, a waxer and a number of stacked buckets. A mop stood in the top bucket. DeKok lifted the mop and smelled it. The smell immediately confirmed his suspicions.

He thought about his next step. The mop seemed too important a piece of evidence to use as bait. The risk was too great. If the mop was lost, he would have lost his proof and that was less easily forgiven than an unauthorized breaking and entering.

"Hold this a moment," he said.

Henkie took the mop from him.

"Damn," he said with a disgusted face, "this thing stinks."

DeKok nodded sympathetically.

"I was sure it would."

He looked around the deep closet. A new mop was hanging from a nail. He took it down and went looking for a sink. A bit further down the corridor he found a small, old fashioned sink built into the wall. He kept the mop under the faucet, squeezed it more or less dry and walked back to the closet. Quickly he exchanged the new mop part for the old. Taking the handle from Henkie, he handed him the dirty mop. He placed the new mop, now attached to the handle, in the bucket.

"And what about this, then?" asked Henkie, holding the dirty mop as far from himself as possible.

"Hold on just a little longer," chuckled DeKok. "I'll relieve you of it, in just a moment."

He went to the private office, switched the lights off and closed the door. In the cupboard with the dusty files he found a large, yellow envelope. He took the mop from Henkie and placed it inside the envelope.

Henkie looked at him.

"Whadda you want with that dirty thing?"

DeKok did not answer. He looked around and oriented himself. He was satisfied with what he saw. The janitor's closet was next to the stairs to the upper floors. He walked up the stairs. At the top of the flight of stairs he stopped, turned around and looked down.

"Light up that door for me, will you?"

Henkie complied willingly.

"Excellent," murmured DeKok, "really excellent."

Slowly he descended the stairs. A satisfied look on his face.

"Now what?" asked Henkie.

"Now, nothing. We're going."

"You mean," asked Henkie, surprised, "That we cracked this place just for a dirty mop? You gotta be kidding!"

"No, that's the reason."

Confused and astonished, Henkie shook his head. He was speechless. Nobody saw them as they left. They closed the front door behind them and walked down the canal quay. DeKok stopped on the corner of the Gentlemen Street.

"I'll wait for you here," he said, "until you've put your tools back in the attic."

Henkie gave him a mocking look and walked away toward his mother's house, his briefcase under one arm. A few minutes later he was back.

"You wanna check it out?" he asked defiantly.

"But why? I trust you."

Henkie looked offended.

"Listen, DeKok," he said, irritated. "I just cracked that door for you, as a sorta favor, you know, because of old friendships, you know what I mean? I don't do breakies no more, not for years. And iffen you think I'll start again, you just go get them tools. You knows where they is, now."

DeKok sighed patiently.

"I didn't mean anything by it. I told you I trusted you. I mean that. You really believe I would have pulled such a stunt, otherwise?"

Henkie face cleared.

"You'd never have done it with someone else, right?"

DeKok smiled.

"No way. I would have worried that they would use it against me, later. Would have taken advantage of me, you understand?"

Henkie nodded thoughtfully.

"Then that woulda been a dirty trick," he declared solemnly.

"Exactly," agreed DeKok, "a dirty trick."

He patted Henkie confidentially on the shoulder.

"Come on, Henkie, I still have a lot of work to do. I'll take you home."

"To my second hand Rose?" joked Henkie.

DeKok winked at him.

"A jewel," he said, "a great girl. Believe me."

Henkie was satisfied with the praise.

* * *

Considering it was Christmas, it was busy in the large detective room. Jan Klaassen, Vledder, Femmy Weingarten and Tom Weick. They were spread around the room and did not speak with each other. Klaassen was seated behind DeKok's desk as if he belonged there. Vledder straddled a chair next to the window, his arms resting on the back of the chair. Tom Weick fiddled with the knob of a radiator and Femmy stared somberly in the distance. There was an atmosphere of tense expectation.

Klaassen was least affected by the atmosphere. He had done his duty. After he had warned Vledder and that worthy had appeared, accompanied by the lady and the soldier, he had gone to the railroad station. He had found the waiter almost immediately. The waiter did remember the girl and the soldier.

No problem there, thought Klaassen. She had been with a soldier, just like DeKok had said. The soldier had left first. The girl had asked for a telephone. That was all the waiter remembered.

Klaassen did not know if it was important. He really could not care less about that, he reflected. He admired DeKok immensely and he was quite open about his admiration. DeKok would decide, he thought, about the importance, or not, of his findings. Why should he worry about it?

From the railroad station he had gone to the service station. The mechanic could remember all about the broken heater and the repair. He remembered the man and his car very well. He had taken the money out of his wallet and added a fat tip. No, no ticket had been written. Why? Klaassen understood why not. A little extra for the mechanic, the boss did not need to know everything. Anyway, that was none of his business. He had checked what he could.

The telephone call to the Hoorn police had been unproductive. Sure, they knew about the Weingarten family. A normal, respectable family. The daughter worked in Amsterdam. That was all.

Jan Klaassen had put it all down on paper. He would turn it in to DeKok.

Vledder was less satisfied with himself. He had that feeling again. The feeling that he was outside the case. It was DeKok's fault, he thought. He seemed to stumble around. Vledder could never discover the reason for DeKok's actions. Why summon the girl to the station? What did DeKok want with Femmy? He *had* interrogated her. And what about Tom Weick? How did the two connect? DeKok apparently knew that the soldier could be found at Femmy's place. Had he arranged that? Had he sent Weick to see Femmy? It was possible. You could expect anything from DeKok, thought Vledder sourly. With a deep sigh he stood up and started to pace up and down the room.

"How long do you expect me to wait here?" asked Femmy impatiently.

"Until my partner gets here."

"And how long is that supposed to take?"

"Who knows," answered Vledder, irritated. "He'll be here when he gets here."

"Well," she said rebelliously, "I don't plan to wait much longer."

Klaassen moved from behind the desk.

"Listen to me, miss," he said threateningly. "If DeKok orders you picked up, then there's a reason for it. And don't think," he continued, shaking his head, "that we'll let you leave without his permission."

Femmy's face became red and her eyes, behind the horn rimmed glasses, flashed dangerously. Abruptly she stood up.

"I would like to see," she said determinedly, "who'd try to stop me!"

Before either Klaassen, or Vledder, could react, she was on her way to the door. She almost walked straight into DeKok's arms.

"Hello, Miss Weingarten," he said in a friendly way. "Surely you're not leaving us already? Especially since I have such a nice surprise for you, shortly."

12

"Was it her suitcase?"

"Yes, I showed it to Femmy. She identified it immediately as Helen's suitcase."

"Any peculiarities?"

"No, nothing. It was found near the side of the road. Most likely tossed from a car. I did have a little problem locating the finder. That's why it took so long."

DeKok nodded.

"Some things take time," he said philosophically.

Vledder yawned.

"I'm starting to get hungry."

"The Christmas bread my wife gave me for you, is still in the glove compartment. Perhaps you'll feel like eating it now."

Vledder took the paper bag out of the compartment and bit greedily into the special bread.

"What do you hope to gain from our visit to Dolman?" he asked with his mouth full. "He'll not be able to tell us much more than Femmy did."

DeKok did not answer at once. He took a firmer grip on the wheel and thought about the best way to conduct the interview with Dolman.

"He was her employer," he said after a while. "He's got a right to know what happens to his employees."

Vledder looked at him in surprise.

"We haven't even notified her parents."

"You're right," sighed DeKok. "You can do that tomorrow. Then you'll be able to arrange for the official identification at your leisure. Be careful, take your time. It'll be difficult for the parents. As far as I know, Ellen was an only daughter."

Vledder turned toward him,

"Why don't you do it yourself? You're much better with those things than me. You've a gift for putting people at their ease."

"I hope not to be available tomorrow."

"What!?"

"No, *one* Christmas day is enough."

Vledder was speechless.

* * *

"But it's terrible, just terrible."

Mr. Dolman had received the two detectives condescendingly—a bit irritated about the disturbance—and had led them to a comfortable room where, with an expansive gesture, he offered them a chair. DeKok had exploded the news of Ellen's death as if it were a bomb.

"But it's terrible, just terrible," repeated Dolman and rose from his easy chair. "Who could have expected it." he paced the room, wringing his hands. He looked genuinely shocked. "Murdered. The poor child. Her parents will be inconsolable. I feel a deep sympathy. They're such respectable people." Depressed, he shook his head. "I don't dare to face them, anymore," he concluded.

"Come, come," said DeKok, "after all, it isn't *your* fault."

"You don't understand," he cried, apparently stricken with grief. "I feel responsible. Ellen wanted so much to work in Amsterdam. Therefore I offered her a job in the office. Her parents did not object, because they knew me. And now this."

He sighed deeply and pressed the palms of his hands against his temples.

DeKok perched on the edge of the impressive chair, his hat on his knees. He was not comfortable. His knees pressed against his abdomen. He could easily have assumed a more comfortable

position, but he did not want to do that. He was consciously trying to create the impression that he was not at ease, that he was impressed by the luxurious surroundings, the rich materials, the expensive furniture and the condescension of the important, theatrical Mister Dolman.

"We were of the opinion," he said meekly, "that it was our duty to inform you. It was not our intention to upset you. But, you see, she worked for you, and if she had not shown up for work, after the Holidays, you might have wondered, you . . ." His tone of voice was downright unctuous.

A faint smile marked the handsome face of Mr. Dolman. He hooked his thumbs in the loud, Scotch plaid vest.

"I don't blame you at all, gentlemen." His tone was friendly, almost jovial. The landlord speaking to his tenants. "Of course, I appreciate your good intentions, but, you understand . . . the sudden shock."

DeKok nodded.

"I understand, sir," he said. "It doesn't happen every day that one of your employees is murdered."

Mr. Dolman raised both hands in despair.

"No, no. Thank God. No, not at all."

DeKok grinned sheepishly.

"That was a dumb remark," he said apologetically. "Very dumb."

Mr. Dolman seemed to have recovered from the shock. He sat down again in his easy chair. He now seemed a bit amused, even.

"Are you making any progress with the case?" he asked calmly.

"Not much," answered Vledder. "We . . ." he halted momentarily. There was a warning light in DeKok's eyes. " . . .we . . . eh, try our best," he concluded lamely.

"Yes," amplified DeKok. "That goes without saying. But it's a rather hopeless case. The girl seems to have been strangled and there are generally few clues in cases of strangulation."

Mr. Dolman looked serious, sympathetic.

"I don't envy you, gentlemen," he said. "It seems to be a difficult problem."

"That's so," sighed DeKok. He fiddled bashfully with his hat. "There are just no starting points, no solid indications."

"And there's nothing that can help you come closer to a solution?"

DeKok shrugged his shoulders.

"We still have a chance. A small chance. Maybe."

"And what is that?"

DeKok smiled sadly.

"It doesn't mean much. It wouldn't interest you."

Mr. Dolman pushed himself slightly forward in his chair.

"On the contrary, I'm very much interested. Sometimes I read detective stories, you know," he said it as if he was admitting a hidden vice. "And I have a deep admiration for the sleuth, the detective. What sort of chance do you have?"

DeKok sighed.

"Strangulation," he said reluctantly, "causes death by suffocation. The victim cannot breath and in nine out of ten cases this results in voiding the bladder. Especially if the bladder is full, this can result in a large quantity of liquid. We do know that Ellen, shortly before her death, consumed a large amount of coffee, several cups. Therefore it's possible that, at the point of death, she voided her bladder. If she was killed in the street, we'll never find the traces. But if she was killed inside, in a house, then, yes, then we have a small chance to bring this case to a satisfactory conclusion."

"How's that?"

"Well, of course, the perpetrator will carefully remove all traces of the deed. But usually he, or she, forgets the mop, or the rags, used for cleaning up the spill, removing the urine. It's just thrown in a corner, or stored wherever it was found."

Mr. Dolman laughed nervously.

"But what use can such a mop be?"

DeKok turned his hat in hands.

Oh," he said, "you shouldn't underestimate the importance of such a find. The laboratory guys are pretty sharp, these days and they can draw on a complete array of equipment and methods. A mop like that can tell stories. Can identify a person. Urine, you see, consists of a complicated mixture of ingredients. The exact composition can differ greatly from one person to another."

"Amazing."

DeKok nodded.

"Of course, that's nice," he said soberly, "But first you have to find the mop. And the way things are, right now . . ." He made a desperate gesture and stood up. "You'll have to excuse us, I hope, but we better get going."

"No, no, not at all," answered Dolman, confused. "I won't keep you." Hastily he rose himself and accompanied them to the front door.

"I . . . eh, I wish you success," he said by way of farewell.

"Thank you," said DeKok simply. "Thank you."

Vledder and DeKok stepped outside, but before Dolman had a chance to close the door behind them, DeKok turned and said:

"Oh, I almost forgot. Tomorrow morning I'd like to take a look around the office. Perhaps there are some personal possessions in her desk."

"Tomorrow morning?"

"If it's convenient."

Dolman seemed startled.

"Yes, well, yes," he said hesitantly. "Yes, that'll be all right."

Politely DeKok lifted his hat.

"Excellent, really excellent. Then we'll see you tomorrow morning, Mr. Dolman."

* * *

As soon as they were out of sight, DeKok became remarkably active: As fast as his legs could carry him, he ran toward the side street where they had parked the car.

DeKok almost never ran. He did not have the figure for it. His upper body was too heavy and, in comparison, his legs were too short.

205

DeKok at speed was a comical sight.

But this time he ran. His hand on his hat and his coat tails streaming behind him. Considering his ungainly gait, he made good time.

Young Vledder was mystified. He exerted himself in a short sprint and pulled level with DeKok.

"What's got into you?" he asked while keeping pace.

"I'm in a hurry," answered DeKok.

"Yes, I can see that."

"Then why do you ask? Surely you don't think I'm training for the Olympics?"

Vledder remained silent.

When they arrived at the car, DeKok handed the keys to Vledder.

"There you go, my boy," he panted. "You drive. You're a better driver."

They entered the car and Vledder started the engine.

"Where to?"

"To the Emperor's Canal and as fast as this bucket of rust will make it."

Vledder applied his foot to the gas pedal and pulled the car, at times with howling tires, through the quiet streets and country lanes of the suburb where Dolman lived.

Vledder was indeed an experienced driver and within the shortest possible time they had reached the edge of town. Meanwhile Vledder wondered what DeKok could be up to. He also criticized, to himself, DeKok's behavior at Dolman's. He had been so dull, so servile, so different from his normal behavior. It had flashed through his mind: DeKok is getting old. But he had immediately abandoned that thought when he caught the warning flicker in DeKok's eyes. The glance that cautioned him to stay out of it. Choosing the better part of valor, he had obeyed the unspoken command. Meanwhile he had listened to the meaningless babbling about rags, mops and voided bladders. Strange though, he thought, they had not discussed it together. Not once. As far as he knew, there was no mop in the scenario. He wrinkled his forehead and looked sideways at his passenger.

DeKok had slid down in the seat. His face was serious. The green light of the communication gear lit his face from below. It made his normally so good natured boxer face look sinister.

"What ... eh," began Vledder with a certain amount of diffidence, "what did you mean, about that mop?"

DeKok sighed.

"Exactly what I said."

"You mean that Ellen voided her bladder when she was strangled?"

"Yes, that's what I mean. If you had given me an accurate report of the autopsy, I would probably have thought about it a lot sooner." He shook his head. "But you were so erratic, this morning . . ."

Vledder looked straight ahead, all his attention on the road. It was still rather busy in the inner city. He had to drop his speed. Traffic lights and Sunday drivers blocked his progress. He had to remain alert on the icy roads.

"Yes, her bladder was empty," he said after a long silence. "Dr. Rusteloos pointed it out to me. But I didn't think it was all that important, otherwise I would certainly have mentioned it to you." He turned off the main thoroughfare into a side street and reached the Emperor's Canal. "Actually, to be frank, I don't see what difference it makes to this case."

DeKok grinned.

"I really thought that my explanation was clear enough. In any case, I hope Mr. Dolman realizes the importance."

He pulled himself up out of his seat and sat more upright.

"I'll explain it all, soon. Park the car on the Gentlemen's Canal, close to the Gentlemen Street. Find a place under the trees an park as close to the water's edge as possible. I'd rather avoid being seen by our Mr. Dolman. He might change his mind."

* * *

About five minutes later they were both seated on the top step of the stairs to the third floor. They had used the front door, so conveniently opened by Henkie and just as conveniently blocked from locking by a piece of tape, supplied by DeKok. This time

DeKok had made sure that the door was securely locked after they entered. Then, followed by Vledder, he had made his way to the top of the stairs, to the spot he had selected as a convenient look-out post.

He had told Vledder about his friend, Handy Henkie, about the burglary on his responsibility, about the discolored part of the parquet floor and about the mop in the bucket in the janitor's closet.

With mounting amazement, Vledder had listened.

"And you think he'll come?"

DeKok rubbed his hands over his face in a weary gesture.

"If he killed her, there's a chance." He remained silent for a while. Then he added: "That is to say . . ."

"That is to say . . . what!?"

DeKok sighed.

"That is to say, he mustn't think about it too long."

"But why?"

DeKok snorted.

"If he thinks about it, he stays home."

Vledder was getting impatient.

"But what about the mop?"

DeKok shook his head.

"That mop, my boy, that mop doesn't mean a thing. Not by itself. The only thing the sharp brains in the lab can tell us with certainty, is that the mop had been contaminated with human urine. And with a little bit of luck, they might even be able to identify the blood group of the person who produced the urine. But that is then just about all. There's not much additional information to gain from it."

"You mean that the mop, by itself, is not sufficient, conclusive evidence?"

"No . . . at most it can be contributing evidence. But with just the mop . . ." DeKok sighed. "Just think about it, my boy. A mop is seldom, if ever, washed. At most it's rinsed, from time to time. The janitor uses the mop everywhere. The corridors, the stairs, floors, also the bathrooms. I bet that you can find traces of urine in almost every mop. A lawyer with just a modicum of experience, wipes the floor with that kind of evidence." He smiled at the involuntary pun. "It might not even be admitted as evidence. It leaves you nowhere."

"But yet, you expect him to show up?"

"Yes, I expect him to show up."

Vledder sighed.

"He didn't seem that dumb."

"No, he isn't dumb. Business people are seldom dumb . . . when it comes to business. But their interests are limited. Maybe, every once in a while, a detective thriller about some super sleuth, who solves the most complicated cases with a minimum of clues, or help." He rubbed his chin, felt the stubble. "I just hope he's read a lot of books like that."

Vledder laughed.

"You're a gambler, DeKok, an incurable gambler."

DeKok grinned.

"Well, I told Dolman we had a chance, a small chance . . . and he'll decide who will win the jackpot."

* * *

Time passed slowly.

They had come closer together for warmth, because it was chilly and damp at the top of the stairs in the empty office building. They did not speak, but listened to the noises made by the building. It was pitch black. Every once in a while they heard tiny feet tripping along the marble corridor. No canal house is ever completely free of rats. The woodwork creaked as it expanded and contracted in response to hidden pressures and temperature changes.

DeKok wondered if Klaassen would be able to keep Femmy at the station for the time needed. Legally, there was no way to keep her any longer. If she insisted on leaving, there would be no way to keep her, unless she was formally charged with an offense. He gambled on Jan's inventiveness and hoped he would succeed. He needed her for the finishing touches, a kind of dramatic finale. Not because of the inherent theatricals, the drama, but in order to convince the perpetrator he had no hope left, to deny any false illusions.

Suddenly they heard the sound of the lock, followed by footsteps in the ground floor corridor. With bated breath they listened intently and they soon heard the creaking of the stairs leading to the floor below.

DeKok felt Vledder's muscles tense.

A light was switched on, on the second floor, and the footsteps came closer. A strange excitement came over him. All thoughts of tiredness and cold vanished.

The footsteps stopped in front of the janitor's closet. Vledder and DeKok watched the tall, lean figure of the man below. His facial features could not be discerned. He opened the closet door and leaned forward. They heard the slight rattle of buckets. For just a moment DeKok restrained Vledder, then they both stormed down the stairs.

Paralyzed with shock, the man saw them approach. His face was gray and his mouth fell open. He backed up against the wall and watched the detectives with wide, frightened eyes. The mop fell from his hand.

DeKok looked at him, head slightly cocked to one side, a sad look on his face.

"Good evening, Mr. Dolman," he said. "I thought our appointment was for tomorrow morning."

Dolman did not resist. He knew he had been defeated. Defeated by this commonplace man, this nondescript civil servant with the friendly face of a good natured boxer. 'Inspector DeKok, with . . . eh, kay-oh-kay,' he had introduced himself. He would never forget that name again. Submissively he allowed himself to be led away.

Flanked by the two detectives, he walked to the police car. It was cold outside, bitter cold. The quays along the canals were deserted. People had withdrawn into the cozy warmth of their homes. Nobody observed the small drama. Candles on Christmas trees glistened behind some frosted windows in the Gentlemen Street. Dolman looked at them and bowed his head.

* * *

The moment Vledder and DeKok, with Dolman between them, entered the detective room, Femmy jumped out of her chair. It was as if she had waited for this moment. Ignoring everything else, she approached Dolman with quick, determined steps. She drummed on his chest with her tiny fists. Her suppressed emotions seemed to discharge all at the same time.

"Murderer!" she screamed. "Murderer! You killed her! You killed her, killed . . ."

Klaassen and Vledder wanted to intervene, but DeKok held them back. From a distance he looked on, resigned, unemotional. His face was a pitiless mask. He noticed that Dolman did not defend himself. There was a painful expression on the man's face. Femmy cursed him, screamed at him and struck him, again and again. DeKok calmly allowed her to relieve her feelings.

After a while he took her by the arm and led her to a different room.

"We'll have to talk later. Calmly and in detail." He took his second clean handkerchief from his pocket and dried her tears. Then he left her and returned to Dolman and the others.

"How old are you?" he asked. His voice was sluggish.

"Forty five," answered Dolman.

"And how old was Ellen?"

"Nineteen."

DeKok sighed.

"If my information is correct, you have a daughter of your own of about nineteen. I'm sure you can understand the feelings of Ellen's parents."

Dolman nodded vaguely.

DeKok remained silent for a long time. His chin rested in his hands.

"Have you ever heard," he asked finally, "of an-eye-for-an-eye and a-tooth-for-a-tooth?" He shook his head slowly. "An atrocious legal concept, don't you think? Happily for you, we have progressed beyond that."

* * *

"I still can't get over Femmy's outburst." Vledder shook his head as he recollected the incident. "I thought she was going to rip him apart."

211

"I take it you made sure she arrived safely in Hoorn?"

"Yes, her parents were a bit surprised when we showed up in the middle of the night. But you were right. It was the best solution. We could hardly have left her in Amsterdam, under the circumstances."

"No," sighed DeKok. "That would have been impossible."

They were seated in front of the open hearth in DeKok's snug and comfortable living room. DeKok had opened his best bottle of cognac, because it was still Christmas, but also because he felt pretty good about himself. He was well satisfied with the developments. He lolled lazily in his chair, his feet in roomy, old slippers.

His wife came from the kitchen.

"I didn't understand it all," said Mrs. DeKok. "What did Femmy have to do with the murder?"

DeKok took a long, luxurious sip from his cognac.

"Femmy," he said, "Femmy is the most pathetic figure in this tragedy. Also a strange figure, hard to understand. Only four, or five, years ago she was a lovely, attractive girl occupied with day dreams and fantasies about Love, with a capital L. In Hoorn, during a sailing contest, she met Dolman, who presented himself passionately as a rich bachelor. Femmy fell in love. Dolman seemed the fulfillment of her dreams, the answer to all her prayers."

Thoughtfully, Dekok took another sip. Then he continued:

"When she discovered that he had been married for years she called him to account. Dolman promised to get a divorce. Of course, it would take a little time before he could marry her, but she could depend on him. Then followed the usual excuses. After about two years she became pregnant. She urged a quick divorce, but Dolman made it clear to her that he had no intention at all, at all, of divorcing his legal spouse. He offered her a compromise. She could remain in the office, at a higher salary that would afford her the means to take care of their child. Of course, with the understanding that she would never ask him for anything else and, just in case, would deny any rumors about their relationship."

He drained his glass and replaced it on the little table next to him.

"Femmy agreed," he went on. "She had no other choice. The pregnancy was too far advanced. There was no other way. But her hatred of Dolman, all men in fact, originates from that date. She suppressed her female vanity and hid her attractiveness behind loose sweaters, black knit stockings and shapeless, low shoes. She even masked her alluring face behind thick, heavy glasses which she really didn't need at all. It was a defense. She built a cocoon around herself to protect herself from the opposite sex."

DeKok paused. Vledder and Mrs. DeKok listened intently. Seldom had either one heard DeKok speak so long at one time, and with so much detail. They were spellbound.

"When Ellen appeared in the office," said DeKok, "and told Femmy about the way she had gotten the job, Femmy immediately understood the background. Femmy tried to protect Ellen. She took Ellen under her wing, so to speak, helped her find a room and told her about her own experiences. She warned her time and again."

He paused again, briefly, while he poured another generous measure of the fine cognac, his favorite beverage.

"When Ellen broke off her engagement after just a few months, Femmy was very upset. She feared that Ellen, too, would be made very unhappy because of a similar, hopeless relationship with Dolman, who would never, ever divorce his wife. Femmy knew this from bitter experience. Perhaps she noticed Ellen's pregnancy even before Ellen herself was aware of it. In any case, when she was certain, Femmy went to Dolman and told him in no uncertain terms that he had to break off his relationship with Ellen. She also told him that he had to take care of the abortion."

He took a careful sip from his glass.

"Understand," he resumed, "she was not motivated by jealousy. Her love for Dolman had died long ago. No, she was motivated by concern for Ellen. She wanted to spare her. She wanted to spare Ellen for an eventual marriage to Tom Weick. That's the way she talked to Ellen. Ellen finally agreed. She would resume the engagement as soon as she had her abortion. We now know that the conversation with Tom, in the railroad restaurant, resulted in a telephone conversation with Dolman. It became the immediate prologue to her death."

213

Another pause, another sip.

"Dolman *did* confess to the conversation he had with Ellen. She told him that he had to pay for the abortion. She was already three months pregnant and there was little time left."

He glanced at Vledder, lifted the bottle in a questioning gesture and, upon Vledder's nod, refilled the empty glass next to the young man. After reflecting on his words, DeKok sniffed the aroma of the precious liquid in his own glass, took a sip and continued:

"Dolman faced a difficult decision. First Femmy and now Ellen had threatened him with public exposure if he did not take care of things. Dolman took the threats seriously, as well he should. He was a member of a number of important committees, was represented on several Boards of Directors, was a member of the governing body of his church and was widely known as an ethical business man, a respectable husband and a good father. The abortion itself was not the problem, but he had to find a way to keep his name out of it. As you know, although the parents, or husband, do not need to be notified, the doctor will insist on the name of the father. That is an administrative requirement. And Dolman wanted to avoid being listed as such."

DeKok refused to drink while talking. He warmed the glass in his hand while he spoke, but took the time to sip and savor his drink. He felt that cognac deserved proper attention. After the proper reverence had been made to his drink, he went on:

"So Dolman began to ask around, carefully, if there was a way that his name could be kept out of the abortion process altogether. If someone would treat Ellen without insisting on the name of the father. But he simply did not have the right connections to get that information. Also, he was afraid to ask questions that might be too obvious. After the telephone conversation, he drove to the station to pick up Ellen. Possibly he had hinted that he finally had found someone to take care of things and leave his name out of it. We can't be sure of that. Dolman himself maintains that he just wanted to talk things over with her. Anyway, he took Ellen directly from the station to the office and strangled her. He cried over her corpse for a long time, so he says. Only later did he worry about how to dispose of the body. He was afraid to drop it in the Emperor's

Canal. Too close to the office, he thought. But it was also a bit risky to drive around too long with a corpse in the car. That's why he dumped the body in the Gentlemen's Canal. It was less obvious in relation to the office."

DeKok drained his glass, enjoying the amber liquid as it worked its warm, glowing way down to his stomach.

"After he had disposed of the corpse, he drove back to the Emperor's Canal to remove the traces of the killing. But he forgot Ellen's handbag; it remained on the back seat of the car. It fell victim to Henkie's quick fingers."

DeKok's wife rested her hands in her lap.

"So Femmy," she stated, "was really not involved with the actual murder."

DeKok stared in his empty glass.

"Not directly," he answered pensively. "But I can't help but wonder about her motives. Were they really as pure as she wanted us to believe? Last night she told me about an incident on the beach, near Seadike. Apparently Dolman had tried to strangle her, at the time. It struck me. Not the fact by itself so much, as the way in which she told the story. It showed a certain duality of spirit and I immediately thought about her professed concern for Ellen. It gave me a uncomfortable feeling. You see, Femmy knew apparently, that Dolman was capable of murder."

About the Author:

Albert Cornelis Baantjer (BAANTJER) first appeared on the American literary scene in September, 1992 with "DeKok and Murder on the Menu". He was a member of the Amsterdam Municipal Police force for more than 38 years and for more than 25 years he worked Homicide out of the ancient police station at 48 Warmoes Street, on the edge of Amsterdam's Red Light District. The average tenure of an officer in "the busiest police station of Europe" is about five years. Baantjer stayed until his retirement.

His appeal in the United States has been instantaneous and praise for his work has been universal. "If there could be another Maigret-like police detective, he might well be Detective-Inspector DeKok of the Amsterdam police," according to *Bruce Cassiday* of the International Association of Crime Writers. "It's easy to understand the appeal of Amsterdam police detective DeKok," writes *Charles Solomon* of the Los Angeles Times. Baantjer has been described as "a Dutch Conan Doyle" (Publishers Weekly) and has been called "a new major voice in crime fiction in America" (*Ray B. Browne*, CLUES: A Journal of Detection).

Perhaps part of the appeal is because much of Baantjer's fiction is based on real-life (or death) situations encountered during his long police career. He writes with the authority of an expert and with the compassion of a person who has seen too much suffering. He's been there.

The critics and the public have been quick to appreciate the charm and the allure of Baantjer's work. Seven "DeKok's" have been used by the (Dutch) Reader's Digest in their series of condensed books (called "Best Books" in Holland). In his native Holland, with a population of less than 15 million people, Baantjer has sold more than 5 million books and according to the Netherlands Library Information Service, a Baantjer/DeKok is checked out of a library more than 700,000 times per year.

American reviews suggest that Baantjer may become as popular in English as he is already in Dutch.

DeKok and Murder in Ecstasy
Baantjer

The driver is killed, shot down, during the assault on an armored truck. An especially cowardly act, according to eye witenesses. The robber made a special effort to turn back and fire two bullets through the head of the victim. Within an hour after the event, DeKok is already in the middle of the investigation. Is it a coincidence that the transport was carrying an unusually large amount, this time? DeKok, like most policemen, does not believe in coincidences. He fears that the affair is less simple than it appears. He *knows* that the hunt for the murderer is just the beginning and the driver is not going to be the only victim in this macabre dance for more than $3 million. He looks at Vledder, his assistant, who is composing the text of the All-Points-Bulletin: "You know, Dick," he says sadly, "money . . . money is an invention of the devil. Some are possessed by it."

Also a major motion picture, directed by Hans Scheepmaker.

ISBN: 1-881164-16-0
LCCN: 97-42994
$9.95

TWISTED

CAHROUL CRAMER

As the Chief of Homicide, the newly promoted Lieutenant Turner Fleece was expected to act as a supervisor and not as an investigator. But when an up and coming recording artist and her lover are brutally murdered in the woman's San Francisco home, the thrill of the hunt is more than Fleece can resist. He is seductively led through a maze of deceit and corruption. And at the very moment when it seems he has untangled the mystery, he realizes it has only become more twisted.

SBN 1-886411-82-9
LCCN: 97-42995
$9.95

VENGEANCE: Prelude to Saddam's War
by Bob Mendes

Shocking revelations concerning his past move Michel Moreels, a Belgian industrial agent and consultant, to go to work for the Israeli Mossad. His assignment is to infiltrate a clandestine arms project designed to transform Iraq into a major international military power. Together with his girlfriend, Anna Steiner, he travels to Baghdad and succeeds in winning the trust of Colonel Saddiq Qazzaz, an officer of the *Mukhabarat*, the dreaded Iraqi Secret Police. At the risk of his own life and that of Anna, he penetrates the network of the illegal international arms trade, traditionally based in Brussels and the French-speaking part of Belgium. He meets American scientist Gerald Bull, a ballistic expert. Gradually it becomes clear to Michel that neither Bull, nor Anna, are what they appear to be. The more he learns about international secret services and the people who are determined to manipulate him, the more his Iraqi mission takes on a personal character: one of Vengeance!

A "faction-thriller" based on actual events in Iraq and Western Europe.
A Bertelsmann (Europe) Book Club Selection.
First American edition of this European Best-Seller.

ISBN 1-881164-71-3 (**$9.95**)

Bob Mendes is the winner of the (1993) "Gouden Strop" (Golden Noose). The "Golden Noose" is an annual award given to the best thriller or crime/spy novel published in the Dutch language. "An intelligent and convincing intrigue in fast tempo; in writing *Vengeance*, Bob Mendes has produced a thriller of international allure." **(From the Jury's report for the Golden Noose, 1993)** . . . Compelling and well-documented—Believable—a tremendously exciting thriller—a powerful visual ability—compelling, tension–filled and extremely well written—rivetting action and finely detailed characters—smooth transition from fact to fiction and back again . . . **(a sampling of Dutch and Flemish reviews)**.

DEADLY DREAMS
by Gerald A. Schiller

It was happening again . . . the mist . . . struggling to find her way. Then . . . the images . . . grotesque, distorted figures under plastic sheeting, and white-coated, masked figures moving toward her . . .

When Denise Burton's recurring nightmares suddenly begin to take shape in reality, she is forced to begin a search . . . a search to discover the truth behind these horrific dreams.

The search will lead her into a series of dangerous encounters . . . in a desert ghost-town, within the restricted laboratories of Marikem, the chemical company where she works, with a brutal drug dealer and with a lover who is not what he seems.

A riveting thriller.

A thriller of fear and retaliation, *Gary Phillips,* **author of Perdition, USA**; . . . promising gambits .. a *Twilight Zone* appetizer, **Kirkus Reviews**; . . . a brisk, dialogue-driven story of nasty goings-on and cover-ups in the labs of a giant chemical works with a perky, attractive, imperiled heroine, *Charles Champlin* [Los Angeles Times].

ISBN 1-881164-81-0 / $9.95

Gerald Schiller's latest book, **DEATH UNDERGROUND,** will be available in Spring, 1999.

The Cop Was White As Snow

Joyce Spizer

THE COP'S SUICIDE on a lonely beach confirmed his guilt. He had been skimming cocaine from police impounds and selling it to drug dealers to support his own habit and a growing taste for luxury. But he was Mel's Dad, and she was not about to accept this for a minute. Her Dad was no dirty cop!

THE COP WAS WHITE AS SNOW is a fast read. Spizer does a good job of keeping the action coming. Her insight as an investigator resonates throughout the book.
—Barbara Seranell, author of **No Human Involved**

JOYCE SPIZER is the shamus she writes about. The novels in the Harbour Pointe Mystery Series are fictionalized accounts of cases she has investigated. A member of Sisters in Crime, she hobnobs regularly with other mystery writers. She lives in Southern California with her husband and co-investigator, Harold.

SBN 1-886411-83-7
LCCN: 97-39430
$10.95